D1512719

GARMAN AND WORSE

LECTOR HOUSE PUBLIC DOMAIN WORKS

This book is a result of an effort made by Lector House towards making a contribution to the preservation and repair of original classic literature. The original text is in the public domain in the United States of America, and possibly other countries depending upon their specific copyright laws.

In an attempt to preserve, improve and recreate the original content, certain conventional norms with regard to typographical mistakes, hyphenations, punctuations and/or other related subject matters, have been corrected upon our consideration. However, few such imperfections might not have been rectified as they were inherited and preserved from the original content to maintain the authenticity and construct, relevant to the work. We believe that this work holds historical, cultural and/or intellectual importance in the literary works community, therefore despite the oddities, we accounted the work for print as a part of our continuing effort towards preservation of literary work and our contribution towards the development of the society as a whole, driven by our beliefs.

We are grateful to our readers for putting their faith in us and accepting our imperfections with regard to preservation of the historical content. We shall strive hard to meet up to the expectations to improve further to provide an enriching reading experience.

Though, we conduct extensive research in ascertaining the status of copyright before redeveloping a version of the content, in rare cases, a classic work might be incorrectly marked as not-in-copyright. In such cases, if you are the copyright holder, then kindly contact us or write to us, and we shall get back to you with an immediate course of action.

HAPPY READING!

GARMAN AND WORSE

ALEXANDER LANGE KIELLAND,
W. W. KETTLEWELL

ISBN: 978-93-5342-461-9

First Published: 1855

© LECTOR HOUSE LLP

LECTOR HOUSE LLP
E-MAIL: lectorpublishing@gmail.com

GARMAN AND WORSE

A NORWEGIAN NOVEL

BY

ALEXANDER L. KIELLAND

AUTHORIZED TRANSLATION
BY W. W. KETTLEWELL

1885

CONTENTS

CHAPTER I.

Nothing is so boundless as the sea, nothing so patient. On its broad back it bears, like a good-natured elephant, the tiny mannikins which tread the earth; and in its vast cool depths it has place for all mortal woes. It is not true that the sea is faithless, for it has never promised anything; without claim, without obligation, free, pure, and genuine beats the mighty heart, the last sound one in an ailing world. And while the mannikins strain their eyes over it, the sea sings its old song. Many understand it scarce at all, but never two understand it in the same manner, for the sea has a distinct word for each one that sets himself face to face with it.

It smiles with green shining ripples to the barelegged urchin who catches crabs; it breaks in blue billows against the ship, and sends the fresh salt spray far in over the deck. Heavy leaden seas come rolling in on the beach, and while the weary eye follows the long hoary breakers, the stripes of foam wash up in sparkling curves over the even sand; and in the hollow sound, when the billows roll over for the last time, there is something of a hidden understanding--each thinks on his own life, and bows his head towards the ocean as if it were a friend who knows it all and keeps it fast.

But what the sea is for those who live along its strand none can ever know, for they say nothing. They live all their life with face turned to the ocean; the sea is their companion, their adviser, their friend and their enemy, their inheritance and their churchyard. The relation therefore remains a silent one, and the look which gazes over the sea changes with its varying aspect, now comforting, now half fearful and defiant. But take one of these shore-dwellers, and move him far landward among the mountains, into the loveliest valley you can find; give him the best food, and the softest bed. He will not touch your food, or sleep in your bed, but without turning his head he will clamber from hill to hill, until far off his eye catches something blue he knows, and with swelling heart he gazes towards the little azure streak that shines far away, until it grows into a blue glittering horizon; but he says nothing.

People in the town often said to Richard Garman, "How can you endure that lonely life out there in your lighthouse?" The old gentleman always answered, "Well, you see, one never feels lonely by the sea when once one has made its acquaintance; and besides, I have my little Madeleine."

And that was the feeling of his heart. The ten years he had passed out there on the lonely coast were among the best of his life, and that life had been wild and adventurous enough; so, whether he was now weary of the world, or whether it was his little daughter, or whether it was the sea that attracted him, or whether it was something of all three, he had quieted down, and never once thought of leaving the lighthouse of Bratvold. This was what no one could have credited; and when it was rumoured that Richard Garman, the *attaché*, a son of the first commercial family of the town, was seeking the simple post of lighthouse-keeper, most people were inclined to laugh heartily at this new fancy of "the mad student." "The mad student" was a nickname in the town for Richard Garman, which was doubtless well earned; for although he had been but little at home since he had grown to manhood, enough was known of his wild and pleasure-seeking career to make folks regard him with silent wonder.

To add to this, too, the visits he paid to his home were generally coincident with some remarkable event or another. Thus it was when, as a young student, he was present at his mother's funeral; and even more so when he came at a break-neck pace from Paris to the death-bed of the old Consul, in a costume and with an air which took away the breath of the ladies, and caused confusion among the men. Since then Richard had been but little seen. Rumour, however, was busy with him. At one time some commercial traveller had seen him at Zinck's Hotel at Hamburg; now he was living in a palace; and now the story was that he was existing in the docks, and writing sailors' letters for a glass of beer.

One fine day Garman and Worse's heavy state carriage was seen on its way to the quay. Inside sat the head of the firm, Consul C.F. Garman, and his daughter Rachel, while little Gabriel, his younger son, was sitting by the side of the coachman. An unbearable curiosity agitated the groups on the quay.

The state carriage was seldom to be seen in the town, and now at this very moment the Hamburg steamer was expected. At length an *employé* of the firm came to the carriage window, and, after a few irrelevant remarks, ventured to ask who was coming.

"I am expecting my brother the *attaché*, and his daughter," answered Consul Garman, while with a movement peculiar to himself he adjusted his smoothly shaven chin in his stiff neckcloth.

This information increased the excitement. Richard Garman was coming, "the mad student," "the *attaché*" as he was sometimes called; and with a daughter, too! But how could they belong to each other? Could he ever have been really married? It was hardly likely.

The steamer came. Consul Garman went on board, and returned shortly after with his brother and a little dark-haired girl, who doubtless was the daughter.

Richard Garman was soon recognized, although he had grown somewhat stouter: but the upright, elegant bearing and the striking black moustache were still the same; while the hair, though crisp and curling as in the old days, was now slightly necked with grey at the temples. He greeted them all with a friendly smile as he passed to the carriage, and there was more than one lady who felt that the glance of his bright brown eye rested smilingly on her for a moment.

The carriage rolled off through the town, and away down the long avenue which led to the large family mansion of Sandsgaard.

The town gossipped itself nearly crazy, but without any satisfactory result. The house of Garman took good care of its secrets.

So much was, however, clear: that Richard Garman had dissipated the whole of his large fortune, or else he would never have consented to come home and eat the bread of charity in his brother's house.

On the other hand, the relation between the brothers was, at least as far as appearances went, a most cordial one. The Consul gave a grand dinner, at which he drank his brother's health, adding at the same time the hope that he might find himself happy in his old home.

There is nothing so irritating as a half-fulfilled scandal, and when Richard Garman a short time afterwards calmly received the post of lighthouse-keeper at Bratvold, and lived there year after year without a sign of doing anything worthy of remark, each one in the little town felt himself personally affronted, and it was a source of wonder to all how little the Garmans seemed to realize what they owed to society.

As far as that went, Richard himself was not perfectly clear how it had all come about; there was something about Christian Frederick he could not understand. Whenever he met his brother, or even got a letter from him, his whole nature seemed to change; things he would otherwise never have thought of attempting appeared all at once quite easy, and he did feats which afterwards caused him the greatest astonishment. When, in a state of doubt and uncertainty, he wrote home for the last time, to beg his brother to take charge of little Madeleine, his only thought was to make an end of his wasted life, the sooner the better, directly his daughter was placed in safety. But just then he happened to get a remittance enclosed in an extraordinary letter, in which occurred several puzzling business terms. There was something about "liquidation," and closing up an account which required his presence, and in the middle of it all there were certain expressions which seemed to have stumbled accidentally into the commercial style. For instance, in one place there was "brother of my boyhood;" and further on, "with sincere wishes for brotherly companionship;" and finally, he read, in the middle of a long involved sentence, "Dear Richard, don't lose heart." This stirred Richard Garman into action: he made an effort, and set off home. When he saw his brother come on board the steamer the tears came to his eyes, and he was on the point of opening his arms to embrace him. The Consul, however, held out his hand, and said quietly, "Welcome, Richard! Where are your things?"

Since then nothing had been said about the letter; once only had Richard Garman ventured to allude to it, when the Consul seemed to imagine that he wished to settle up the accounts that were therein mentioned. Nothing could have been further from the *attaché's* thoughts, and he felt that the bare idea was almost an injury. "Christian Frederick is a wonderful man," thought Richard; "and what a man of business he is!"

One day Consul Garman said to his brother, "Shall we drive out to Bratvold, and have a look at the new lighthouse?"

Richard was only too glad to go. From his earliest days he had loved the lonely coast, with its long stretches of dark heather and sand, and the vast open sea; the lighthouse also interested him greatly.

When the brothers got into the carriage again to drive back to the town, the *attaché* said, "Do you know, Christian Frederick, I can't imagine a position more suitable to such a wreck as myself than that of lighthouse-keeper out here."

"There is no reason you should not have it," answered his brother.

"Nonsense! How could it be managed?" answered Richard, as he knocked the ashes off his cigar.

"Now listen, Richard," replied the Consul, quickly. "If there is a thing I must find fault with you for, it is your want of self-reliance. Don't you suppose that, with your gifts and attainments, you could get a far higher post if you only chose to apply for it?"

"No; but, Christian Frederick--" exclaimed the *attaché*, regarding his brother with astonishment.

"It's perfectly true," replied the Consul. "If you want the post, they must give it to you; and if there should be any difficulty, I feel pretty certain that a word from us to the authorities would soon settle it."

The matter was thus concluded, and Richard Garman was appointed light-house-keeper at Bratvold, either because of his gifts and attainments or by reason of a timely word to the authorities. The very sameness of his existence did the old cavalier good; the few duties he had, he performed with the greatest diligence and exactitude.

He passed most of his spare time in smoking cigarettes, and looking out to sea through the large telescope, which was mounted on a stand, and which he had got as a present from Christian Frederick. He was truly weary, and he could not but wonder how he had so long kept his taste for the irregular life he had led in foreign lands. There was one thing that even more excited his wonder, and that was how well he got on with his income. To live on a hundred a year seemed to him nothing less than a work of art, and yet he managed it. It must be acknowl-edged that he had a small private income, but his brother always told him it was as good as nothing; how much it was, and from what source it was really derived, he never had an idea. It is true that there came each year a current account from Garman and Worse, made out in the Consul's own hand, and he also frequently got business letters from his brother; but neither the one nor the other made things clearer to him. He signed his name to all papers which were sent to him, in what appeared the proper place. Sometimes he got a bill of exchange to execute, and this he did to the best of his ability; but everything still remained to him in the same state of darkness as before.

One thing, however, was certain: Richard got on capitally. He kept two assis-tants for the lanterns; he had his riding horse Don Juan, and a cart-horse as well. His cellar was well filled with wine; and he always had a little ready money at hand, for which he had no immediate use. Thus, when any one complained to him of the bad times, he recommended them to come into the country; it was incredible how cheaply one could live there.

In the ten years they had passed at Bratvold, Madeleine had grown to woman-hood, and had thriven beyond general expectation; and when she had got quite at home in the language (her mother had been a Frenchwoman), she soon got on the best of terms with all their neighbours. She did not remain much in the house, but passed most of her time at the farmhouses, or by the sea, or the little boat haven.

A whole regiment of governesses had attempted to teach Madeleine, but the task was a difficult one; and when the governesses were ugly her father could not abide them, and when one came who was pretty there were other objections. Richard paid frequent visits to Sandsgaard, either on Don Juan or in the Garmans' dogcart, which was sent to fetch him. The chilly, old-fashioned house, and the reserved and polished manners of its inmates, had made a repellant impression on Madeleine. For her cousin Rachel, who was only a few years her elder, she had no liking. She preferred, therefore, to remain at home, and her father was never absent for more than a few days at a time. She spent most of her time on the shore or in the neighbouring cottages, in the society of fishermen and pilots. Merry and fearless as she was, these men were glad to take her out in fine weather in their boats. She thus learnt to fish, to handle a sail, or to distinguish the different craft by their rig.

Madeleine had one particular friend whose name was Per, who was three or four years older than herself, and who lived in the cottage nearest to the light-house. Per was tall and strongly built, with a crop of stiff, sandy hair, and a big hand as hard as horn from constant rowing; his eyes were small and keen, as is often seen among those who from their childhood are in the habit of peering out to sea through rain and fog.

Per's father had been a widower, and Per his only child, but he managed to get married again, and now the family increased year after year. The neighbours were always urging Per to get his father to divide the property with him, but Per preferred to wait the turn of events. The longer he waited the more brothers and sisters he had to share with. His friends laughed at him, and somebody one day called him "Wait Per," a joke which caused great amusement at the time, and the nickname stuck to him ever afterwards. Beyond this, Per was not a lad to be laughed at; he was one of the most active boatmen of the community, and at the same time the most peaceable creature on earth. He did not trouble to distinguish himself, but he had a kind of natural love for work, and, as he was afraid of noth-ing, the general feeling was that Per was a lad that would get on.

The friendship between Per and Madeleine was very cordial on both sides. At first some of the other young fellows tried to take her from him, but one day it so happened that when she was out with Per, a fresh north-westerly breeze sprang up. Per's boat and tackle were always of the best, so that there was no real danger; but nevertheless her father, who had seen the boat through the big telescope, came in all haste down to the shore, and went out on to the little pier to meet them.

"There's father," said Madeleine; "I wonder if he is anxious about us?"

"I think he knows better than that," said Per, thoughtfully.

All the same the *attaché* could not help feeling a little uneasy as he stood watching the boat; but when Per with a steady hand steered her in through the fairway, and swung her round the point of the pier, so that she glided easily into the smooth water behind it, the old gentleman could not help being impressed by his skill. "He knows what he's about," he muttered, as he helped up his daughter; and instead of the lecture he had prepared, he only said, "You are a smart lad, Per; but I never gave you permission to sail with her alone."

There was no one near enough to hear the old gentleman's words, but when the spectators who were standing near saw that Per shook hands with both Madeleine and her father in a friendly manner, they could all perceive that Per was in the lighthouse-keeper's good books for the future, and from that day it was taken for granted that Per alone had the right to escort the young lady.

Per thought over and over whom he should take with him in the boat. He saw well enough that the whole pleasure would be spoilt if one of his friends came with them. At length he hit upon a poor half-witted lad, who was also hard of hearing into the bargain. No one could make out what Per wanted with "Silly Hans" in his boat; but there! Per always was an obstinate fellow. Both he and Madeleine were well contented with his choice; and when, a few days after, she put her head in at the door, and called to her father, "I'm just going for a little sail with Per," she was able to add with a good conscience, "Of course, he has got some one with him, since you really make such a point of it." She could not help laughing to herself as she ran down the slope.

Richard, in the mean time, betook himself to the big telescope. Right enough: Per was sitting aft, and he saw Madeleine jump down into the boat. On the forward thwart there sat a male creature, dressed in homespun, with a yellow sou'wester on its head.

"*Bien!*" said the old gentleman, with a sigh of relief. "It is well they have got some one with them--in every respect."

CHAPTER II.

The highest point on the seven miles of flat, sandy coast was the headland of Bratvold, where the lighthouse was built just on the edge of the slope, which here fell so steeply off towards the sea as to make the descent difficult and almost dangerous, while in ascending it was necessary to take a zigzag course. The sheep, which had grazed here from time out of mind, had cut out a network of paths on the side of the hill, so that from a distance these paths seemed to form a pattern of curves and projections on its face.

From the highest and steepest point, on which the lighthouse was built, the coast made a slight curve to the southward, and at the other end of this curve was the large farm of Bratvold, which, with its numerous and closely packed buildings, appeared like a small village.

On the shore below the farm lay the little boat harbour, sheltered by a breakwater of heavy stone.

The harbour was commanded by the windows of the lighthouse, so that Madeleine could always keep her eye on Per's boat, which was as familiar to her as their own sitting-room. This was a large and cheerful room, and into its corner was built the tower of the lighthouse itself, which was not higher than the rest of the building. The room had thus two windows, one of which looked out to sea, while from the other was a view to the northward over the sandy dunes, which were dotted with patches of heather and bent grass. In the sitting-room Madeleine's father had his books and writing-table, and last, but not least, the large telescope. This was made to turn on its stand, so that it commanded both the view to the north and that out to sea. Here also Madeleine had her flowers and her work-table; and the tasteful furniture which Uncle Garman had ordered from Copenhagen, and which was always a miracle of cheapness to her father, gave the room a bright and comfortable appearance.

In the long evenings when the winter storms came driving in on the little lighthouse, father and daughter sat cosy and warm behind the shelter of their thick walls and closed shutters, while the light fell in regular and well-defined rays over the billows, which raged and foamed on the shore below. The ever-changing ocean, which washed under their very windows, seemed to give a freshness to their whole life, while its never-ceasing murmur mingled in their conversation and their laughter, and in her music.

Madeleine had inherited much of her father's lively nature; but she had also a kind of impetuosity, which one of her governesses had called defiance. When she grew up she showed, therefore, the stronger nature of the two, and her father, as was his wont, gave way. He laughed at his little tyrant, whose great delight was to ruffle his thick curling hair. When, in his half-abstracted way, the old gentleman would tell her stones which threatened to end unpleasantly, she would scold him well; but when, from some cause or other, he was really displeased with her, it affected her so much that the impression remained for a long time. Her nature was bright and joyous, but she yearned for the sunshine, and when her father was out of spirits she could not help fancying that it was her fault, and became quite unhappy.

Madeleine had also her father's eyes, dark and sparkling, but otherwise her only resemblance to him lay in her slight figure and graceful carriage. Her mouth was rather large, and her complexion somewhat dark. None could deny that she was an attractive girl, but no one would have called her pretty; some of the young men had even decided that she was plain.

One fine afternoon early in spring, Per lay waiting with his boat off the point of the Mole. Silly Hans was not with him, for both he and Madeleine had agreed that it was not necessary when they were going only for a row; and to-day all there was to do was to provide the lobster-pots with fresh bait for the night.

One after another the fishermen rowed out through the narrow entrance. Each one had some mischievous joke to throw on board Per's boat, and more than once the annoying "Wait" was heard. He began to lose his temper as he lay on his oars, gazing expectantly up at the lighthouse.

But there all was still. The solid little building looked so quiet and well cared for in the bright sunshine, which shone on the polished window-panes and on the bright red top of the lantern, where he could see the lamp-trimmer going round on his little gallery, polishing the prisms.

At last, after what seemed endless waiting, she came out on to the steps, and in another moment she was across the yard, over the enclosure which belonged to the lighthouse, out through the little gate in the fence, and now she came in full career down the slope. "Have you been waiting?" she cried, as she came on to the extreme point of the breakwater. He was just going to tell her not to jump, but it was too late; without lessening her speed, she had already sprung from the pier down into the boat. Her feet slipped from her, and she fell in a sitting posture on the bottom of the boat, while part of her dress hung in the water.

"Bother the women!" cried Per, who had told her at least a hundred times not to jump; "now you have hurt yourself."

"No," answered she.

"Yes, you have."

"Well, just a little," she replied, looking stubbornly at him as the tears came into her eyes; for she really had bruised her leg severely.

"Let me see," said Per.

"No, you shan't!" she answered, arranging her dress over her.

Per began to make for the shore.

"What are you going to do?"

"Going to get some brandy to rub your foot."

"That you certainly shan't."

"Well, then, you shan't go with me," answered Per.

"Very well, then; let me get out."

And before the boat quite touched the ground, she sprang on to the shore, climbed on to the breakwater, and went hurriedly off homewards. She clenched her teeth with the pain as she went, but still without raising her eyes from the ground she followed the well-known path. As she passed in front of the boat-houses, she had to step over oars, tar-barrels, old swabs, and all sorts of rubbish, which was scattered among the boats. All around lay the claws of crabs and the half-decayed heads of codfish, in which the gorged and sleepy flies were crawling in and out of the eye-sockets.

She reached the lighthouse without turning her head; she was determined not to look back at him. At the top, however, she was obliged to pause to get her breath; she surely might look and see how far he got. Madeleine knew that the other fishermen had had a long start, and expected, therefore, to find Per's boat far behind, between the others and the shore. But it was not to be seen, neither there nor in the harbour. All at once her eye caught the well-known craft, which was not, however, far behind, but almost level with the others. Per must have rowed like a madman. She was well able to estimate the distance, and could appreciate such a feat of oarsmanship, and, entirely forgetting her pain and that she was alone, she turned round as if to a crowd of spectators, and pointing at the boats she said, with sparkling eyes, "Look at him! that's the boy to row!"

Meanwhile Per sat in his boat, tearing at his oars till all cracked again. It was as though he wished to punish himself by his gigantic efforts. Her form grew smaller and smaller as he rowed out to sea, till at length she was out of sight; but he had deserved it all. "Deuce take the women!" and each time he repeated the words he sprang to his oars and rowed as if for bare life.

The next day the same lovely weather continued, and the sea lay as smooth as oil in the bright sunshine. An English lobster-cutter was in the offing, with sails flapping against the mast, and the slack in the taut rigging could be seen as the craft heaved lazily to and fro on the gentle swell. Madeleine sat by the window; she did not care to go out. Her eye followed the lobster-cutter, which she knew well: it was the *Flying Fish*, Captain Crab, of Hull.

So Per must have been out with lobsters that morning: she wondered if he had caught many. Perhaps he might have done himself harm by his efforts of yesterday. She went out on to the slope, and looked down into the harbour. Per's boat was there; it was quite likely he was not well.

Suddenly Madeleine made up her mind to run down and ask a man whom she saw by the boat-houses, but half-way down the slope she met some one who was coming upwards. She could not possibly have seen him sooner, because he was below her at the steepest part of the hill, but now she recognized him, and slackened her pace.

Per must also have seen her, although he was looking down, for at a few paces from her he left the main path, and took one that was a little lower. When therefore they were alongside each other, she was a little above him. Per had a basket on his back, and Madeleine could see there was seaweed in it.

Neither of them spoke, but both of them felt as if they were half choking. When he had got a pace beyond her, she turned round and asked, "What have you got in the basket, Per?"

"A lobster," answered he, as he swung the basket off his back and put it down upon the path.

"Let me see it," said Madeleine.

He hastily drew aside the seaweed, and took out a gigantic lobster, which was flapping its broad, scaly tail.

"That is a splendid great lobster!" she cried.

"Yes, it isn't a bad un!"

"What are you going to do with it?"

"Ask your father if he would like to have it."

"What do you want for it?" she asked, although she knew perfectly well that it was a present.

"Nothing," answered Per, curtly.

"That is good of you, Per."

"Oh, it's nothing," he answered, as he laid the seaweed back in the basket; and now, when the moment came to say good-bye, he said, "How's your foot?"

"Thanks, all right. I got the brandy."

"Did it hurt much?" asked Per.

"No, not very much."

"I am glad you did that," he said, as he ventured to lift his eyes to the level of her chin.

Now they really must separate, for there was nothing more to be said, but Madeleine could not help thinking that Per was a helpless creature.

"Good-bye, Per."

"Good-bye," he answered, and both took a few steps apart.

"Per, where are you going when you have been up with the lobster?"

"Nowhere particular," answered Per.

He really was too stupid, but all the same she turned round and called after him, "I am going to the sand-hills on the other side of the lighthouse, the weather is so lovely;" and away she ran.

"All right," answered Per, springing like a cat up the slope.

As he ran he threw away the seaweed so as to have the lobster ready, and when he got to the kitchen door he flung the monster down on the bench, and cried, "This is for you!" as he disappeared. The maid had recognized his voice, and ran after him to order fresh fish for Friday, but he was already far away. She gazed after him in amazement, and muttered, "I declare, I think Per is wrong in his head."

Northward stretched the yellow sand-hills with their tussocks of bent grass as far as the eye could reach. The coast-line curved in bights and promontories, with here and there a cluster of boats, while the gulls and wild geese were busy on the shore, and the waves rolled in in small curling ripples which glistened in the' clear sunshine. Per soon caught up Madeleine, for she went slowly that day. She had pulled a few young stalks of the grass, which, as she went, she was endeavouring to arrange in her hat.

The difference of the preceding day hung heavily over both of them. It was really the first time that anything of the sort had occurred between them. Perhaps it was that they felt instinctively that they stood on the brink of a precipice. They therefore took the greatest pains to avoid the subject which really occupied their thoughts. The conversation was thus carried on in a careless and desultory tone, and in short and broken sentences. At last she made an effort to bring him to the point, and asked him if he had caught many lobsters that night.

"Twenty-seven," answered Per.

That was neither many nor few, so there was no more to be said about that.

"You did row hard yesterday," said she, looking down, for now she felt that they were nearing the point.

"It was because--because I was alone in the boat," returned he, stammering. He saw at once that it was a stupid remark, but it was said and could not be mended.

"Perhaps you prefer to be alone in the boat?" she asked hastily, fixing her eyes upon him. But when she saw the long helpless creature standing before her in such a miserable state of confusion, strong and handsome as he was, she sprang up, threw her arms round his neck, and said, half laughing, half crying, "Oh, Per! Per!"

Per had not the faintest idea how he ought to behave when a lady had her arms round his neck, and so stood perfectly still. He looked down upon her long dark hair and slender figure, and, trembling at his own audacity, he put his heavy arm limply round her.

They were now out on the dunes, and she sat down behind one of the largest tussocks, on the warm sand. He ventured to place himself by her side, and looked vacantly around him. Every now and then he cast his eye upon her, but still doubtfully. It was clear that he did not grasp the situation, and at length he appeared to her so absurd that she sprang up, and cried, "Come, Per, let's have a run!"

Away they went, now running, now at a foot's pace. His heavy sea-boots made a broad impression upon the sand, and the mark of her shoe looked so tiny by the side of it that they could not help turning round and laughing. They jested and laughed as if they knew not that they were no longer children, and she made Per promise to give up chewing tobacco.

Away along the curving shore, with the salt breath of ocean fresh upon them, went these young hearts, rejoicing in their existence, while the sea danced in sparkling wavelets at their feet.

The *attaché* had just finished a letter to his brother; it was one of these wearisome business letters, enclosing some papers he had had to sign. He never could make out where the proper place was for him to put his name on these tiresome, long-winded documents. But, wonderful to relate, his brother always told him that it was perfectly correct, and Christian Frederick was most particular in such matters. The old gentleman had just sent off the letter, and was beginning to breathe more easily, when he went to the window and looked out. He discovered two forms going in a northerly direction over the sand-hills.

Half abstractedly, he went to the other window and directed the large telestope upon them.

"Humph!" said he, "I declare, they're there again."

Suddenly he took his eye from the telescope.

"Hulloa! the girl must be mad."

He put his eye down again to the telescope, and threw away his cigarette. There was no doubt about it--there was his own Madeleine hanging round Per's neck. He rubbed the glass excitedly with his pocket-handkerchief. They were now going respectably enough side by side; now they were among the grassy knolls, and behind one of them they disappeared from his sight. He thoughtfully directed the telescope to the other side of the hillock and waited. "What now?" muttered he, giving the glass another rub. They had not yet come from behind the hillock. For a few minutes the father was quite nervous. At last he saw one form raise itself, and immediately after another.

The telescope was perfect, and the old gentleman took in the situation just as well as if he had himself been sitting by their side.

"Ah! it's well it's no worse," he murmured; "but it's bad enough as it is. I shall have to send her off to the town."

When they were at dinner, he said, "You know, Madeleine, we have long been talking about your staying a little while at Sandsgaard."

"Oh no, father," broke in Madeleine, looking beseechingly at him.

"Yes, child; it's quite time now in my opinion." He spoke in an unusually determined tone.

Madeleine could see that he knew everything, and all at once the events of the morning stood in their true light before her. As she sat there, in their well-appointed room, opposite her father, who looked so refined and stately, Per and the shore, and everything that belonged to it, bore quite a different aspect, and instead of the joyful confession she had pictured to herself as she went homewards, she looked down in confusion and blushed to the very roots of her hair.

The visit was thus arranged, and Madeleine was delighted that her father had not observed her confusion; and he was glad enough to escape any further explanation on the subject, for it was just in such matters that the old gentleman showed his weakest point. The next day he rode into the town.

CHAPTER III.

"Avoir, avant, avu--that's how it goes! That's right, my boy; *avoir, avant."*

The whole class could see clearly that the master was lost in thought. He was pacing up and down, with long steps and half-closed eyes, gesticulating from time to time, as he kept repeating the ill-used auxiliary. On the upper benches the boys began to titter, and those on the lower ones, who had not such a fine ear for the French verbs, soon caught the infection; while the unhappy wretch who was undergoing examination, sat trembling lest the master should notice his wonderful method of conjugating the verb. This unfortunate being was Gabriel Garman, the Consul's younger son. He was a tall, slender boy of about fifteen or sixteen, with a refined face, prominent nose, and upright bearing.

Gabriel was sitting in the lower half of the class, which was, in the opinion of the master, a great disgrace for a boy of his ability. He was, however, a curious, wayward boy. In some things, such as arithmetic and mathematics generally, he distinguished himself; but in Greek and Latin, which were considered the most important part of his education, he showed but little proficiency, although he was destined for a university career.

At last the general mirth of the class burst out in sundry half-stifled noises, which roused the master from his reverie, and he again resumed the book, to continue the examination. As ill luck would have it, he once more repeated, *"Avoir, avant,"* and then half abstractedly, *"avu."* "Ah, you young idiot!" cried he, in a discordant voice, "can't you manage *avoir* yet? Whatever is to become of you?"

"Merchant," answered Gabriel, bluntly.

"What do you say? You dare to answer your master? Are you going to be impertinent? I'll teach you! Where's the persuader?" and the master strode up to his seat, and, diving down into his desk, began routing about in it.

At this moment the passage door opened, and an extraordinary and most unscholarly looking head intruded itself into the room. The head had a red nose, and wore a long American goat's-beard and a blue seaman's cap. "Are you there?" said the head, addressing Master Gabriel in a half-drunken voice. "Is that where you are, poor boy? Bah! what an atmosphere! I only just came in to tell you to come down to the ship-yard when you get out of school; we are just beginning the planking."

He did not get any further, for at the sight of the long-legged master, who stalked down from the desk, quite scandalized at this disturbance of order, the head suddenly stopped in its harangue, and with a hearty, "Well, I'm blest! what a ghost!" disappeared, closing the door after it,

It did not take very much to provoke the laughter of the boys, and when at the same moment the bell rang to announce that the school-hour was over, the class broke up in confusion, and the master hastened, fuming with rage, to complain to the rector.

Gabriel hurried off as fast as he could, in hopes of catching up his friend who had caused the disturbance, but he had already disappeared; he had probably gone down to the town to continue his libations. This friend was a foreman shipwright, who, since his return from America, had borne the name of Tom Robson. His real name when he left home was Thomas Robertsen, but it had got changed somehow in America, and he kept to it as it was.

Tom Robson was the cleverest foreman on the whole west coast, but his drinking propensities tried to the utmost both the patience and the firmness of his employers. He had already built several vessels for Garman and Worse, but he was determined that the one he was now superintending at Sandsgaard should be his masterpiece.

This vessel was of about nine hundred tons burden, and was the largest craft that had been built at that port up to the present time, and Consul Garman had given orders that nothing should be spared to make it a model of perfection.

Tom Robson was thus only able to get drunk by fits and starts, which he did when they came to any important epoch in the building. On that day, for instance, the time had just arrived for beginning to lay the planking upon the timbers.

As Gabriel neither found his friend nor saw anything of the carriage from Sandsgaard, which generally met him on his way from school, he set off to walk homewards, down the long avenue which led to the family property. It was a good half-hour's walk, and while he sauntered along, swinging his heavy burden of the books he so cordially hated, he was lost in gloomy thought. Every day, on his way from school, he met the younger clerks going to their dinner in the town. They looked tired and weary, it is true; still, he envied them their permission to sit working the whole day in the office--a paradise with which he, although his father's son, had no connection whatever. He was obliged to confine his energy to the building-yard, where there were plenty of hiding-places, and where the Consul was seldom seen of an afternoon. The ship on the stocks was at once his joy and his pride; he crept all over her, inside and out, above and below, scrutinizing every plank and every nail. At length he had begun to have quite a knowledge of the art of ship-building, and had gained the friendship of Tom Robson, Anders Begmand, and the other shipwrights. The ship was to be the finest the town had yet produced, and when this fact came into his thoughts it almost enabled him to forget his burden of Greek and Latin.

From conversations he had partly overheard at home, Gabriel knew that there had been a difference of opinion between his father and Morten, the eldest son, who was a partner in the firm, ever since the building of this ship was first mentioned.

Morten maintained that they ought to buy an iron steamer in England, either on their own account or in partnership with some of the other houses of the town. He insisted, particularly, that the time could not be far distant when sailing ships would be entirely superseded by steamers. But the father held by sailing ships on principle; and, moreover, the idea that Garman and Worse should have anything in common with the mushroom houses of the town was to him quite unbearable. In the end, the will of the elder prevailed; the ship was built of their own materials, in their own ship-yard, and by the workmen who from generation to generation had worked for Garman and Worse.

When Gabriel reached the point from which he could see down into the bay on which lay the property of Sandsgaard, the ship was the first thing which caught his eye. She stood on the slip below the house, and he could not help remarking the beauty of her bow, and the elegant rake of her stern. It was the dinner-hour, and all the workmen were either at home, in the cottages which stretched along the west side of the bay, or lay asleep among the shavings. As he stood on the crest of the rising ground, which sloped gradually down towards the buildings, and gazed at all these dominions, which from time out of mind had belonged to Garman and Worse, Gabriel became more and more out of spirits.

There lay the old-fashioned house, with white painted walls, and its blue slate roof, which was adorned by dormers and gables. In front of the house, on its southern side, lay the garden, with its paths and clipped hedges, and the little pond half overgrown by sedge and thick bushes. On the northern side, towards the sea, he could discern the carriage drive, and the extensive level yard with the ancient lime tree standing in the middle of it. Beyond that came four warehouses standing in a row, all painted yellow, with brown doors; and further on still, close down to the innermost curve of the bay, was the building-yard. Higher up, on the road which led to the southward along the coast, lay the farm, as it was called. This consisted of a byre, the bailiff's house, and other buildings; for the property of Sandsgaard was extensive, and comprised a mill, a dairy, and such like.

That part of the property had never had much interest for Gabriel, but all the same, if he had only been allowed to be a farmer, he could have turned his attention to agriculture, and still have been near the counting-house, the ships, and the sea; but he was destined for the university, and there was no possibility of escape.

It was not easy to persuade Consul Garman. His father had brought up his elder son to the business, and sent the younger to the university, and he was determined to do the same. The thought sometimes occurred to the wilful Gabriel, that Uncle Richard had had but a poor return from his university career, but he did not dare to express his thoughts openly.

Mrs. Garman believed firmly that it was most desirable, as a cure for self-will, that a young man should battle against his inclinations; nothing could be more baneful than pampering the flesh. No help, then, was to be expected from any quarter.

Gabriel was sauntering down the alley, quite crestfallen under his heavy burden of books, when at some distance his eye caught sight of some one on horseback, whom he soon recognized, and who was coming along the road behind the farm. It was Uncle Richard on Don Juan.

Gabriel started off at once, forgetting in a moment his heavy burden of books and care, and thinking only on the merriment and good cheer which Uncle Richard always brought with him. He determined to hasten off to the kitchen to tell Miss Cordsen, and then to go in to his father; for Gabriel knew well that the bearer of the news of his uncle's arrival was always welcome.

"Lord save us!" cried Miss Cordsen. "Make up the fire, Martha;" and off she ran to get a clean cap.

"All right, my boy!" said Consul Garman, giving Gabriel a friendly nod.

Gabriel was well pleased at the effect of his intelligence. He had actually surprised Miss Cordsen into an impropriety, in which he seldom succeeded; and his father, who was generally undemonstrative, had greeted him with more than usual warmth.

The young Consul, as he was generally called from the time when his father, the old Consul, was alive, was not so tall as his younger brother, and while the latter had grown stouter in the course of years, the former seemed to have got thinner and smaller. His hair was smooth, thin, and slightly grey, carefully brushed so as to make the most of it. His eyes were keen, and of a light blue colour; and his lower jaw was somewhat prominent. Smoothly shaved and well brushed, with stiff white neckcloth, shining boots, and silver-headed cane, there was something about his whole appearance which told of prosperity. Every word, every movement, even the peculiarly characteristic one with which he adjusted his chin in his stiff neckcloth, was the picture of propriety and precision. Precision was, in fact, a word which seemed made for the young Consul; both his appearance and his career reflected it to the uttermost fibre.

With his extensive business and large fortune, Consul Garman had also inherited a boundless admiration and respect for his father, Morten W. Garman, the old Consul, who had come into the property of Sandsgaard at a time when it was of little value, and considerably encumbered by debts, and when the business itself was in rather a confused condition. In order to keep the business afloat during the disastrous years of the war, Morten W. Garman took into partnership a rich old skipper, by name Jacob Worse, from whence sprang the name of the firm. Thanks to old Worse's money, life came again into the tottering business, and Garman's great ability made the firm, in a few years, one of the most important on the west coast. But when old Worse died, and his son took his place in the firm, it was soon evident that Morten Garman and young Worse would not be able to work together. Under a friendly arrangement, therefore, Worse retired with a considerable fortune, while Garman retained the business and the old family property of Sandsgaard.

It was from that time that the great wealth of the Garmans really dated, while Worse in a few years squandered his money and died insolvent.

It was whispered that Worse had left the business rather hastily, just as the good times were beginning, but that was the usual luck of the Garmans.

At first it looked as if Worse's widow and son, who carried on a small business in the town, would work themselves up again, and this was especially the case in recent years. Whatever might be the opinion as to the arrangement between Garman and Worse, no one could ever accuse Morten Garman of any want of straightforwardness in his business arrangements; and his son Christian Frederick followed closely in his steps, observing always the maxim, "What would father have done under the circumstances?"

All went on thus prosperously and uniformly, until the young Consul began to get old, and his elder son Morten came home from abroad and became a partner in the firm. From that time many changes showed themselves. The son had his head full of new foreign ideas; he was all for rushing about, writing and telegraphing, ordering and counter-ordering--a course of action that was quite foreign to Garman and Worse's mode of procedure.

"Let them come to us," said the Consul.

"No, my dear father," answered Morten. "Don't you see that the times are leaving you behind? It's of no use in these days to sit still; you must keep your eyes open, or else run the risk of losing the best of the business, and get nothing but just the residue."

Morten so far prevailed that the Consul was at length obliged to let him set up an office in the town, but under his own name; for Garman and Worse were still to be found only at Sandsgaard, and there those who wished to do business with the firm had to betake themselves.

Meanwhile a considerable amount of business passed through Morten's office in the town. This did not altogether please the Consul, but he felt bound to uphold his son, which was what his father had always done, and the firm thus became mixed up in many transactions which the father would never have cared to enter upon.

To the clerks the young Consul was a being of quite another sphere. Every head was bowed to him whenever he passed through the office, and each one seemed to feel that the cold blue eyes penetrated everything and everywhere--books, accounts, and letters, even into their own private secrets. It was believed that he knew every page in the ledger, and that he could quote intricate accounts, column by column, and if there was even the slightest irregularity to be found anywhere, they would wager that it could not escape the young Consul's eye. The general conviction was, that if every creditor of the firm, or even the devil himself, should some day take it into his head to come into the office, there would not be found even the slightest error in one of the ponderous and well-bound account books.

There was, however, one account which was a sealed book to them all, and that was the one of Richard Garman. No mortal eye had ever seen it. Some thought it might possibly be in the Consul's own red book; others thought that no such thing existed. True it was undoubtedly, that the chief carried on personally all the correspondence with his brother; and, wonderful to relate, these letters were never copied. This was food for much speculation among the clerks, and at last they came to the conclusion that the young Consul did not wish any one to know in what relation Richard Garman stood to the firm.

One thing was plain, and confirmed by long experience, and that was, that the Consul attached great importance to the letters that came from his brother. He read them before the rest of the post, and if any one happened to come in when he was thus engaged, he always covered the correspondence with a sheet of paper. One of the younger clerks once asserted that he had seen a bill of exchange in one of the aforesaid letters, but the statement found but little credence in the office; for it was a recognized fact that not one single paper existed which bore Richard Garman's signature. Another story, which was even less worthy of credit, was one told by the office messenger, who stated that one day he had brought a letter from Bratvold, and that as he came in with the portfolio he had found the young Consul standing by the key-drawer, with a letter in one hand and two bills of exchange in the other, quite red in the face, and apparently bent double, as if he was on the point of choking. The messenger thought at first that it was a fit, but it was plain to the meanest understanding that there was not a word of truth in the story, for the messenger had the audacity to aver that he had heard the young Consul give vent to a short but unmistakable laugh. There was plainly a misapprehension some-where; every one knew that the young Consul was unable to laugh.

CHAPTER IV.

When Gabriel had shut the door after announcing his uncle's arrival, the Consul got up and went off to the key-drawer, from whence he took a gigantic key, to which was attached a wooden label black with age. He then brushed his coat, and, after adjusting his chin in his neckcloth and arranging his scanty locks, left the office.

The house was large and old fashioned, with long passages and broad staircases. In the western wing were the offices, having a separate entrance on the side towards the sea. On the southern side, and overlooking the garden, were the bedrooms of the family, and the apartments which were generally used as sitting-rooms.

The second floor consisted entirely of reception-rooms, which were so arranged as to have the large ballroom in the middle, with *salons* at the side. In one of these rooms the family generally dined on Sunday, or when they had guests, and it was the small *salon* at the north-west corner, looking over the building-yard and the sea, in which the dinner was usually served.

On the third floor, or, more correctly, in the garrets, was an endless number of spare rooms, whose windows looked out of the quaint dormers which embellished the roof.

The furniture was mostly of mahogany, now dark with age, while chairs and sofas were covered with horsehair. Against the walls stood tall dark presses, and mirrors with the glass in two pieces, and having their gilded frames adorned with urns and garlands. The rooms were lit by old-fashioned chandeliers and girandoles.

The Consul met one of the servants in the passage. "Has Mr. Garman arrived?"

"Yes, sir; and he has gone upstairs, to my mistress," answered the girl.

When the weather was warm, Mrs. Garman usually preferred one of the airy rooms upstairs. She was a very fat lady, who lived in a continual state of strife with dyspepsia. From whatever side you looked at her, she presented a succession of smoothly rounded curves covered with shining black silk.

It was wonderful that Mrs. Garman got so stout; it must have been, as she herself said, "a cross" she had to bear. She seemed to eat very little at her meals, and could not control her astonishment at the appetites of the rest of the company. Only at times, when she was alone in her room, she seemed to have a fancy for some little delicacy, and Miss Cordsen used to bring her a little bit of just what happened to be handy.

When the Consul entered her room, his wife was sitting on the sofa, engaged in conversation with her brother-in-law.

"How are you? how are you, Christian Frederick?" said Richard, gaily. "Here I am again!"

"You are welcome, Richard. I am charmed to see you," answered the Consul, keeping his hands behind his back.

Richard seemed quite confused, as he generally was when he met his brother, who sometimes could be as gay and cheerful as when they were boys, and at others would put on his business manner, and be cold, repellant, and so abominably precise.

"Is any one coming to dinner to-day, Caroline?" asked Consul Garman.

"Pastor Martens has announced his kind intention of introducing the new school inspector to us," answered the lady.

"Yes, I dare say, another of your parson friends," said the Consul, drily; "then, I'll just send the coachman with the carriage for Morten and Fanny, and ask them to bring some young people with them: they might find Jacob Worse, perhaps."

"What for?" answered the lady, in a tone which showed an inclination to dispute the proposition.

"Because neither Richard nor I care to have our dinner with nothing but a lot of parsons," answered the Consul, in a tone which brought his wife to her senses. "And will you be so kind as to arrange with Miss Cordsen about the dinner?"

"Oh! the dinner, the dinner!" sighed Mrs. Garman, as she left the room. "I cannot understand how people can think so much about such trifles."

Uncle Richard followed his sister-in-law to the door, and when he turned round after making his most polite bow, he saw his brother standing in the middle of the room, with his legs far apart, and one hand behind his back. With the other he held up the monster key like an eyeglass before his eye, and through it he regarded his brother with a knowing look.

"Do you know that?" asked the Consul.

"*Mais oui!*" answered Richard, in a tone which showed his delight at finding his brother in a mood which betokened a visit to the wine-cellar.

The two old gentlemen went off arm-in-arm, until they reached the top of the kitchen stairs. At the kitchen door they stopped, and the Consul called for the lights. A commotion was heard inside, and in a few seconds Miss Cordsen appeared with two ancient candlesticks.

Each took his own light--they never made any mistake as to which was which--and descended the stairs which led to the dark cellar. They first arrived at a large outer cellar, where it was comparatively light, in which were stored the wines which were in ordinary use, such as St. Julien, Rhine wine, Graves, and brandy. This was all under the charge of Miss Cordsen, who, in accordance with the *régime* which had come down from the old Consul's time, produced the different wines according to the number and importance of the guests. In the darkest corner of the cellar there was an old keyhole, only known to the Consul, but he could find it in the dark. All the same, both of them held out their lights to look for it, and the young Consul never omitted to remark upon the clever way in which his father had concealed the secret door.

The key turned twice in the lock with a rusty sound, which the brothers could distinguish from any other sound in the world, and an atmosphere redolent of wine and mould met them as they entered. The Consul shut the door, and said, "There now, the world will have to get on without us for a little while." The inner wine-cellar looked as if it were considerably older than the house itself, and the groined roof had a resemblance to the cloister of an old monastery. It was so low that Richard had to bend his head a little, and even the Consul felt inclined to stoop when he was down there.

In the old bins lay bottles of different shapes covered with dust and cobwebs, and in the recess of what had been a grated window, but was now walled up on the outside, there stood two old long-stemmed Dutch glasses, while in one corner there lay a large wine-cask. In front of the cask was placed an empty tub, between an armchair without a back, and from the seat of which the horsehair was protruding, and an ancient rocking-horse that had lost its rockers.

The brothers put down their lights on the bottom of the tub, and took off their coats, which they hung each on their own peg.

"Well, what's it to be to-day?" said Christian Frederick, rubbing his hands.

"Port wouldn't be bad," suggested Richard, examining the bin.

"Port wine would be first-rate," answered the Consul, holding out his light. "But look, there's a row of bottles lying in here that we have never tried. I should like to know what they are."

"I dare say it is some of my grandmother's raspberry vinegar," suggested Richard.

"Nonsense! Do you suppose father would have hidden away raspberry vinegar in this cellar?"

"Perhaps he was as fond of old things as some other people I know," answered Richard.

"You always are so sarcastic," muttered the Consul. "I wish we could get at these bottles."

"You'll have to creep in after them, Christian Frederick. I am too stout."

"All right," answered his brother, taking off his watch and heavy bunch of seals. And the old gentleman crept into the bin with the utmost care. "Now I've got one," he cried.

"Take two while you are about it."

"Yes; but you will have to take hold of my legs and pull me out."

"*Avec plaisir!*" answered Richard. "But won't you have a drop of Burgundy before you come out?"

There must have been some joke hidden in the question, for the Consul began to laugh; but before long he stammered out, "I am choking, Dick; will you pull me out, you fiend?"

The joke about the Burgundy was as follows. Once when the young Consul had crept in among the bottles, to look for something very particular, he managed to knock his head against one which lay in the rack above so hard that it broke, and the whole bottle of Burgundy ran down his neck. Every time any allusion was made to this mishap, a meaning smile passed between the brothers, and Richard was even so careless as sometimes to allude to it when others were present. For instance, if they were sitting at dinner, and the conversation turned upon red wines, he would say, "Well, my brother has his own peculiar way of drinking Burgundy;" and then would follow a series of mysterious allusions and laughter between the two, which usually ended in a fit of coughing.

The young people had several times tried to get at this joke about the Burgundy, but always in vain. Miss Cordsen, who had been obliged that day to get a clean shirt for the Consul, was the only one in the secret; but Miss Cordsen could hold her tongue about more serious matters than that.

At last the Consul came out again, laughing and sputtering, his waistcoat covered with dust, and his hair full of cobwebs. When they had had a good laugh over their joke--it was well the walls were so thick--Richard, on whom the duty always devolved, uncorked the first bottle with the greatest care and skill.

"H'm! h'm!" said the Consul, "that is a curious bouquet."

"I declare, the wine has gone off," said Richard, spluttering.

"Bah! right you are, Dick," said Christian Frederick, spluttering in his turn.

Uncle Richard opened the second bottle, put his nose to it, and said approvingly, "Madeira!" and in a moment the golden wine was sparkling in the old-fashioned Dutch glasses.

"Ah! that's quite another thing," said the young Consul, taking his usual place astride of the old rocking-horse.

The rocking-horse was a relic of their childhood. "They used to make everything more solid in those days," said Christian Frederick; and when some years previously the horse had been found amongst a lot of rubbish, the Consul had had it brought down to the cellar. For many a long year he had sat on this horse, drinking the old wine out of the same old glasses with his brother, who sat in the rickety armchair, which cracked under his weight, laughing and telling anecdotes of their boyhood. He never got such wine anywhere else, and no room ever appeared so brilliant in his eyes as the low-vaulted cellar with its two smoky lights.

"I declare, it's a shame," said the young Consul, "that you have never had your half of that cask of port. However, I will send you some wine out to Bratvold one of these days, so that you may have some, till we can get it tapped."

"But you are always sending me wine, Christian Frederick. I am sure I have had my half, and more too, long ago."

"Nonsense, Dick! I declare, I believe you keep a wine account."

"No, I am sure I don't."

"Well, if you don't, I do; and I dare say you've remarked that in your account for last year--"

"Yes; that's enough of that. Here's to your health, Christian Frederick," broke in Uncle Richard, hastily. He was always nervous when his brother began about business.

"That's a great big cask."

"Yes, it is a very big one."

And the two old gentlemen held out their lights towards it, and each of them thought, "I am glad my brother does not know that the cask is nearly empty;" for it returned a most unpromising sound when it was struck, and the patch of moisture beneath it showed that it had evidently been leaking for many years.

At the end of the bottle, they got up and clinked their glasses together. They then took each his bottle of Burgundy for dinner, hung their coats on their arms, and went up into the daylight. It was strictly forbidden for any one to meet them when they came out of the cellar, and Miss Cordsen had trouble enough to keep the way clear. They presented a most extraordinary spectacle, especially the precise Christian Frederick, coming up red and beaming, in their shirtsleeves, covered with dust, and each carrying his bottle and his light.

An hour later they met at the dinner-table--Richard, trim and smart as usual, with his conventional diplomatic smile; the Consul precise, haughty, and correct to the very tips of his fingers.

CHAPTER V.

Dinner was served in the small room on the north side of the house, and the company assembled in the two so-called Sunday-rooms, which looked over the garden.

Mrs. Garman always dressed in black silk, but to-day she was more shining and ponderous than usual. She had been looking forward to a nice quiet little dinner with Pastor Martens and the new school inspector; and now here came a whole posse of worldly minded people. Mrs. Garman was thus not in the best of tempers, and Miss Cordsen had to display all her tact. But Miss Cordsen had had long practice, for Mrs. Garman had always been difficult to manage, especially of late years since "religion had come into fashion," as the careless Uncle Richard declared.

Mrs Garman did not really manage her own house; everything went on without change, according to the immutable rules which had come down from the old Consul's time, and she very soon gave up the attempt to bring in new ideas, according to her own pleasure. But now, since she was as it were without any positive influence, she contented herself with saying "No" to everything that she observed the others wished to do. In this way she acquired a kind of negative authority, for although her "No" did not always prevail, it still seemed to give her a right to show her annoyance, by meeting it with an expression full of unmerited suffering and Christian forbearance.

It was thus, with this expression, that Mrs. Garman was listening to Mr. Aalbom, the tall assistant master, who was holding forth about the delicacy and effeminacy of the rising generation. Mrs. Aalbom sat by the window, pretending to listen to the Consul, who was describing with great clearness, and in carefully chosen language, how the garden had been arranged in his late father's time. But the lady was in reality listening to her husband, for whom she had a most unbounded admiration. Mrs. Aalbom was extremely tall, lean, bony, and angular; her lips were thin, and her teeth long and yellow.

The pastor and the carriage from the town had not yet arrived. The Consul's only daughter, Rachel, was standing by the old-fashioned stove, talking merrily with Uncle Richard, and as the door opened, and the pastor and the new inspector entered the room, she was laughing still more gaily, and her mother gave her a reproving look.

As this was Mr. Johnsen's first visit to Sandsgaard, Mr. Martens took him round and introduced him to each guest in succession, beginning with the ladies. When they came to the fireplace, Uncle Richard received them with his usual affability; but Rachel only gave a momentary glance at the new acquaintance, and, almost without turning her head, continued her conversation with her uncle. To her astonishment, however, she remarked that the strange gentleman still remained standing by her side, and, raising her calm blue eyes, she looked fixedly at him. What followed was for her most unusual: she was obliged to withdraw her glance, for, contrary to her expectation, she did not find Mr. Johnsen shy, awkward, and impressed with the strange surroundings. It was plain, however, that he was conscious that his behaviour was unconventional, but he did not therefore desist. This caused Rachel to lose somewhat of her usual self-possession.

"Have you been on the west coast before?" said Uncle Richard, coming to her assistance.

"Never," replied the young man; "all I have as yet seen of the sea has been Christiana Fjord."

"And what do you think of our scenery?" continued the old gentleman. "I have no doubt that you have already seen some of the finest views in the neighbourhood."

"It has made a deep impression on me," answered Mr. Johnsen; "but Nature here is so grand and so impressive as to make one feel insignificant in its presence."

"Perhaps you find it too dull here?" said Rachel, a little disappointed.

"Oh no, not exactly that," replied he, quietly. "The idea I wished to convey is that Nature here has something--how shall I express it?--something exacting about it, by which one seems, as it were, impelled to activity, to perform some deed which will make a mark in the world."

She looked at him with astonishment; but her uncle said good-humouredly--

"For my part, I find our desolate and weather-beaten coast tends rather to lead the mind to meditation and thought than to excite it to activity."

"When I come to your years," answered Mr. Johnsen, "and have done something in the world, I dare say I shall look upon life as you do."

"I hope not," sighed Uncle Richard, half smilingly and half sadly. "As to having done anything, I--"

At that moment the door opened and young Mrs. Garman entered the room. She looked so lovely that all eyes were turned upon her. Her French grey silk with its pink trimmings had a cut quite foreign to those parts, and it was difficult to look at her or her toilette without feeling that both were out of the common in that society.

But the first glance told that the beautifully fitting dress, and the graceful and bright-eyed woman who wore it, were well suited to each other; and as she stepped lightly across the room and gave a sprightly nod to her uncle, there was a natural ease about her gait and manner which contrasted favourably with the self-consciousness with which young ladies exhibit themselves and their smart dresses when first entering into society.

"I declare, she has got another new one!" muttered Mrs. Aalbom.

"Mais, mon Dieu, comme elle est belle!" whispered Uncle Richard, enchanted.

After Fanny followed the short but active-looking Mr. Delphin, secretary to the resident magistrate, then Jacob Worse, and lastly Morten Garman.

Morten was tall and stoutly built. It would appear that he had inherited something of his mother's "cross," which did not, however, seem to oppress him. He had a good-looking face, which was, however, rather weak; and his eyes were too prominent and slightly bloodshot.

George Delphin had been about six months in the town, as secretary to the magistrate, and since Fanny Garman was the magistrate's daughter, Delphin soon got an *entrée* into the Garmans' house, and was a frequent guest at Sandsgaard. Morten had picked him up at his father-in-law's office, when the carriage was sent to the town to find the young people; they had met Jacob Worse accidentally, and Fanny had called to him when they were already seated in the carriage.

Morten had no great liking for Jacob Worse, although they had been much thrown together in their boyhood. Consul Garman, on the other hand, was particularly well disposed towards him, and there were some who maintained that the young Consul would gladly have the name of Worse back in the firm, perhaps as his son-in-law; who could tell?

But those who had an opportunity of closer observation declared that there was no truth in the story. Rachel herself appeared to dislike Jacob Worse, and Mrs. Garman could not bear the sight of him, since Pastor Martens had assured her that he was a freethinker.

The Consul took in Mrs. Aalbom, and George Delphin was so fortunate as to get Fanny Garman. Rachel, to his astonishment, turned to her uncle and said, "I beg pardon, but I am going to ask you to-day to give me up to our new acquaintance. Mr. Johnsen, will you be so kind?"

He offered her his arm stiffly, but not awkwardly, and they followed the others into the dining-room.

"What can be up with Rachel?" muttered Morten to Worse; "she generally can't bear these parsons of mother's."

Jacob Worse made no reply, but, with a polite bow, gave his arm to Miss Cordsen.

For the *habitués* of the house, it was not difficult to foresee what the *menu* would be. It consisted of Julienne soup, ham, and pork cutlets with *sauer kraut*; then roast lamb and roast veal, served with chervil and beet-root; and lastly, meringues and Vanilla cream.

At the head of the table the conversation was mostly carried on between Mr. Aalbom and Delphin, both of whom came from the neighbourhood of Christiania, and Aalbom tried his best to induce the other to say something disparaging of the west coast and its surroundings. This he did in the hope that it would cause annoyance to the Consul and his brother, and also that it would put the speaker, as a new guest at Sandsgaard, in an unfavourable light. Delphin was, however, too quick for him. Either he noticed his intention, or else he really meant what he said. The scenery, he declared, was most interesting, and he was particularly pleased with the acquaintances he had hitherto made in the neighbourhood.

Richard Garman had his usual place on the left of the Consul, who sat at the head of the table, and, leaning over beyond Rachel and Mr. Aalbom, who sat next to him, and raising his glass to the new school inspector, he said--

"As you are of the same opinion as Mr. Delphin with regard to our scenery, I hope you will also receive the same favourable opinion of our society. May I have the honour of drinking your health?"

The Consul regarded his brother with some astonishment. It was seldom that he took much notice of the young people who came to the house, especially if they belonged to the Church.

"Well, you see," whispered Uncle Richard, "I don't think this one's so bad."

Fanny also noticed the attention that was shown to the new guest, who sat opposite to her, and, glancing at him, thought he might prove not interesting. True, he was not so refined as Delphin, nor so good looking as Worse, but still her eyes often wandered in his direction. Neither Worse, who sat on her right hand, nor Delphin, who was on her left, had much attraction for her. Worse, although perfectly polite, paid her but little attention; and that Delphin was at her feet was only natural--it was a fate that, without exception, had befallen all her father's secretaries since her girlhood.

Mr. Johnsen was now drawn into the conversation. Delphin met him at first with an air of superiority, but after receiving a few cutting answers, he was glad to draw in his horns and become more affable. Aalbom, on the contrary, did not change his manner so readily. He was annoyed that Delphin had not fallen into the trap he had laid for him, and was now eager to break a lance with the new guest. He began his attack on the inspector in a half-respectful, half-jesting tone, and with the greater gusto because he knew the aversion which the two Mr. Garmans had to the clergy generally, and Mrs. Carman was deep in conversation with Pastor Martens, who was sitting beside her at the other end of the table.

"I dare say you expect a rich harvest out here, now that there is so much religious excitement," said Aalbom, with a grin to the others.

"Harvest?" asked Johnsen, shortly.

"Or draught of fishes; I don't know under which simile you prefer to regard your calling," replied Aalbom.

"I regard my calling very much in the same light as you do yours. We are both here to teach the young, and I prefer to see my duty plain before my eyes without any simile," answered Johnsen, quietly; but there was something in his voice which rather disconcerted his opponent.

Fanny and Delphin could not restrain a slight laugh; and Mrs. Aalbom muttered, "To think of answering a man in my husband's position in that way!"

The Consul now endeavoured to give a peaceable direction to the conversation, by consulting Johnsen on several matters relating to the National School. Mr. Garman had been for some years chairman of the school committee; for Sandsgaard was included within the limits of the town, although it was situated at a considerable distance from it.

Rachel heard with pleasure the terse and forcible answers which her neighbour gave to the Consul's questions. She was especially pleased to hear the new inspector insist upon certain changes being made in the school, and upon an increase of expenditure, which her father thought unnecessary and altogether too lavish.

It was not often Rachel had met a man who showed such power and energy as their young guest, and each time he spoke as to the necessity of something or another being done for the school, she could not help looking half disdainfully at Delphin, who was now quite taken up with teaching Fanny a trick with a piece of cork and two forks. But when her eye fell on Jacob Worse, an inquiring expression seemed to come over her face, to which, however, he appeared to pay little attention. He was quite occupied in talking half jestingly with old Miss Cordsen.

Ever since Jacob Worse had begun to be a constant guest at Sandsgaard, quite a friendship had sprung up between him and the old lady. She was usually cold and reserved in her manner, but he had a particular knack of getting her into conversation, so that he became quite a favourite of hers.

Aalbom was so annoyed that he ate nearly all the beet-root, and Uncle Richard was amusing himself by quietly working him up. Gabriel, too, devoted all the time that he could spare from his dinner to staring at the master; and every time the latter looked over to that part of the table where Gabriel was sitting, by the side of Miss Corsden, the young scapegrace took up his glass and emptied it with a careless, grown-up air, which he knew would irritate his natural enemy.

Morten, who sat between Mr. Johnsen and Pastor Martens, amused himself by keeping both their glasses well filled. He paid otherwise but little attention to what went on at the table, especially as he had managed to get one of the bottles of Burgundy close by his side.

It was a still, warm day in spring, and at dessert the sun, which shone in obliquely through the two open windows, just reached as far as the table. First it was reflected from Mrs. Garman's black silk, and then shed a faint halo around Pastor Martens's blond head. The rays fell on those of the company who were sitting with their backs to the light, and, casting their shadows over the white cloth, sparkled in the polished decanters. Morten held up his glass to the light, and enjoyed its brilliancy.

"See how lovely your sister-in-law looks in the sunlight!" whispered Delphin to Fanny.

"Oh! do you really think so?" she answered.

Shortly after she told one of the maid-servants, who was waiting, to pull down the blind a little, as she did not like the glare in her eyes.

The conversation now became lively at the upper end of the table. The subject on which it turned was education. Aalbom held forth on his hobby, which was, that it was quite impossible for young people to get a proper insight into learning without the use of corporal punishment, and maintained that there would be an end of all intellectual cultivation if a limit were not placed to modern humanitarianism, which he preferred to call indulgence. His wife took the same side from conviction, and Richard Garman from mischief, while the Consul was impartial. He set the greatest store by the good old times, but still he could not help thinking that they might get on with a little less of the stick than he had experienced. Johnsen was very strong on the importance of religious instruction and home influence.

"As to home influence," broke in Mrs. Aalbom, "school and home ought to go hand-in-hand."

"Of course they ought," rejoined her husband. "If a boy is punished at school, he ought to be punished also at home."

"But then, homes are so different," said Johnsen. This was the first time he had made a remark that Rachel found rather feeble.

"Well, I don't know," cried Mrs. Aalbom, putting her head on one side and looking up to the ceiling. "It is possible to have too much of natural affection, mother's influence, home feeling, and that sort of thing."

"It entirely depends what sort of home it is, Mrs. Aalbom," broke in Jacob Worse, suddenly.

Every eye was turned upon him. He had drawn himself up, and his face was red and his eyes gleaming.

There came a slight pause in the conversation, of which the Consul availed himself, and, taking up his glass, he said, with a smile, "Now we must mind what we are about. This is not the first time I have seen Jacob Worse join in a conversation like this; and if we do not want him to make it too warm for us, we had better change the scene of action to another room, where we can carry on the conflict in the shade. So if the ladies and gentlemen are of the same opinion as myself, we had better retire."

The company broke up. Uncle Richard laughed heartily as he thanked Worse, while they were going downstairs, for having joined in so opportunely. Worse himself could not help a laugh, in which all joined, except Aalbom and his wife, who were too much annoyed to do so.

Rachel was quite astonished at the anxiety displayed by her father when Worse began to speak. She had herself once or twice heard him take part in a discussion, and had been surprised at the way in which his feelings suddenly seemed to get the better of him. There was, it is true, an originality in his views; but for all that there was no reason why he should be silent, and she thought it mean of Jacob Worse to allow himself to be put down so easily.

During dinner Pastor Martens had made several attempts to state his views on the subject, but hitherto without success. The others were too much taken up with their new and interesting guest, and besides, his neighbour fully engrossed his attention. After dinner was over, he had again to take his place beside Mrs. Garman on the sofa, while the young people went down to the croquet lawn, which was shaded by the dense avenue of limes.

Mr. Aalbom was walking up and down the broad path in front of the house, encircled by his wife's bony arm, as Mr. Delphin kindly put it, while they were waiting for coffee. He was still annoyed at his failure, and at the slights he had endured, and his wife was doing her utmost to pacify him.

"How can a man of your standing bother about such nonsense? These young upstarts will only be here for a time. They will soon make themselves unwelcome in some way or another. There is no doubt that we are considered superior to the rest. You must have noticed that the Consul took me in to dinner."

"Nonsense!" answered her husband. "What have I in common with these tradesmen and their moneybags? But for a man of my intelligence, and of my attainments in literature and education, to have to put up with such impertinent answers from a set of youngsters, from such--" and from his rich *répertoire* of abuse the master poured out a choice stream of invective, which afforded some relief to his feelings.

The Aalboms lived about half-way between Sandsgaard and the town, which had been the original cause of their being invited to the Garmans' house.

Since then they had shown themselves such good neighbours that the Garmans were generally glad to fall back upon them when they wanted to get a few people together in a hurry. Mr. Garman had also assisted the master in some unexpected difficulties he had encountered in writing a short paper on the origin of the French language, and its connection with history. The pamphlet was headed "For Use in Schools," but from want of perception and appreciation on the part of the authorities, this pearl of literature had not been taken into use in a single school in the country.

Both the elder Garmans were in the habit of retiring to their rooms and taking a short nap after dinner; but on this occasion they did not sleep long, as they were engaged in talking over Madeleine's projected visit to the town. It was arranged that she was to come in two or three days, and have a room upstairs, close by Miss Cordsen's.

Gabriel, having annexed a cigar, had wandered off to the ship-yard, in a happy and contented mood, to make an inspection of the vessel and talk English with Mr. Robson.

CHAPTER VI.

The first acquaintance Madeleine made in her new home was with the sewing-maid, for naturally there were a good many repairs of various kinds to be seen to. She had already made some acquaintance with the family by previous short visits to Sandsgaard, and the same impression of coldness which she had hitherto received from her relations still oppressed her. Not that Madeleine was of a timid nature--far from it; but the change from a free and open-air life to the regularity of a well-ordered house was too abrupt. She tried in vain to adapt herself to her new surroundings, and during the first few weeks she fretted herself quite out of health. For a reason she could scarcely define, she concealed this fact from her father when writing to him.

Her cousin Gabriel was the only person who seemed to have a friendly word for Madeleine; the others were so reserved that she could not help thinking they were selfish. With Rachel she could never get on friendly terms, and the two cousins had but little in common. Although Rachel was only a few years the elder, she was greatly superior to her cousin in knowledge and experience. Whilst Madeleine was bright and radiant as sunshine, there was something in Rachel's cold and commanding nature which betokened an uneasy longing for employment, and a desire to take an active part in whatever she could find to occupy her.

Not long previously Rachel had had a sharp dispute with her father. She came one day into the office, and desired him to give her some employment in the business. Consul Garman never lost his self-command, but on this occasion he was on the very point of doing so. The dispute was short, it is true, and soon ended, like every other conflict that was carried on against the father's principles, in a decided victory for his side; but from that time the daughter became still more cold and reserved in her manner.

It was a light task for Rachel to read her little country cousin through and through, and when she made up her mind that Madeleine had nothing in her except perhaps some undefined longings, but at the same time no real desire for work, she let her go her own way, and the relation between them became almost that of a child to a grown person--friendly, but without intimacy.

Mrs. Garman was not particularly well disposed towards her new guest, because she had not been originally consulted as to her visit; and even the good-natured Miss Cordsen frightened Madeleine at first, with her tall, spare figure and well-starched cap-strings.

The sewing-maid was a pale, weakly creature, with large wondering eyes which wore a deprecatory expression. She was still pretty, but the first look told that her face had once been still prettier, and there was something stunted and faded about her appearance. Her cheeks were somewhat sunken, and it could be seen that she had lost some of her teeth.

During the first few days Madeleine had to spend much of her time with the sewing-maid, for Mrs. Garman was anxious that her dress should be in keeping with the rest of the establishment, and the Consul had given Miss Cordsen strict orders on the subject. It was a great relief to Madeleine, in her loneliness, to show herself kindly and almost affectionately disposed towards the timid girl. One evening when she had gone, Madeleine asked Miss Cordsen who she was, and the old lady, after scrutinizing her sharply, answered, "that Marianne was a granddaughter of old Anders Begmand, and that some years before she had had a baby. Her sweetheart," said Miss Cordsen, fixing her eyes again sharply on Madeleine, "had gone to America, and the child was dead, and as she had been in service at Sandsgaard, the Garmans had had her taught dressmaking, so that now she had constant employment in the house."

This was all Madeleine found out, and she did not ask any more questions on the subject, which was a relief to Miss Cordsen.

The old lady's story was, however, not Strictly correct in its details; a secret of the Garman family was hid in the sempstress's history--a secret which Miss Cordsen concealed with the greatest jealousy.

As Marianne went home that evening this event came into her thoughts; it was, in fact, never entirely absent from them. The bright and friendly manner of Madeleine, who was so unlike the rest of her family, had awoke in her many reminiscences. She felt quite sure that Madeleine did not as yet know all her history; it was impossible that she could know it, for she seemed so kindly disposed towards her, and Marianne dreaded that any one should tell her. There were, indeed, plenty of people who could tell her story, but none knew what she had suffered. As she went on her way all the sad events of her life's misfortune seemed to pass in review before her. Her first thought was, how handsome he looked when he came home from abroad, before there was any talk about his marriage with the magistrate's daughter! how long he had prayed and tormented her, and how long she had striven against him; and then came the dreadful day, when she had been called into the Consul's private office. She never could imagine how any one had found it out; the only one who could know anything was Miss Cordsen: but still less could she now understand how she had allowed herself to be talked over, and compelled to agree to what had since been arranged. There must be truth in what people said, that it was impossible to resist the young Consul, and so she allowed herself to be betrothed to Christian Kusk, one of the worst men she knew, who shortly after went to America; then the child was born, and was christened Christian. Then again she recalled that night when the child died; but all further impressions became indistinct and hazy as mist. She had hoped that her shame might kill her, but it had only tortured her. To Sandsgaard, where she had vowed never again to set her foot, she now went daily. Whenever she chanced to meet one of the family, and especially Fanny, her heart seemed to cease beating; but they passed her with as much unconcern as if they knew nothing, or as if she had nothing to do with them.

Many a time also she had met him. At first they passed each other hurriedly, but after a time he also seemed to have forgotten, and now he greeted her with a friendly nod, and the well-known voice said, "How are you, Marianne?"

It was as if these people lived surrounded by a thick wall of indifference, against which her tiny existence was shattered like fragile glass.

Marianne took a short cut through the ship-yard, where the carpenters were busy dividing the shavings and putting them into sacks. She found her grandfather, who had finished his work in the pitch-house, and they set off homewards together.

Anders Begmand lived in the last of the little red-painted cottages which lay below the steep slope on the western side of the bay of Sandsgaard. The road along the shore was only a footpath leading to the door of each cottage, and then on to the next. Seaweed and half-decayed fish refuse lay on the shore, while at the back of the houses were heaps of kitchen refuse, and other abominations. The path itself consisted of a row of large stones, on which people had to walk if they wished to keep out of the accumulation of dirt. The houses were mostly crowded, but especially so in the winter, when the sailors were home from sea.

They were all in the employ of Garman and Worse, and the firm owned everything they possessed, even to their boats, their houses, and the very ground under their feet. When the boys grew old enough, they went to sea in one of the vessels belonging to the firm, and the brightest of the girls were taken into service, either at the house or at the farm. Otherwise the cottagers were left pretty much to themselves. They paid no rent, and there was no interference on the part of the firm with the "West End," which was the name by which the little row of cottages was generally known amongst the workpeople.

Anders Begmand's house was both the last and the smallest, but now that he was alone with his two grandchildren, Marianne and Martin, he did not require much room. Before, when his wife was alive, and they had three grown-up sons at home, one of whom was married, it was often close work enough; but now all were dead and gone. The wife lay in the churchyard, and the sons in the deep sea.

Anders was an old man, bent by age. His curly white hair covered his head like a mop, and stood out under his flat cap, which looked more like the clot of pitch it really almost was, than anything else. In his youth Anders had made one voyage to the Mediterranean, in the *Family Hope*, but he had then been discharged; for he had a failing, and that was--he stammered. Sometimes he could talk away without any hesitation, but if the stammering once began, there was nothing for it but to give up the attempt for that time. There he would stand, gasping and gasping, till he got so enraged that he nearly had a fit. When he was young it was dangerous to go near him at such times, for the angrier he got the more he stammered, and the more he stammered the more his anger increased. There was only one way out of it, and that was by singing; and so whenever anything of more than usual importance refused to come out, he was obliged to sing his intelligence, which he did to a merry little air he always used on these occasions. It was said that he had to sing when he proposed to his wife, but whether there was any truth in the statement is not quite clear. It was certain, however, that he did not often have to sing, and woe to any one who dared to say, "Sing, Anders." This was, of course, when he was young; he was now so broken down that any one could say what they liked to him. There was, therefore, no longer any pleasure in teasing him, and he was allowed to go in peace. Among the workmen he was held in the greatest respect, not only because he had been in the shop for more than fifty years, but because he had had so much sorrow in his old age, and especially because of the misfortune of Marianne, who was the apple of his eye and the light of his life. Martin, too, had brought him nothing but trouble: he was quite hopeless, and the captain with whom he had returned on his last voyage had complained of him, and refused to take him out again; so now he stayed at home, drinking and getting into mischief.

The evening was dull and rainy, and a light already shone in the cottage as Begmand and Marianne approached.

"There they are, drinking again," said she.

"I believe they are," answered Begmand.

She went to the window, the small panes of which were covered with dew, but she knew one which had a crack in it, through which she could look.

"There they are, all four of them," whispered Marianne. "You'll have to sit there, in front of the kitchen door, grandfather."

"Yes, child; yes!" answered the old man.

When they entered the room, there was a pause in the conversation, which was carried on by four men who sat drinking round the table. They had not long begun, and were only in the first stage of harmless elevation.

Martin greeted them in a cheerful tone, which he thought would hide his guilty conscience. "Good evening, grandfather. Good evening, Marianne, Come, let me offer you a drop of beer."

The thick smoke from the freshly lighted pipes still lay curling over the table, and round the little paraffin lamp without a globe. On the table were tobacco, glasses, matches, and half-empty bottles, while on the bench stood several full ones awaiting their fate.

Tom Robson, who sat opposite the door, lifted the large mug which had been standing between him and his friend Martin, and, with his hand on his heart, began to sing--

"Oh, my darling! are you here,
Marianne I love so dear?"

He had composed this couplet himself, in honour of Marianne, to the great annoyance of the hungry-looking journeyman printer who sat in the corner close by him.

Gustaf Oscar Carl Johan Torpander was a most remarkable Swede, inasmuch as he did not drink; but otherwise there was about him that exaggerated air of politeness, and that imitation of French manners, which seems generally to attach to the shady individuals of that nation. He had risen when Marianne came into the room, and was now making a low bow, with his shoulders, and especially the left one, well over his ears. His head was on one side, and he kept his eyes the whole time fixed on the young girl. While Tom Robson was singing his poetry, the Swede shook his head with a sympathetic smile to Marianne, by which he meant to express his regret that they met in such bad company.

The fourth person of the group was sitting with his back to the door, and did not move, for he was deaf; but when at length the Swede, who was still bowing, attracted his attention, he turned round heavily on his chair and nodded deafly to the new-comers. This person's real name had almost disappeared from the memory of man, for he had been nicknamed "Woodlouse" among his acquaintance. Mr. Woodlouse passed his time in a dingy den in the magistrate's office, where he either slept or occupied himself in sorting documents and papers. But there he had grown to be almost a necessity, for he had the special gift of knowing the contents of every paper, and the name of every single person who for years had sought information at the office. He could stand in the middle of the room and point to the different shelves, and say, apparently without effort, what each contained, and what was missing. He had thus gone down as a kind of living inventory from magistrate to magistrate, and as his special knowledge increased he endeavoured to get his salary raised, so that he might give himself up recklessly to his two ruling passions, which were drinking beer and reading novels at night.

As Marianne went through the room she moved her grandfather's chair close to the kitchen door, and gave him a meaning look. He nodded to show that he understood her wishes. She then said good night to the old man, and went into the kitchen, from whence a little dark staircase led upstairs to her room.

Marianne locked her door and went to bed. She was so tired every night that she could scarcely keep her eyes open while she undressed, and she fell asleep the moment she got into bed. Under her the noise of voices continued, varied by quarrelling and cursing, which mingled with the dreams of her heavy and broken slumber. In the morning her hair and pillow were damp with perspiration; she was chilled with cold, and was even more tired than when she went to rest.

The talking soon went on again as briskly as ever. Martin related how he had been up to the office that morning, intending to speak to the young Consul personally. He wished to complain of the captain who had told tales about him.

He did not, however, get so far as the Consul, but one of the clerks, a stupid lout with an eyeglass, had come out and told him that he would get no employment on a ship belonging to the firm, until he had been to the Seamen's school, and gave up drinking. As he told his story there was an evil glare in his eyes, which were large and bright like Marianne's, but piercing and cruel. In the pale face there was also the same trace of weakness as in his sister's; but Martin was tall and bony, and his arms were strong and powerful, and he gesticulated with them as he talked, and gave force to his words by striking the table with his fist. He became every moment more violent, as he got heated by drink and argument.

He was not going to the school to please Garman and Worse; and as to his drinking, what had the young Consul got to do with that? But they should see what he would do. And with a mighty oath, he shook his clenched fist in the direction of Sandsgaard.

"Right you are, my boy!" cried Tom Robson, laughing; "good again. Let us see what you are made of."

Robson was never so happy as when he could get Martin to talk himself into a fury, which was not a very difficult task.

Ever since his childhood Martin had shown himself of a worthless and cross-grained nature. His character at school was, that he was one of the cleverest and at the same time the most quarrelsome among the boys, and since then he had done nothing but fall foul of everything and everybody he came in contact with. Martin did most of the talking of the four, who already began to be excited by drink. It would perhaps be more correct to say, of the three, for Torpander was not there to drink, but only to be near Marianne. Woodlouse did not say much, for he heard but little; and when Mr. Robson, who had taken on himself the duty of chairman, gave him an opportunity of speaking, Woodlouse used so many strange expressions that the others did not understand him.

Neither did Torpander do much of the talking: for him the event of the evening was Marianne's return, after which he preferred to sit in silent rapture. This afternoon, however, Torpander joined Martin in his attack on the Garmans, whom he also hated, and poured forth a lot of newspaper tirade about the tyranny of capital, and such like.

"Oh, stop that infernal Swedish jargon!" cried the chairman, "and let us hear what Woodlouse is mumbling about."

"You see, gentlemen," began Woodlouse, eagerly, "the right of the proletariat--"

"What does he mean?" shouted Martin.

Woodlouse did not hear the remark, and paused in his speech, as his eyes wandered inquiringly from one to another to see if they were listening.

But Martin could not keep silent any longer, and broke out into a volley of oaths and curses against Garman and Worse, capital, captain, and the whole world, only interrupting himself occasionally to take a drink or light his pipe over the lamp.

Old Anders had at first taken his place by the kitchen door, but that evening they seemed to be pretty quiet, and he was always anxious to hear what they said when the conversation turned upon the firm. He therefore left the door and came up to the table, where Tom Robson made room for him, and at the same time offered him a drink from his mug.

"Thanks, Mr. Robson," said Begmand, as he put the mug to his lips.

Tom Robson was not only the chairman, but at the same time the host of the company, for it was he who paid for the liquor. By his side on the bench he kept a bottle of rum, from which he every now and then poured out a glass for each. He generally put a good drop of rum into his own beer, "to kill the insects," he said. He was now occupied in cutting up some cake tobacco to fill his pipe.

"Beautiful tobacco that, Mr. Robson," said Begmand.

"Take a bit," answered Tom, good naturedly.

"Thanks, Mr. Robson," said the old man, overjoyed, as he took out his pipe, the stem of which was not more than half an inch long, while the whole was as black as everything else which belonged to Anders.

He pressed down the moist tobacco as hard as he could, in the hope of getting as much as would last for a day or two; he then picked up a burning ember from the turf fire, which he applied to the bowl.

It was no easy matter to get the tobacco to light, but the smoke, when it began to draw, seemed warm and comforting to the old man. He sat there, crouching on the edge of the bench, eagerly watching Tom each time he passed him the mug, and not forgetting to say "Thank you, Mr. Robson," before he took his drink.

Martin grew more and more violent. "Isn't it enough," he yelled, "for us to work ourselves to death for these creatures? Are they going to watch every bit we eat, and every drop we drink? Just look at their houses! look how they live up there! Who has got all that for them? We, I tell you, grandfather; we who have been toiling here fishing, and going to sea year after year, son after father, in storm and tempest, watching night after night in wind and snow, so as to bring back wealth for these wretches! Just look what we get for it all! What a pig-stye we live in! And even that does not belong to us. Nothing does! It all belongs to them--clothes, food, and drink, body and soul, house and home, every bit!"

Begmand sat rocking himself to and fro, and drawing hard at his pipe. Wood-louse saw that there was a pause, and so began again.

"Property is robbery--"

But Martin would not let him continue. "There is no one in the whole world," he shouted, "who puts up with what we do! Why don't we go up and say, 'Share with us, we who have done all the work'? There has been enough of this blood-sucking! But no; we are not a bit better than a lot of old women; not one of us! They would never put up with that sort of thing in America."

"Ha! ha! good again!" laughed Tom Robson. "I dare say you think people are willing to share like brothers in America? No, my boy; you would soon find out you were wrong."

"Do you mean to tell me that workmen in America live like we do?" asked Martin, somewhat abashed.

"No; but they do what you can't do," answered Tom.

"What do they do?" asked Martin.

"They work; and that is what you and no one else does here!" shouted Tom, bringing his fist down heavily on the table. He was beginning to feel the effects of the rum.

"What's that about work? Do you mean to say--?" began the Swede.

"Hold your jaw!" cried Tom. "Let the old un have his say!"

"You are quite wrong, Martin," said Begmand, and this time without stammering. The watery look of his old eyes told that the beer was beginning to work. "It's shameful of you to talk like that about the firm. They have given both your father and your grandfather certain employment; and you might have had the same if you had behaved yourself. The old Consul was the first man in the whole world, and the young Consul is a glorious fellow too. Here's his health!"

"Oh!" broke in Martin, "I don't know what you are talking about, grandfather. I don't see that you have got much to boast of. What about my father, and Uncle Svend, and Uncle Reinert,--every one lost in the Consul's ships; and what have you got by it all? Two empty hands, and just as much food as will keep body and soul together. Or perhaps you think," continued he, with a fiendish laugh, "that we have some connection with the family because of Marianne!"

"Martin, it's--it's--" began the old man, his face crimsoning up to the very roots of his hair, and struggling vainly with his infirmity.

"Have a drink, old un," said Tom, good naturedly, handing Begmand the mug.

The old man paused for breath. "Thanks, Mr. Robson," said he, taking a long breath.

Tom Robson made signs to the others to leave him alone. Begmand put his pipe into his waistcoat pocket, got up, and went into the little room by the kitchen, where he slept. The unwonted drink had roused again the fire of his youth, and never had he felt his helplessness so keenly as he did that evening.

The others still sat drinking till there was no more, and the lamp began to grow dim as the oil gave out. Then they staggered off; Woodlouse away through West End, while Tom clambered up a steep path that led over the hill at the back of Begmand's cottage. He lived with a widow in a small house near the farm buildings of Sandsgaard.

Torpander went with Robson, because he was afraid to go through West End alone, and because he wanted to have a last glance at Marianne's window, which looked on to the hillside.

Martin shut the door after them, and managed to lift up the lid of a sort of locker in which he was going to sleep. He did not see that there were some empty bottles on the locker, and they rolled down on the floor, and one of them was broken against the spittoon. The lid slipped out of his hand, and, without trying to undress, he let himself fall just as he was into the bedclothes.

The last remaining drop of oil in the lamp was now gone, and the last blue flame flickered up through the chimney and was quenched. Then followed a thick grey smoke, which came curling up from the still glowing wick, and wreathed itself in graceful spirals through the glass and glided out into the room, until it looked like a maze of fairy threads in the faint light from the window.

Nothing was heard but the sound of heavy breathing. The old man's respiration was short and broken, while Martin, after turning over a few times, lay quiet, and at length began to snore. Before long he started up again uneasily, heated as he was by drink and passion.

Still a little longer smouldered the red glow of the wick, while the smoke wreathed up thinner and thinner through the glass and spread itself in the darkness.

CHAPTER VII.

Fanny Garman had from the first shown herself particularly well disposed towards Madeleine, and had more than once invited her to come and pay her a visit in the town. Nothing had hitherto come of the invitation, for even Madeleine, unversed as she was in the ways of society, could see that nothing more was meant than a compliment.

One Sunday, however, Madeleine was standing before the looking-glass, only partially dressed, and with her thick dark hair hanging in curls over her shoulders. Fanny happened to pass, and caught sight of her reflection by the side of Madeleine's. She stopped and noticed the contrast. The dark hair and slightly gipsy complexion of her cousin set off her own fair skin and light hair most admirably. It is true that Madeleine was taller, and her figure rather more stately, but the face itself had only very slight pretensions to beauty. Fanny closely observed the effect as she helped Madeleine to arrange her hair, and when she had finished her observations she threw her arm round Madeleine's waist, and they left the room together.

"Listen now, my dearest Madeleine," began she, arching her eyebrows. "I am really very much annoyed with you, for never coming down to see us in the town. As a punishment, I shall take you with me this afternoon. Morten can sit on the box."

Madeleine looked into the small and delicate face, and could not help thinking how lovely it was. The large blue eyes looked so charmingly out through their lashes; the pose of the head was so elegant; while round the mouth played so many changing expressions, which seemed to rivet the attention when she was speaking.

"What are you staring at?" asked Fanny, mischievously.

"You really are too pretty," answered Madeleine, with sincerity.

"Well, that's a rustic compliment," laughed her cousin, turning colour a little, but looking still more charming.

Madeleine went down with them to the town, and stayed a few days; afterwards she paid short visits there more frequently. Fanny took her to the few amusements the town offered, and occasionally there were small *réunions* either in their own house, or in those of some of their acquaintances. Wherever they went the two seemed to set each other off by the wonderful contrast in their appearance, or by some coquettish similarity or difference in their toilets.

It was the rule in the Garmans' house, that any one who was staying there could do exactly as they liked. They could come or go, ride or drive, just as the fancy took them. The house was so large, and there were so many guests, and so many business acquaintances who came either to dinner or supper, that the absence of any particular person attracted but little attention. Madeleine, therefore, soon perceived that no one seemed to miss her very much if she was away. Mrs. Garman was as usual more or less peevish; and Rachel kept to herself, which Fanny maintained was because she had taken up with a new father confessor.

The Consul was the only person who seemed to care for her, and when she came back from a visit in the town, he would pat her on the head and say, "Well, my dear, I am glad to see you back again."

One day, just as she was getting into Fanny's carriage to drive down to the town, the Consul happened to pass the door.

"Are you going to run away from us again?" said he, with a friendly smile, as he passed.

Madeleine felt she had a guilty conscience, and, after much stammering and hesitation, she at last managed to ask her uncle if he did not like her to go.

"Oh no! I didn't mean that," said the Consul, as he patted her on the cheek. "I wish you always to do exactly what you like best."

As Madeleine sat in the carriage she could not help thinking that she was one of the dullest creatures on earth. How could she be so foolish as to imagine that any one in the house cared whether she were there or not? More probably she was only in the way. She could not help regretting her defective education, and a few days after, when she returned to Sandsgaard, she noticed that her uncle did not pat her on the cheek. The fact was, she did not yet quite understand her new life; everything had turned out so different to what she had expected.

When Madeleine and her friend Per had met for the last time, but few words had passed between them, but when he went down the hill towards Bratvold, she stood gazing after him till he was out of sight. She had then made a vow to keep true to him, no matter what her relations might say, and she knew well enough they would all be against her; but as she looked over the sea, she felt herself so strong and so determined, that she could not doubt her courage and her constancy to her first love.

But now, as it so turned out, her constancy was never called in question. She felt certain that a rumour of her connection with Per must have reached Sandsgaard, for she well knew that there were stories enough about her free and unrestrained life at Bratvold, and so at first she always dreaded the slightest allusion to it. She had at the same time quite made up her mind to confess openly how matters stood, and to say plainly that although he was nothing but a simple peasant and fisherman, she, Madeleine Garman, would be true to him. But in the course of conversation she could not discover even the most distant hint at her adventure; it did not even appear that anything really was known about it; her past life was, in fact, never mentioned in any way, and it seemed to be taken for granted that she could never have conducted herself otherwise than naturally became a Miss

Garman. It was this very assumption that seemed to shake her in her resolution.

Everything about Fanny's pretty and artistic house was always kept in the best of order. Old mahogany and horsehair were here quite inadmissible.

The furniture, which was mostly of carved walnut, and plush, had all come from Hamburg. *Portières* hung before the doors, and the windows and the corners of the rooms were gay with *jardinières*, and vases containing flowers and choice foliage plants; while small tables and luxurious armchairs were grouped about the room. The rooms were not large, but when all the doors stood open the general effect was very pleasing, enhanced by its china, paintings, bright carpets, and gilded mirrors.

Sandsgaard, with its large and lofty rooms, where the furniture was all arranged round the walls, was so cold and stiff that Madeleine could not help feeling she must move about noiselessly, or sit demurely in a corner. At Fanny's her feelings were very different; everything seemed so inviting; and the difficulty was to choose a seat among the many comfortable armchairs and sofas.

Morten never seemed to be perfectly at home in his own house, where his heavy form was quite out of place. Fanny took but little notice of him, and his opinion was never consulted. However, he was easy-going, and preferred to keep pretty much to himself.

Morten Garman had the reputation of being a good-natured fellow, but at the same time of not being very easy to get on with. To do business with him required the greatest circumspection; a single word might spoil everything, and if once anything upset him, it was almost impossible to get him right again. Old-fashioned people, therefore, preferred going out to Sandsgaard, and dealing with the young Consul personally; it was a slower process, but the result might be reckoned on with the greatest certainty. The young man had a habit of suddenly looking at his watch, breaking off the negotiations, getting into his carriage, and driving off to Sandsgaard or elsewhere, leaving behind him nothing but loose statements and half-concluded business.

Fanny had never troubled her husband with any demonstrative affection, and certainly never with jealousy. She understood him well enough to know that if at any time she should have occasion for his forbearance, there were quite faults enough on his side to weigh down the balance in her favour.

"There goes your admirer, Pastor Martens. Look, Madeleine, how he is eyeing us, the worthy man! He is taking off his hat.--Good morning," said Fanny, bowing, and at the same time beckoning to him to come in.

The pastor was at the other side of the narrow street, and seemed to consider a moment before he made up his mind to cross. In the mean time Fanny rang the bell and ordered chocolate. She dearly loved these morning visits, with a cup of chocolate or a glass of wine, and accordingly always kept her eye upon the street. Martens, who was the resident chaplain, was among her most frequent guests, especially since she had taken it into her head that he admired Madeleine. There was nothing remarkable that Fanny should have her attention taken up in finding a suitable *parti* for the chaplain. The whole congregation was, in fact, busy in the same direction; for Martens was a man of about thirty, not otherwise than prepossessing in appearance, and it was now more than a year and a half since he had lost his first wife, so that nothing could be more natural than that he should be thinking about another.

"Good morning, ladies; good morning, Miss Garman. I hope you are both well," said the chaplain, as he came into the room. "I could not resist your kind invitation, although I knew by experience that a visit to you is far too agreeable to be of very short duration."

"You are really too kind, Mr. Martens; and your complaisance to such a child of the world as I am, always causes me great astonishment," said Fanny, giving Madeleine a look.

"A great many people are astonished at it," answered the chaplain, not understanding her meaning.

"No, really! Who? who?" cried Fanny, curiously.

"Ah, you can scarcely understand," Martens began to explain, "to what an extent we poor clergymen are observed by the hundred eyes of our congregation; and the fact is, there are several most respectable old ladies who have taken offence at my frequent visits to Sandsgaard and to yourself."

"No! How amusing! Do listen, Madeleine!" cried Fanny, beaming.

"It's all very well for you to laugh," said the chaplain, good humouredly; "but it might be very embarrassing for me, were it not that I can rely on the support of the good dean."

"So Dean Sparre and you get on now. I was under the impression that the relation--"

"Yes, at first; only just at first. But I am not ashamed to confess that the fault was on my side. You see, when I first came I took up with some of our so-called Evangelical neighbours; respectable, worthy people, too--I should be sorry to say otherwise--but still, not exactly such--such--"

"*Comme il faut*?" suggested Fanny.

"Well," answered he, smiling, "that was not exactly the expression I was looking for; but still, you understand what I mean."

"Perfectly!" said Fanny, laughing, as she took the cup of chocolate which Madeleine had poured out for her.

"I am sorry to say I took up a false position with regard to the dean, which led to many annoyances until I learnt to know him; then everything smoothed itself down so nicely that, if I may venture to say so, the relations between us became almost that of father and son. He is an extraordinary man," repeated the chaplain several times.

"Yes, is he not?" said Fanny. "I think he is the nicest clergyman I have ever seen; and if one did not understand a word of his sermon, it would still be most edifying only to hear him read the service. Then the charming poems he writes!"

"Yes. For my part, I consider his last poem, 'Peace and Reconciliation,' the best thing of the kind that has appeared in our literature for the last ten years. Can you imagine anything more charming than the lines--

"'I sat, in silent peace of even,
    On humble bench before my cot'?"

"Was he poor once?" asked Madeleine, quickly.

Fanny laughed; but the chaplain explained, in a clear and good-natured way, that the poem had been written after Sparre had become dean, and that the cottage was merely a poetical way of expressing his great simplicity.

Madeleine felt that she had asked a foolish question, and went to the window and looked out into the street.

"Yes," continued the chaplain, "there is something about the dean I can never quite understand. I never can quite make up my mind exactly where it lies; but when you are face to face with him, you feel his power and superiority. I might almost say he seems to fascinate you. When he is made a bishop--"

"A bishop?" asked Fanny.

"Yes, indeed; there is no doubt that the dean will have the first bishopric that becomes vacant. I have heard it publicly mentioned."

"No, really! I should never have thought of it," said Fanny. "But you are quite right. Won't he look noble with his imposing figure and white hair, and the gold cross shining on his breast? It is a pity ours is not a cathedral town; a bishop is really so interesting. For instance, in 'Leonardo.' Madeleine, have you ever seen a bishop?"

Madeleine turned towards her with a deep blush on her face, as she stammered out, "What were you asking, Fanny?"

But Fanny's quick eye had already caught sight of Delphin, who was coming over from the other side of the street. She returned his bow, and, observing Madeleine closely, said to her, "Will you be so good as to go and get a cup for Mr. Delphin?"

"Is he coming in?" said the chaplain, looking for his hat.

"Yes. But I have not given you leave to go, Mr. Martens; we were getting on so nicely."

Delphin came in, and Fanny gave him a friendly nod, and continued, "Now, in your position as clergyman, you really must assist us to effect Mr. Delphin's conversion."

"No necessity! no necessity, I assure you, Mrs. Garman," said Delphin, gaily. "My conversion is already about as perfect as it can be. Mr. Johnsen and I have been conversing on the subject in a most serious manner for the last half-hour."

"We were also talking on religious subjects," said Fanny.

"Have you just left Mr. Johnsen?" asked the chaplain, who had got his hat, and was on the point of taking his leave.

"I walked with him a little way on the road to Sandsgaard. It appears that he had an invitation to go there," answered Delphin.

"To-day, again!" said Fanny.

"Good morning, ladies, good morning! No, you really must allow me. I have already been here longer than I ought. Good morning, Miss Garman."

Madeleine was just coming into the room, and the chaplain took a step towards her in order to shake her hand; but, as she was carrying the tray with the cups upon it, he was obliged to content himself with giving her a warm and respectful look. As he went downstairs, he thought how unfortunate it was that Delphin should always be coming in his way.

Severin Martens was naturally very good-natured, but Delphin was a man he could not bear. If the two got into conversation, everything seemed to go wrong for the chaplain. The other had a particular way of taking up his words, turning them into ridicule, and exciting laughter among the hearers, which was most unpleasant. The chaplain did not care very much, either, for Mr. Johnsen. That apparently helpless young man had shown that he knew how to look after himself only too well. "Invited nearly every day to Sandsgaard! Hum!" muttered Martens, as he went down the street.

No sooner had Delphin taken the clergyman's place, than the conversation changed its tone.

"Our worthy chaplain did not much like Johnsen's going to Sandsgaard," said Fanny.

"That was just the reason I mentioned it," said Delphin.

"Yes, I could see that very well. You are always so dreadfully mischievous. But can you make out what is the matter with my learned sister-in-law? Rachel, who is generally as cold and unsympathetic as an iceberg, becomes all at once quite taken up with what appears to me the most unlikely person."

"Your sister-in-law always appears attracted towards any one who shows originality."

"Well," objected the lady, "I don't see much in him; at first I thought he was rather interesting. He reminded me somewhat of Brand in Ibsen's play, or something of that sort; but really, how tiresome he is, with his short, cutting remarks, which come plump into the middle of a conversation like so many stones!"

"I am a man of the people! my place is among the people!" said Delphin, imitating Johnsen's voice and manner.

Fanny laughed, and clapped her hands. Madeleine laughed too; she could not help it when Delphin said anything amusing. It is true she liked him better when he was serious, as he was when they were alone; he had then a frank, genuine manner that she found particularly attractive. She could talk to Mr. Delphin on many subjects which she would never have had the courage to mention to others. It was plain enough--that is to Fanny, though not to Madeleine--that he always paid his visits, quite accidentally, of course, whenever Madeleine was in the town.

As they sat chatting merrily on different subjects, Fanny, who always kept her eye on passers-by, suddenly cried, "Just look! there is Jacob Worse. I declare, he is passing the house without looking up; but I saw him speak to some one at the door. I wonder who it could have been?" and, with a woman's curiosity, she hurried over to the window.

"Ah!" said she, laughing, "I declare it was my little Frederick he was talking to. Freddy," she cried, looking out of the window, "come up to mother, and you shall have some chocolate."

Little Christian Frederick, a white-haired, sturdy little fellow of between six and seven, came scrambling up the stairs. The maid opened the door for him, and his mother asked, as she poured him out some chocolate, "Who was it my Freddy was talking to downstairs there by the door?"

"It was the big man," answered the child, looking at the cup with eager eyes.

"The big man is Jacob Worse, and the little man is yourself, Mr. Delphin," explained Fanny, laughing. "My son's manners are not yet quite perfect. Did the big man ask who was up here with mother?"

"He asked if Aunt Rachel was in town," answered the child, putting out his hand for the cup.

Madeleine did not exactly see what the others found so amusing, but she joined in the laugh, because little Freddy was her darling.

"You are a dangerous woman," said George Delphin, as he took his leave; "I must go and warn my friend Worse."

"Yes, you dare!" cried Fanny, holding up her taper finger threateningly at him.

There was something which Madeleine could not exactly define, that she did not quite like, about Fanny. She noticed it most when they were in the society of men, but even when they were alone the same unpleasant manner would sometimes appear. She was not accustomed to all these questions, innuendoes, and allusions, which always seemed to take the same direction; but at last she became so fascinated by her lively and talkative friend, that she began to lose some of her self-possession, and a feeling of anxiety which she could not comprehend, came over her lest some fate was in store for her which she was unable to avert.

Fanny stood by the window, looking at Delphin as he left the house. He was not such a little man, after all! He had a nice figure, and his clothes fitted as if he had been melted into them. There was an air of distinction about his black moustache and curly hair. He was, in fact, a man that you would look twice at anywhere. It was wonderful she had never remarked it before!

Fanny turned to Madeleine, who was clearing the table, and observed her narrowly.

CHAPTER VIII.

"I notice, Mr. Johnsen," said Rachel, "that in almost all the conversations we have had on serious subjects, we seem to come to some point or another which all at once gives rise to a whole army of doubts and questions in us both; or perhaps, to speak more correctly, in you rather than in myself."

"The reason is that your extraordinary acuteness leads the conversation into certain lines of thought," answered the inspector.

Rachel paused for a moment, and looked at him. At every turn of their interesting acquaintance she had been on her guard against any word which had the slightest resemblance to a compliment. But when she saw before her the earnest and somewhat plain features of her friend, she felt that her caution was unnecessary, and she answered, "It does not require any extraordinary acuteness to perceive that when two people make an attempt in common to thoroughly understand any subject, they are more likely to be successful than if each were to work for himself. But what appears to me most remarkable is really this, that you did not long ago work out these problems for yourself."

"You have opened my eyes to many things which hitherto--"

"But hear what I have to say," broke in Rachel, with some impatience. "We have been going backwards and forwards here certainly for half an hour, talking about the many difficulties which must beset a clergyman, who is at the same time the servant of both God and the State, and continually, or at least several times, you have told me that I was right, or that you had not thought of such and such things before, or something of that sort." Rachel stopped in the broad path between the hedges in front of the house, where they were walking, and, looking him full in the face, said, "How is it possible, Mr. Johnsen, that you who have studied theology, and intend in the course of time to take priest's orders, have not already long ago made the subject clear to yourself, and taken your line accordingly?"

Johnsen's eyes fell before her clear and penetrating glance as he answered, "I have been quite enough troubled by doubts and anxieties, which are things none of us can escape; but if it now appears to you--and I must confess that it is the fact--that I have neglected certain points, I must plead that this negligence has been caused by my peculiar education. I come from a poor home, a very poor home"--he seemed to regain his confidence as he spoke--"and I have raised myself, without any special abilities, by sheer hard work. My time has, therefore, been fully occupied during my studies, and, as far as my opinion goes, a person who is working in real earnest has but little time for speculation. Besides, there is something about the subject itself, and about the men with whom one is brought into contact--something, what shall I call it?--something soothing, reassuring, which has the effect of making the doubts which from time to time appear bring, as it were, their own solution with them. But life's experience, and even more, my aquaintance with you, Miss Garman, has caused me to waver on many points."

"Do you remember our first conversation?" she asked.

"I don't think I have forgotten a single word that has passed between us."

"It was one of the first Sundays you were at Sandsgaard."

"The conversation at dinner turned upon the subject of war. Was not that the day you mean?" asked he.

"Yes, exactly," answered Rachel. "Mr. Delphin was maintaining, in his foolish, superficial way, that the spirit of the time would soon get rid of the evil of war, if we could only have done with kings and priests. You may remember Mr. Martens got quite excited, and insisted that priests were distinctly men of peace, and that their work was the work of peace. And then Mr. Delphin made the adroit answer, that any one who liked could go to church any Sunday, and hear how devoutly this man of peace, Mr. Martens, prays for the arms of the country by land and by sea."

"I remember it very well," answered Johnsen, with a smile; "it was just there I joined in the conversation."

"Yes; you declared that you would never, if you were ordained, mention the arms of the country in your prayers."

"Neither will I; nothing shall ever make me."

Rachel looked at him: he was in just the humour she liked to see him.

"I bring this to your recollection," she went on, "because I know now that there are many other duties which fall to the lot of a clergyman, that you will not be able altogether to reconcile with your convictions. In the course of our conversations you have expressed many decided opinions--for instance, about the Marriage Service, about Absolution, Confirmation, and several other matters; so that it now appears clear to me that you must either give up the idea of being ordained, or else be false to yourself."

"False to myself I cannot be," cried he; "I would rather give up my future prospects."

"But is that sufficient?"

"I don't understand you, Miss Garman."

"Do you think that you would be doing yourself justice by thus evading the responsibility that your convictions give rise to? If I were a man"--Rachel drew herself up--"I would go and seek the conflict, and not shirk it."

"Neither will I shirk it, Miss Garman," answered Johnsen.

"I hope you won't; there are quite enough who do." She looked towards the house to which they were approaching, and through the open window saw Fanny and Delphin carrying on a flirtation. Pastor Martens and Madeleine were going towards the croquet lawn, and Jacob Worse stood watching them with a cigar in his mouth.

Rachel turned quickly round to her companion and said, "I don't know anything more despicable than when a man does not dare, either by word or deed, to declare plainly what he feels in his inner consciousness to be in opposition with generally received opinions. A man who sneaks through life in this manner is, in my opinion, a coward."

She went towards the house, and Johnsen remained standing for a moment, and then wandered down the path again, lost in deep thought.

Jacob Worse said to her as she passed him, "Would you like to join the croquet? I hardly think it is right to leave your cousin to play alone with the chaplain."

"I think you might have spared yourself that well-meant remark, Mr. Worse," answered Rachel, in a tone which made him look at her with astonishment. "It seems to me, on the contrary, that Madeleine is in very good company--just the company that suits her."

"I beg your pardon," answered Worse, good humouredly. "I did not mean to be indiscreet; but I cannot help feeling that your cousin is in reality of such a lively nature, it is hard for her to find vent for her spirits."

"I did not know that Madeleine had such a concealed fund of spirits. As a general rule, I do not much care for people who are afraid to show their feelings."

"Afraid?" asked he, in astonishment.

"Yes; I said afraid. What else is it but want of courage which makes a man sit down quietly and hide his thoughts, conceal his convictions, live a false life, and play a part from morning to night? It were better to do like your friend out there"--and she gave a toss of her head towards Delphin--"to talk so grandly about one's principles, and to illustrate them by paradoxes and witticisms."

Jacob Worse now saw that he had found Rachel in a more earnest mood than he had expected.

"I have often observed," said he, seriously, "that you always think that it is a man's duty to speak out boldly when he finds his convictions are in danger; but allow me to explain--"

"I don't want to hear any explanations," rejoined Rachel, "and you are not bound to give me any; but I repeat what I said. It is cowardly."

She regretted the word the moment it was spoken. She said it because she had just used the same expression in her conversation with Johnsen; but, however, without saying anything further, she went into the house.

Jacob Worse remained thoughtfully contemplating his cigar. At last, then, the storm had burst. The ill humour he had so long noticed in her had found vent. He knew she meant what she said. She thought he was a coward. There had hitherto been a kind of friendly comradeship between them, which excluded any attempts at courtesy. She had told him that their friendship must be on this footing, if he wished it to continue. He had accepted his position, and they had often talked freely together, but latterly less than had formerly been the case.

Jacob Worse turned round, and found himself face to face with Mr. Johnsen, who was coming up the path with his eyes fixed on the ground. He at once perceived that here was to be found the cause for Rachel's extraordinary conduct, and the discovery did not tend to put him in a better humour.

Mr. Hiorth the magistrate, and Mr. Aalbom the schoolmaster, were seated together in the old summer-house near the pond. They were generally to be found together on these Sunday afternoons at Sandsgaard. The opportunity for talking scandal was one not to be neglected.

Hiorth's family had been for a long time in the service of the State, a fact of which he was not a little proud; and after his daughter's marriage with Morten Garman, who was one of the most eligible young men of the district, his somewhat sensitive feelings began to revolt against the self-satisfaction which the Garman family seemed to have inherited with their solid prosperity.

Aalbom was, therefore, not afraid to give free play to his bitter tongue, and after a good dinner he was just in the vein for so doing.

"They are asleep," said he. "I dare bet they are both of them fast asleep. Have you not noticed that both the Consul and his brother disappear after dinner every Sunday?"

"Yes, I have remarked that I don't generally see them when the coffee comes; but it is only for about a quarter of an hour," answered the magistrate, as he brushed some cigar-ash off his coat, just where his new North Star Order hung.

"They are not treating you properly," continued Aalbom; "especially when Richard calls himself an *attaché*, and has some pretensions to good manners."

"Oh! well, as far as he is concerned," answered the other, "he means to show his contempt for people in office. Richard Garman, like all people who have led shady lives, is an ultra-Radical."

"No doubt, sir. And I am not very certain about the Consul either; he has no respect for a cultivated intellect."

"But can you expect anything better from a man in trade?"

"A shopkeeper, you might say," whispered Aalbom, looking cautiously around. "There, now," he added, "I declare if it is not raining! Just what one might have expected. We had a little sunshine in the morning, and so of course it must rain in the afternoon. What a climate! what a country!" and, amid a torrent of ejaculations and anathemas, they both went hurriedly round the pond, and reached the house just as the rain began to fall in earnest.

The company generally sat downstairs when the weather was fine, in the room with the French windows opening into the garden; but now, as it had begun to rain, and the wind began to rustle through the flowers and the Virginian creeper on the railings, they went upstairs.

Whether it was that the two Garmans had really wished to show their con-tempt for people in office by taking a nap, or whether their absence had been ac-cidental, they had both returned to the company, and Richard was standing with his back to the fireplace, and the Consul was under the old clock, in conversation with Jacob Worse.

It was generally supposed that it was to these Sunday afternoon conversations with Worse that the Consul owed his perfect knowledge of every event that took place in the town.

Madeleine was sitting by the window, looking out at the rain. She was quite astonished to find how agreeable Pastor Martens could be. Her knowledge of cler-gymen had hitherto been confined to her father's descriptions of them, which were amusing enough, but far from flattering.

But Mr. Martens was quite lively, if not merry. He had not attempted to say anything serious, and she had nothing against him except that he hit very hard at croquet; but he played really well, and seemed to enjoy it. It was a pity that the rain had come before they had finished their game.

It was one of those evenings when it is not dark enough to light the candles, but is still too dark for any one to see to work; and a wet evening, even in summer, can become very tiresome before lights, cards, and such like make their appear-ance.

Mrs. Garman and Mrs. Aalbom sat gossiping on the sofa; and Fanny, who in the course of the day had received more than one reproving look from her moth-er-in-law for flirting with Delphin, was now doing penance with the old ladies, to whom Pastor Martens had also attached himself.

Quite a group had gathered round the fireplace by the *attaché*, consisting of the magistrate, Mr. Aalbom, and Delphin. Morten had disappeared, no one knew whither.

Delphin was anxious to slip away, so as to get an opportunity of having a chat with Madeleine; but Richard would not let him go--he was just the man after the *attaché's* heart. He reminded him of his own youth, with his polite assurance and ready wit. The old diplomatist had a weakness for getting up little disputes among his acquaintances, while he himself, by alternately assisting the two sides, took care to preserve the balance between them, and maintain a good tone in the discussion. From this point of view George Delphin was quite a treasure. He had just that irritating manner which sometimes became very nearly offensive, but was at the same time so polished, that it would indicate a want of good breeding to be annoyed at it. It was thus a real treat for Uncle Richard to see the magistrate, with all his aplomb, writhe under Delphin's adroit and sarcastic rejoinders. Aalbom, on the other hand, was not so well bred, and often, therefore, broke through conven-tionalities, to the great delight of both the *attaché* and the magistrate.

Uncle Richard had on this occasion led the conversation in a direction which he knew would be at the same time entertaining and interesting. The subject was the position of the country with regard to other nations. Mr. Hiorth had been in

Paris under Louis Philippe, and Delphin had two years previously made a summer tour through Europe, while the schoolmaster had been at the University of Copenhagen. Delphin's account of his travels was most animated, and culminated in the greatest admiration for Paris. The magistrate maintained that Paris was a dangerous, restless, and vicious town. This was the result of his observation in 1847, and it was generally allowed that since that time it had become even worse. Aalbom vainly tried to get in something about Thorwaldsen's museum.

The conversation began to get lively. The *attaché* distributed his aid with the greatest impartiality, and winked knowingly at Delphin, when to all appearances he had quite gone over to the magistrate's side. Each point as it arose was discussed with the greatest eagerness, until they arrived at woman's position in society. The magistrate was very strong on the subject of French immorality, but he was unluckily obliged to curtail his remarks on account of the ladies. Aalbom, who was able to take up a firm position on the ground of his acquaintance with "The Origin and History of the French Language," came to the assistance of his friend with a string of the most frightful quotations from Rabelais to Zola. Both then began to compare the women of their own country with those of Northern Europe generally, and managed to make the comparison a very favourable one, holding up their countrywomen as veritable heroines; and as both Richard Garman and Delphin were far too gallant to dispute their theory, so the other two had full enjoyment of their triumph.

Jacob Worse now got up and joined the group. He had not been able to help partly overhearing the conversation, and ruffled as he was by Rachel's accusations, he could no longer keep silence. The Consul smiled as he joined the others, and said in a low tone, "I will keep my eye upon you, and if it gets too hot, will come to your assistance."

From the moment Jacob Worse began to take part in the conversation, the *attaché* felt that the reins were slipping out of his hands. Worse went at it hammer and tongs; not that he raised his voice, or used unbecoming expressions, but his views were so subversive and so original, that the others were forthwith reduced to silence. At the first onset he brushed aside all the nonsense about Norwegian women, and that sort of thing, and went on boldly to consider the position of woman generally with regard to man. The magistrate asked him superciliously if he meant them to understand that he was in favour of emancipation; and when Worse answered that he was, the magistrate asked him with a smile how he thought he would be treated by an "emancipated wife." Worse, however, maintained that it was not a question how a man was treated, but what the relation really was which existed between the two. The time must be drawing to a close when the sole consideration was, what a man found most agreeable, and it was to be hoped that the young men of the future would be ashamed to argue from that basis. This was plainly a hit, not only at the magistrate, but at all married men of his generation. Aalbom protested warmly against Worse's theory, and his wife could be heard ejaculating in the distance. Pastor Martens now came and joined the disputants.

Jacob Worse was becoming excited; he spoke hurriedly, and his tone showed that he only restrained himself by an effort. On what absurd principles, he maintained, was the education of women generally conducted! How many thousands ended their career, worn out by the drudgery of household duties! Their intellect was wasted, and their strength exhausted for nothing. It was quite easy to talk so glibly of purity in a state of society where man was to know everything and have a right to everything, while woman was to be debarred from all intellectual knowledge.

At the first pause in the conversation, Aalbom came to the front as woman's champion, and the magistrate and Martens joined him. The conversation now waxed warmer, and Delphin wandered off to Madeleine, leaving Worse struggling alone against the arguments which both sides brought to bear on him. The disputants became heated and excited, and all went on talking at once, without giving time for the others to finish their sentences.

The *attaché* stood with his hands behind his back, regarding with apprehension the storm he had raised, and which was now out of his power to quell.

Mr. Johnsen made several attempts to join in the conversation, which had, however, become so warm that no one could be got to listen to his measured and carefully worded remarks. Rachel followed the arguments with the greatest interest, but she could not help feeling annoyed. She was annoyed when the others said anything stupid, and even still more so when she was obliged to confess that Worse was in the right. Everything seemed to irritate her. She could not bear to hear these men discussing her and her position as if she were some strange animal, and without ever having the grace to ask her opinion. The conversation had now gone far beyond woman's position, although Jacob Worse tried in vain to keep them to the point. Off they went through recent literature, foreign politics, home politics, ever with increasing earnestness, and with the same division of parties. Latterly the pastor had come more to the front. Aalbom's voice began to fail him, and the magistrate was unable any longer to get beyond the beginning of his sentences, and could do little else than point to his decorations and say, "For God and the King!" And before they knew where they were, they found themselves on the subject of modern scepticism.

Jacob Worse protested against this digression; but Martens, whose voice was just as calm as when he began, maintained that this lay at the bottom of the whole question, and that modern unbelief formed, as it were, a background to all the questions they had been discussing, and that all the arguments that were adduced from a "certain point of view" had their roots in this very principle.

The magistrate and Aalbom were agreed on this point, but Jacob Worse, with a pale face and excited gestures, began, "Gentlemen--!"

The Consul here made a sign to Miss Cordsen, who opened the doors into the dining-room, from whence the bright light shone suddenly into the room. The disputants only now remarked that it had become quite dark as they were talking. The company then adjourned to the dining-room, thankful enough to have a little breathing-time, but the voices still retained traces of the excitement.

"Where did you get those splendid lobsters, mother?" asked Morten, who had suddenly turned up, no one knew from whence. He never missed his meals.

"Uncle Richard brought them," answered Mrs. Garman. "I think he has a fisherman at Bratvold, who always brings him the finest lobsters that are to be got." She had taken care to help herself to some of the coral, which looked most appetizing in its contrast to the white meat.

Madeleine got almost as red as the lobster, and bent down over her teacup. Per, and everything connected with her old home, now seemed so distant, that when she thought upon her original intention of making an open confession, the idea seemed mere folly. She was indeed thankful that none of those around her guessed how near she had been to such an absurd engagement.

The two brothers, when they were going to bed that evening, had a chat over the events of the day. Richard's room opened into the Consul's, and notwithstanding that his habit of smoking cigarettes was an abomination to his brother, the door between the rooms always remained open at night. Each had his own particular method of undressing. The Consul took off each garment in due order, folded it up, and laid it in its appointed place. Richard, on the other hand, tore off his things and threw them about anyhow. He then wrapped himself in his dressing-gown, and sat down and smoked till his brother was ready.

"He is the very devil, that Worse!" said the *attaché*, leaning back in the armchair; "but it does me good to hear any one speak out his mind so plainly."

"He is too violent; he forgets conventionalities."

"It is possible to have too much conventionality. It is well for young people to air their views; it does them good."

"What nonsense you are talking, Dick!" cried the Consul, entering his brother's room. "What the deuce would become of the world if youngsters were allowed to jabber like that on every possible occasion?"

But Uncle Richard was not nervous when they were *tête-à-tête*. He got slowly up from his chair, and let his dressing-gown slip off his shoulders; and the two brothers now stood opposite each other, in very different *déshabille*. The young Consul was in his night-shirt, and a pair of flannel drawers tied at the knees with broad tape. His thin legs were thrust into long grey stockings, which Miss Cordsen alone knew how to knit. Richard had a pair of Turkish slippers, thread stockings, which fitted closely to his well-formed leg, and a shirt of fine material stiffly starched, in which he always slept. There were none of his brother's failings which the Consul disliked more than this.

"I tell you what, Christian Frederick," said Uncle Richard, as he laid his hand on his brother's shoulder, "I don't say that young people will do the world a great deal of good by making a noise, but I am quite certain that none of us have done it much good by holding our tongue."

"What do you mean? Nonsense, Richard!" said the Consul, contemptuously, as he turned back into his room.

They both got into bed and put out their lights.

"Good night, Christian Frederick."

"Good night," answered the Consul, rather drily; but just as Uncle Richard was on the point of falling asleep, he heard his brother say--

"Dick, Dick! are you asleep?"

"No, not quite," answered the other, sitting up in bed.

"Well, then, perhaps there was something in what you said just now. Good night."

"Good night," said the *attaché*, lying down with a smile on his face. A few minutes after the two old gentlemen were snoring peacefully in unison.

CHAPTER IX.

Gustaf Torpander was still consumed by his silent passion. Every penny he could save he devoted either to heightening his personal attractions or to treating Marianne's brother; for hitherto he had never had the courage to offer her any presents personally. The circuitous course he was thus driven to follow in his courtship, was not altogether agreeable to the Swede, and the drinking bouts at Begmand's cottage, in which he was obliged to take part in order to get a glimpse of his sweetheart, he found particularly distasteful.

At first Marianne was greatly annoyed by the attentions of the journeyman printer. From her earliest childhood, the knowledge of her exceptional beauty had made her careful to be on her guard against any advances from the other sex; but since her misfortune, she had come to regard every attention as a kind of persecution. But her shyness was generally received with an incredulous smile or a coarse joke. What shocked her most was, that men seemed no longer to believe that she really meant to shun them in earnest, and she was therefore quite nervous if any of them approached her. When, however, she saw that Torpander did not presume on his acquaintance, and preserved his polite and even respectful manner, she became at last used to his society, and had even a kind of sympathetic feeling for him. For Tom Robson she had always an unconquerable aversion. It is true that she saw Tom only from his worst side, when he was drinking. In the morning, when Robson was sober, there was something of the gentleman about him. He was always neatly dressed in a blue serge suit, coloured shirt, and in dry weather wore canvas shoes. It was a great pleasure for the young Consul to go his morning round in the shipyard with Mr. Robson. The work went on bravely, and the ship bid fair to be both handsome and well built. Mr. Garman knew Tom's weakness as well as any one, but as long as he attended to his work he was free to use his leisure as he liked. The firm had always worked on the principle that the less the workpeople were interfered with the better. They worked all the better for it, and gave far less trouble generally.

"I think she ought to be ready next spring," said the Consul one day in the beginning of July.

"In about eight or nine months, if the winter is not too wet," answered Tom.

"I should be very pleased if we could manage to launch her on the 15th of May," said the Consul, in a low tone; "but you must not mention the day to any one; you understand, Mr. Robson?"

"All right, sir," answered Tom.

Tom did not betray the day, even to his friend Master Gabriel; he only said it was to be some time in the spring, and with that Gabriel had to be content: but he still showed great curiosity as to what the name of the ship was to be. Tom swore that he knew nothing about it, and Morten answered that it was "a thing which did not concern schoolboys." From which Gabriel inferred that neither of them knew much about it, and, at all events, not Morten.

During the summer Gabriel got on but poorly at school; it seemed really too hard that he should have to pore over his books, while the work was going on with all its noise and bustle in the ship-yard. His character-book showed a sad spectacle, and each month when he had to take it in to his father, he made up his mind to make a little speech, of which the burden was to be, that he did not wish to continue his studies, but to be employed in the office, or be allowed to go to sea, or anywhere his father chose to send him. But each time when he stood before those cold blue eyes, every word seemed to vanish from his memory, and he looked so helpless and confused that his father shook his head as he left the room, and said--

"I can't make the boy out. I don't think he will ever grow into a man."

When first Madeleine came to Sandsgaard, Gabriel had found it a great relief to confide his woes to her. But now she had got too clever for him, and refused to be frightened by his threats of running away to sea, or giving his master, Mr. Aalbom, some rat-poison in his toddy, and he ended by feeling jealous of Delphin.

Fanny had for some time remarked that Delphin was openly paying his attentions to Madeleine, and the more plainly her sharp eyes took in the situation, the more clearly did she perceive that she had been relegated to the unenviable position of third person. She knew that Delphin had been used to the society of Christiania; he was neither so young nor so green as most of her father's assistants, and she therefore found his society agreeable. But when she found that, as usual, he began at once to show his admiration for her, she thought to herself he was no different to the rest. But now she began to take a little more notice of him; perhaps it was hardly worth while to let him slip entirely out of her hands; and when she looked at herself in the glass, she could not help laughing and thinking how absurd it was for any one, with her pretensions to beauty, to be contented to accept her present humiliating position.

Fanny had arranged that Madeleine should take music lessons in the town, and Delphin had got to know exactly when these music lessons took place. Madeleine met him very frequently, and they generally managed to go a little out of the way on her return, either in the streets, or in the park. Madeleine found these meetings rather amusing, and talked gaily and openly with her admirer.

"Now, Mr. Delphin," she said to him one day, "how is it you are so sarcastic and critical when you are in society? When we are alone you are much more agreeable."

"The reason is, Miss Madeleine, that when I am talking alone with you, I show more of my natural character; when I am in conversation with other people, I rather prefer to conceal my opinions."

"So you conceal your opinions?" said she, laughing.

"Yes. What I mean is, I don't care for every passer-by to pry into my mind. I generally keep the blinds down."

"Yes, now I understand," she answered seriously; not that she remarked the preference shown her, but she could not help thinking how much of her own life was also concealed by a curtain.

In one of the small streets near the sea they had to pass through a crowd of fishermen, who had been out all night, and were carrying home their lines, tarpaulins, and large baskets full of fish.

"Bah!" said Delphin, when they had passed, "I can't bear that smell of fish. But I forgot, Miss Garman; you must have had plenty of it when you lived at Bratvold."

"Oh yes!" answered Madeleine, with some confusion.

"Well, for my part," he continued, in a merry tone, "I can say with truth that I am a friend of the people, but I must confess that when the dear creatures come too near my nose my affection for them somewhat cools. There is something about that mixture of fish, tobacco, tar, and wet woollen clothes that I can't get over."

Madeleine could not but feel what a vivid description this was of the people among whom she had lived, and of him to whom she had so nearly--Ah, it was well she had not betrayed the secret to any one.

As they were crossing the market Delphin pointed to some one going in the direction of Sandsgaard.

"I declare, there is Mr. Johnsen going to Sandsgaard again to-day. Do you know, Miss Garman, he has gone a little wrong in his head?" But Madeleine had heard nothing about it.

"Yes, he is quite wrong in his head," continued her companion; "but it is not yet perfectly clear whether he is in love or whether it is religious mania. In favour of the first theory, that he is in love, we have the fact that he rushes over to Sandsgaard nearly every day, and is seen talking *tête-à-tête* with Miss Rachel. In favour of the other theory, that he has gone wrong on the subject of religion, it is said that he intends to give us no end of a sermon one of these Sundays. Won't you go to hear him?"

"Well, I don't know; but if the others go, I dare say I may go too."

"No! now promise me you will go to church that Sunday," said he, looking at her imploringly.

There was no time for an answer; they were close to the door, and Madeleine had caught a glimpse of Fanny behind the curtains of the sitting-room.

In the mean time Mr. Johnsen went on his way. It was quite true that he was going to Sandsgaard, but Delphin's statement that he was there every day was an exaggeration. Since that Sunday, when the conversation had waxed so warm, he had not been at Sandsgaard; but his thoughts had been occupied ever since by the recollection of his last conversation with Rachel in the garden.

Eric Johnsen came, as he often said, of a poor family. At the Garmans' he was first brought into contact with that luxury which he had hitherto despised, and he had made up his mind beforehand that he would not allow himself to be dazzled by it, and therefore on his first introduction had made his best endeavour to put on an air of severity, and to show himself superior to its attractions. But now he was not only astonished by the well-ordered and unpretentious comfort of the house, but he was also shaken in his preconceived notions about the rich, when he came to make the acquaintance of the Garmans. Johnsen had expected to find something more ostentatious, especially at table; but the solid tone of the household, and the easy and polished manners of the family, perhaps most of all the presence of Rachel, finally caused him to change his original ideas. He regarded with suspicion the satisfaction he felt, after having been at Sandsgaard a few times. He was on his guard against everything that tended to draw him away from his calling. There was one point which he felt of the highest importance, which was, since he had his origin from the poor and indigent, it was among them his work ought to lie, among paupers and in pauper schools.

One day Johnsen actually found himself hesitating before the door of his school, shrinking from going into its tainted atmosphere, when it was not actually necessary for him to do so. The discovery caused him at first the greatest uneasiness. Now, however, Rachel's society was beginning to have more influence over him. It was no longer the comfort of Sandsgaard which attracted him--of that he was quite certain; neither had he any feeling for the young lady except interest, a deep, earnest interest, after all the stirring impressions he had received through her. She had a wonderful power over him. Her words seemed to shed a ray of light over much which he had hitherto overlooked. He had, like the rest of us, the germs of doubt in his heart, and he was still so young and fresh that his aspirations were but loosely covered, and had not yet had time to wither entirely in his heart. When, therefore, he was suddenly thrown into the society of a woman of such intellectual power, his mind seemed as it were to awake, and her influence and his own reviving energies kindled within him a desire for action which increased with each day that passed. The tiresome and uninteresting work of his daily life seemed aimless to him. He must find some other means of publishing his convictions--this was now clear to him. He went, therefore, to his adviser, ready to engage in any combat into which she might think fit to send him.

Rachel generally did at home pretty much as she liked. She disdained all the hundred restraints which are generally considered so necessary for a young girl; they plainly did not apply in her case--she was so different to others. As soon, therefore, as Johnsen had exchanged a few words with old Mrs. Garman, she said, without further ado, "Come, Mr. Johnsen, let us take a turn in the garden," without her mother being in the least astonished. Rachel had grown up quite beyond her power of restraint, and if it came to the worst, thought Mrs. Garman, this unusual *penchant* for a clergyman was not the worst one Rachel could have hit upon.

The two went down into the garden, where they walked as usual up and down the central path. He found it rather difficult to lead the conversation in the direction he wished. His tone was therefore somewhat doubtful, as he said, "I have thought a great deal about our last conversation; in fact, I have hardly thought of anything else since, and, with your permission, I should like to say a few more words on the same subject."

"I am always glad to talk with you," answered Rachel, fixing her eyes upon him. Rachel had the same clear blue eyes as her father, to whom, in fact, she bore considerable resemblance, even in the slight projection of her under jaw. Her dark hair was faintly tinged with red, especially at the temples, and her tall and well-built figure rendered her appearance rather more imposing than attractive. The young men generally were absolutely afraid of her, and she had the reputation of being terribly learned and sarcastic, which was considered to be a great pity, as in other respects she was a most desirable *parti*. Mr. Johnsen did not notice any of these peculiarities: all he thought of was leading the conversation into the direction he desired. At length he was successful. He spoke with ever-increasing earnestness on the change that had taken place in him; how that she had not only roused him to meditation, but had also imparted to him a desire for work, for which he must now find vent. He had come to her to be told how and where he was to begin.

Rachel seemed somewhat embarrassed. "It is not so easy for me," she answered, "who as a woman am debarred from a life of action, if even I had the wish for it, to advise you how you ought to begin."

"I am ready for anything," cried he, excitedly. "I am ready to write or speak against the abuses I see everywhere around me. I am ready to cut myself adrift from the calling I have adopted, if it must be. I will not leave a single corner of my innermost heart concealed, but will lay open my convictions as a man ought to do."

His young friend was too wary to allow herself to be carried away by this sudden outburst, which she could not but regard with some misgiving.

"I think you ought to consider," she began, "that what we have hitherto been speaking of is a mere matter of scattered detail; there is scarcely any irreconcilable want of agreement between your ideas and those of Christianity in general."

"But Christianity requires either an entire belief or else none at all, and I do not care to continue in my doubtful position any longer."

"Yes; and besides," she continued, "I am quite willing to confess that I consider these forms and dogmas of but very slight importance. Our conversation has only turned particularly on these points from the fact that you hold a position in the Church."

"But that is not what we have been talking about," answered he, excitedly; "the real gist of the matter is, that you have been trying to rouse in me a consciousness of the personal responsibility which follows conviction."

"Yes," answered she, "you are quite right; that is exactly what I was aiming at."

"Whether I am in the Church or not, then, is not the question. What is really important is to be a man--man enough to have a conviction, and man enough to stand by it."

His vehemence and honesty overcame Rachel's scruples, and she answered hastily, and almost with a feeling of relief, "Yes, that is the point; it is exactly sincerity which is so rarely met with. This is the principle which I can myself scarcely hope to carry out to its full extent. What weight does the conviction of a woman carry with it, in a society like ours? But my whole sympathy is excited whenever I see sincerity struggling to the light. And that is why I believe that you are on the right path now, that you have entered upon this combat with falsehood. It is better to be utterly beaten in the battle than to lead a peaceful but insincere life."

Her clear blue eyes sparkled as she spoke. He looked at her with rapture, and with a sudden change of manner that was characteristic of him, he said in a calm, quiet voice:

"I will live a life of falsehood no longer!" He took a few steps, and said slowly and with emphasis, "I will ask the provost's permission to preach in the church next Sunday; I have, in fact, already said something to him about it. I want to tell the congregation--"

"It would, perhaps, be scarcely worth while," said Rachel, "to go too much into details."

"No, that was not my intention. I wish to bring forward the importance of sincerity. I will tell them plainly that I have my doubts, and that God is to be found in truthfulness, and not in mere forms; and I wish especially to examine the position of those of my own calling, who even more than others are fettered by forms and ceremonies."

"It may cost you your future; and in any case you will make many enemies."

"But perhaps I may make one friend."

"You shall have my friendship," said she, giving him her hand, "if you find any support in that. You can count upon me, even if all others turn their backs upon you."

"Thank you," said he, with solemnity, as he let go her hand. He left the garden hastily, but without going through the house; he took a side path, and went through the little wicket gate.

Rachel stood gazing after him as he went down the avenue. At last she had met a man who dared to state his convictions. This was more than ever Jacob Worse would have the courage to do.

CHAPTER X.

Jacob Worse's mother was regarded as quite a character in the town. When her husband died, he was about as insolvent as a man could be. For several years he had only kept his business going by means of unlimited credit, but up to the very last he managed to keep one of the gayest houses in the town. Nothing was left but a mass of bills and liabilities when he was gone. People shook their heads, and went one and all to the widow to condole with her. There were both friends and enemies among them, but all alike were creditors. Some were for selling her up at once, and others wished to keep the business going, while one wished to buy the horses privately. The "Boston-parti"[1] to which the deceased belonged, agreed to give the widow a monthly allowance. For a few days Mrs. Worse was quite bewildered and broken down by the ruin she had so little expected. She had never had the slightest knowledge of her husband's affairs, but she was quite convinced that he was very rich. On the evening after the funeral she was sitting alone with her son Jacob, who was a boy of about seven or eight, when a little wizened, grey-haired man came into the room, who, after respectfully wishing Mrs. Worse good evening, laid on the table some account-books and papers. The old man was well known to Mrs. Worse: it was Mr. Peter Samuelsen, commonly known as Pitter Nilken, the manager of the small shop in the back premises. Worse's property had consisted of an entire building, of which the front looked out towards the sea and the quay where the steamers were moored, and at the back was a little dark lane, where Pitter Nilken had his shop. Worse never liked anybody to allude to the shop; he considered that he was far too respectable a man of business for anything of the sort. He used to say that it was mostly for old Samuelsen's sake, that he kept the little shop going; it could have no importance in a concern like his.

Mrs. Worse had also believed this story; but that afternoon she learnt to think otherwise. It was quite clear to her, after hearing Mr. Samuelsen's figures and calculations, that the shop was not at all to be despised, and she came at last to perceive that this was what had really so long kept everything going.

The two sat over their figures far into the night. At first comprehension seemed quite hopeless to Mrs. Worse. The explanations she had heard from her husband's friends and creditors during the last few days were so complicated, and couched in terms beyond her understanding; but with Peter Samuelsen it was quite otherwise. He never went on until he was quite sure that she comprehended what he said. At length it all began to dawn upon her, and she kept on repeating, "I declare, it is all as clear as daylight."

[1] "Boston" is a game of cards, and the "Boston-parti" is a club, the members of which meet and play at each other's houses.

Next morning she ordered her carriage and drove off alone. The scandal this excited in the town was beyond description. To think that she, who scarcely owned the very clothes on her back, should have the audacity to drive in a carriage and pair before the very noses of those whom her husband had swindled! The general feeling towards her had hitherto been favourable, and several people could not help feeling a mischievous delight at the idea of seeing the haughty Mrs. Worse live on a monthly allowance. But now all were as hard as stone. Mrs. Worse herself did not seem to be so nervous as she was the day before, and when she entered Consul Carman's office, with Pitter Nilken's papers under her arm, her step was as firm and confident as a man's.

It was now several years since Worse had left the firm, but some ill-feeling had long remained on both sides, and the deceased and Mr. Garman had never got on well together. It was thus no light matter for the widow to betake herself to Consul Garman; but Mr. Samuelsen had assured her that it was quite out of the question to think of keeping the business going without a guarantee from Garman and Worse.

When the Consul saw Mrs. Worse come into the room, he imagined that she was bringing a subscription-list to raise the means for educating her son, or something of that sort; and, as he offered her a chair on the opposite side of the table, he turned over in his mind how much he should subscribe. But when Mrs. Worse began to give an explanation of her affairs, according to the calculations of Pitter Nilken, the Consul's manner changed, and he got up, walked round the table, and seated himself near her. He calmly and patiently examined each paper, went through the calculations and figures, and at last read the draught of a guarantee which Samuelsen had made, with the greatest attention.

"Who has assisted you with all this, Mrs. Worse?" he asked.

"Mr. Samuelsen," she answered, somewhat anxiously.

"Samuelsen? Samuelsen?" repeated the Consul.

"Yes, that is to say, Pitter Nilken. Perhaps you know him better by that name."

"Ah yes! the little man in the shop. H'm! Does Mr. Samuelsen wish to go into partnership with you?"

"No. I have asked him, but he prefers to remain in his present position, and give me his assistance in the business."

The Consul got up with the guarantee in his hand. It was one of his peculiarities that he could not write the signature of the firm except when he was sitting in his usual place. But as soon as he had seated himself in the old wooden armchair, he wrote in a large and bold hand, "Garman and Worse," taking care to adorn the signature with several flourishes, which he had inherited from his predecessors.

Armed with this document, Mrs. Worse and Mr. Samuelsen set to work at the ruins. The first thing they did was to sell everything there was to sell; but, with the assistance of Mr. Garman, they managed to save the whole of the valuable premises. The front of the house was let, and the old lady moved over to the back, where she took turns in the shop with Mr. Samuelsen. She was at her post from early in the morning till late in the evening, gossiping with her customers, and selling to-bacco, tallow candles, salt, coffee, tar-twine, herrings, train oil, paraffin, tarpaulins, paint, and many other commodities.

In the course of a few years Mrs. Worse quite lost her manners. People in polite society had never forgiven her her drive, but still less were they willing to look over the fact that she, a lady, had not more self-respect than to sink down into the position of a common shop-woman. The lower orders, on the other hand, had quite a fellow-feeling for Mrs. Worse, and the dingy little shop was just to their taste; and thus, contrary to all expectation, Mrs. Worse's business, common little retail affair as it was, went on capitally.

The trustworthy Mr, Samuelsen did the work of three. He was a little grey shrivelled man, with a face like a dried fig. He might be forty, or he might be sixty, it was not easy to tell. In his monotonous life there had only been one single event which he particularly remembered, and that was the afternoon when he had taken his books and calculations in to Mrs. Worse, and since that time he had, with the greatest honesty, helped her to overcome her many difficulties. Mr. Samuelsen had also his own private enemies to contend against, and these consisted of nearly all the school children in the town. It had always been, and was still, a favourite amusement for the children to "Sing for Pitter Nilken." The game was carried on in the following manner. Boys and girls all assembled, the more the merrier, gen-erally in the dusk of the evening, and sneaked quietly down into the alley at the back of the Worses' house, and when they got under Samuelsen's shop-window, they began singing, to a well-known air--

"Little Pitter Nilken,
Sitting on his chair!
He's always growing smaller,
The longer he sits there."

This couplet was repeated again and again, each time in a louder tone, until the tormented man seized his iron ruler and sprang over the counter. Then off flew the crowd, screaming and shouting along the narrow lane, for there was an old tradition that the iron ruler had a rusty stain of blood on it. Samuelsen would then retire quietly to his desk. In the course of years the episode had been of constant occurrence, and he well knew that the only way of getting a little peace was to make this sally with the ruler.

No one could blame Mrs. Worse for making an idol of her son; he was all she had to care for. Although Jacob was a good son, and grew up strong and healthy, he had cost his mother many tears when he came home from school bruised and untidy after a fight. The boy had almost too much spirit, as the principal said, and when he was roused he did not mind tackling the biggest and strongest boys in the school. But he got better as time went on, and when he came home from abroad to take his place in the business, he was, and not only in his mother's opinion, one of the best-looking and most agreeable young men in the town.

Jacob Worse took his father's old office in the front of the house, which looked on to the market and the quay. He carried on a business partly on commission and partly on his own account. He did a good deal of trade, particularly in corn, which had hitherto been almost entirely in the hands of Garman and Worse. The old firm had established itself so securely on every side, that he seemed to meet them whichever way he turned.

Morten wished that Garman and Worse should at once use their strength, and crush their tiny rival before he had had time to become dangerous, but Consul Garman would not hear of it. He seemed to have an extraordinary liking for Worse, and even went out of his way to help him, and latterly "the rival" had become a constant Sunday guest at Sandsgaard.

At first Jacob Worse did not like leaving his mother on Sunday, but Mrs. Worse said, "Go along, you great stupid! do you suppose that Samuelsen and I care to have you sitting and laughing at us when we are playing draughts; and besides," said she, giving him a sly poke with her finger, "don't you know there is somebody out there that expects you?"

"Ah, mother, do stop those insinuations of yours; you know perfectly well nothing will ever come of it."

"Now, Jacob," said Mrs. Worse, with her arms akimbo, "you think yourself very clever, but I tell you you are as stupid as an owl, a barn-door owl, when it is anything to do with women. You ought to see it must all come right some day. I dare say Miss Rachel is a little bit singular, but she is not quite cracked. You see, it will all get straight in the end; it will still all come right some day."

This was the refrain of all Mrs. Worse's observations on this head, and her son saw plainly it was of no use to contradict her. It was of no use either to advise her to give up her shop, or, at any rate, to give up the management to somebody else.

"Why, I should die of dropsy," said she, "and Samuelsen would dry up to nothing in about a fortnight, if we had not got the shop to attend to."

"Yes," suggested Jacob, "but still you need not work any longer: you have earned some rest for your old days; besides, your legs are not so young as they were."

"As to my legs," cried Mrs. Worse, with a gesture of impatience, "my legs are quite good enough for a shop-woman."

"Well, why not get a horse and carriage? You have every right to have one."

"I took a drive once that made stir enough," answered his mother; "I hope to take another some day, but that won't be before everything comes right."

It was no use trying to persuade her, and so she and Samuelsen remained in the back premises they were so fond of, and Jacob set up his establishment in the front.

When Mrs. Worse was in her son's rooms, she used to play the fine lady to her own great edification; but when she got him into her own apartments, her behaviour entirely changed, and her laughter was coarse and noisy. Her manners had really quite gone.

One Saturday afternoon Delphin came into Jacob Worse's office with some books he had borrowed.

"Have you heard that I have bought a horse?" asked he, in a merry tone.

"No," answered Worse. "What new folly now?"

"Well, you see, I have got an idea that it will make a favourable impression on Miss Madeleine if she sees me on horseback. Just fancy me on a horse with a long mane and tail, like the picture of General Prim; there!" and he went cantering round the room, and pulled up suddenly before Worse--"there, like that: a good fierce expression. Is not that it? I believe that will do the business."

Worse could not help laughing, although he did not think much of the frivolous way Delphin had of paying his addresses to Madeleine.

"You are not going to ride up to Sandsgaard this morning?"

"No, not exactly; it would not do. I can't very well go up there dressed for riding, and if I were to ride in these clothes I should look absurd. But I thought of riding out there this evening, somewhere about seven o'clock. Just fancy me coming in over the garden wall with a flying salute, and lighted by the last rays of the evening sun! Why, it would be irresistible."

"Well, I am afraid, or perhaps I ought rather to say I hope, that Miss Madeleine will not fully appreciate your novel way of paying her your addresses," said Worse, half-seriously.

"Ah, my most respected friend, you know very little of woman's heart; and how should you, when your ideal is a woman who goes in for her rights? a tall bony creature with a moustache under her nose, and 'Woman's wrongs' under her arm."

"Leave off, will you?" cried Worse. "You are just in your most disagreeable vein. You had better go off to young Mrs. Garman. She will find you most amusing to-day."

"A good idea, which I was already thinking of," answered Delphin, as he took his hat; "and at the same time I will take a place for myself in her carriage for to-morrow."

"Won't you drive with me?" cried Worse after him.

"No, thanks; I would rather go with Mrs. Garman, if for nothing else than to have the pleasure of seeing her worthy husband on the box," said he, as he went out of the door.

Jacob Worse stood watching him. At first he had been very glad to make Delphin's acquaintance. There were not many young men in the town with whom he could associate. Delphin was intelligent, well read on different subjects, and when alone was good company enough. But by-and-by he showed more of the frivolous side of his character, and Worse began to get a little tired of his friend.

Fanny was sitting all this time in a state of absolute boredom. Little Christian Frederick had gone out with his nurse, and the street was uninteresting, dusty, hot, and thronged by country people making their Saturday purchases. She did not care to look out of the window, but sat leaning back in her most comfortable armchair, yawning in front of the glass. Would it be better to send for Madeleine? it was several days since she had paid her a visit. But then she would have to play the part of go-between again. Or should she begin on her own account? Yes; why not? But then he never came except when Madeleine was there. It really was too tiresome.

When he now came unexpectedly into the room it gave her quite a start, but she still remained leaning back in her armchair, and gave him her left hand, which was the nearest, as she said, "I am glad to see you. I was just thinking of you as I was sitting here all alone."

"It was very kind of you, I am sure," answered he, as he sat down in a chair in front of her.

"Yes; all sorts of foolish things come into one's head when one is sitting alone."

"I hope I was not the most foolish thing that could come into your thoughts," answered Delphin, jestingly. "But it is quite true; you have been left a great deal alone lately."

"Yes; but perhaps I have my own reasons for it."

"May I venture to ask what these reasons are?"

"Perhaps it would be better if I were to tell you," said she, regarding attentively the point of her shoe, which projected from her dress as she lay back in her chair. She had tiny pointed French shoes with straps across the instep, through which appeared a blue silk stocking.

"I assure you I shall be very thankful, and at the same time most discreet."

"Well, then, Madeleine is so young," said Fanny, as if following the train of her own thoughts, "that I feel it to a certain extent my duty to look after her, and--"

"I scarcely see that it is absolutely necessary," answered he.

"Yes; but when a girl so inexperienced as Madeleine is brought into contact with gentlemen who are--well, who are so clever as, for instance, yourself, Mr. Delphin, you see--" She looked at him as she paused in her sentence.

"You are paying me too great a compliment," said he, laughing; "and besides, you can never imagine that I would take advantage--"

"Nonsense!" rejoined Fanny; "I know all about that. You are just like all the rest. You would never hesitate to take advantage of even the slightest opportunity; would you, now? Tell me frankly."

"Well," answered he, rising, "if you really wish for an honest answer, I must confess that when I see a strawberry that nobody else seems to notice, I generally pick it."

"Yes; it is just that greediness that all men have, and which I find, at the same time, so dangerous and incomprehensible."

"Yes; but, Mrs. Garman, strawberries are really so delicious."

"Yes, when they are ripe," answered Fanny.

The words fell from her lips as smoothly as butter. Delphin had taken a few paces across the room, and just turned in time to see the last glimpse of a look which must have been resting on him while she spoke. It was not very often that he lost his self-possession in a conversation of this kind, but the discovery he had made, or thought that he had made, with all its uncertainty, and the feeling of pleased vanity it brought with it, confused him, and he stood stammering and blushing before her. She still lay stretched in the armchair, a position which displayed to the best advantage the lines of her lovely form. Her beauty was fully matured, and showed freedom and elegance in every movement. She could see that she had said enough for the present, and she got up without apparently taking any notice of his confusion.

"You must think," said she quickly, with a smile, "that it is absurd for me to preach you a sermon. We all have to attend to our own affairs; and if you will excuse me, I have to go and try on a dress. Good-bye, Mr. Delphin; I hope you will find your strawberries to your taste."

Delphin was quite confounded; but before he had had time to get his hat she put her head in at the door, still smiling, and cried, "You will drive over with me to-morrow?" and, without waiting for an answer, she nodded her head and disappeared.

Delphin had hardly recovered himself when he went for his ride to Sandsgaard, and he quite forgot about the flying salute over the garden wall, for there was no one to be seen either at the window or in front of the house. The fact was, his adventure had made such an impression on him that he did not take very much notice.

Fanny at first repelled his advances haughtily; but he accepted his fate with resignation. George Delphin was not the man to lose his time or his temper, in a hopeless pursuit. There are many respectable prizes in a lottery without aiming at the first. But now here was the chance of winning the great prize, the charming Fanny, the admiration of all. His heart swelled with pride, and if Jacob Worse could have seen the look with which he regarded the passers-by, it would certainly have reminded him of General Prim.

The next day at Sandsgaard, Fanny and Madeleine were together during the whole afternoon. Delphin could not manage to get an opportunity of talking to either separately. Just once he came upon Fanny in the morning-room at the piano, but she got up and went out hurriedly as he entered. As they drove home that evening scarcely a word passed between them. Fanny kept gazing the whole time over the fjord, of which they caught glimpses from time to time through the trees of the avenue. It was a still, peaceful autumn evening, and Delphin was in an excited mood. Each time he moved he felt the rustle of her silk dress, the folds of which nearly filled the carriage. Both sat quite silent to the end of the drive.

During the next few days Madeleine was again staying with her cousin, whom she found more gracious than ever. Delphin came even more frequently than before; but she did not meet him during her walks, a fact which she related to Fanny. Fanny said with a smile that Delphin was perfectly right, and his conduct was only proper, now that people had begun to talk about their frequent walks together.

Madeleine thought with regret upon how much there is to be careful of in this world; but a short time afterwards she met Mr. Delphin, and during the pleasant walk they had together he was most attentive, and in the best of spirits.

Fanny was now more beaming than ever. Whenever she saw her own and Madeleine's reflection in the glass, which, to tell the truth, was very often the case, a smile of satisfaction would pass over her features. Without Madeleine having a suspicion, the *rôles* had been changed, and the play was ready to begin, now that Fanny had made up her mind that the parts were in the right hands.

CHAPTER XI.

All the Miss Sparres, of whom there were five, rushed to the window.

"It is Mr. Johnsen, the new school-inspector! No, it isn't! Yes, it is! It *is* Mr. Johnsen! Do you think I don't know him, although he has got a new coat? I declare, he is coming in!"

"Clementine, you have taken my cuffs! Yes, you have! They were on the piano. He is only going in to see father. Clara, Clara! you are standing on my dress! Here he is! It is a visit! Who can have taken my cuffs?"

Mrs. Sparre was not long in getting them into order. The street door was opened. There was a moment's breathless expectation in the room. It was agreed that Miss Barbara, the eldest, was to say, "Come in," and as all eyes were fixed upon her, she became quite pale with emotion. A knock at the door was heard; but it was at the study door, and the dean said, "Come in!" The door was heard to open, and a subdued conversation began in the room.

"I told you he was only going to see father."

"Yes, and so did I," another said. "What was the good of rushing about looking for your cuffs?"

"I didn't rush about!"

"Yes, you did!"

"Hush! I wonder what he wants with father?" said Mrs. Sparre. All were silent, but they could not hear anything of the conversation which was going on in the other room.

Mr. Johnsen had come to ask the dean to fulfil the promise he had made to him some weeks previously, and to kindly give him permission to preach in the church the next Sunday. The dean had not forgotten his promise, and was only too glad to have an opportunity of fulfilling it. He also begged to thank Mr. Johnsen for his goodness in offering to assist him in his duties.

As far as that went, answered Mr. Johnsen, he would not conceal from him that it was not so much consideration for the weight of his duties which had impelled him to make the request. He must confess, that it was rather that he wished to have an opportunity of addressing the congregation on a personal matter.

The dean could quite feel that his connection with the school would lead to the desire of speaking a few words to the parents of the children who were entrusted to his care.

But this again was not exactly the subject on which Mr. Johnsen wished to speak. There were many things which might weigh on the mind and oppress the thoughts. It would be better, once for all, to disburden the conscience by coming forward honestly and truthfully.

The dean allowed that the idea was only natural. It was the duty of every Christian, and especially of a clergyman, to speak truthfully. But sincerity was a rare virtue, and was often hidden under the changing circumstances of life. But great care would be necessary. It was of the first importance to examine closely both one's mind and one's composition.

Johnsen was able to say honestly that he had arrived at his conclusions after earnest thought and conscientious inquiry, and that his conviction was the result of many lonely hours of self-examination.

The dean could assure him that he well knew these lonely hours of thought, and great was the blessing that might be found in them; but he would venture to suggest what he knew from his own experience, that the problems which a man worked out alone were not always the most trustworthy. He would, therefore, remind him of the passage where we are recommended to confess to each other, which seemed to suggest working in fellowship, and giving each other mutual assistance.

Johnsen answered that that was the very reason why he wished to speak to the congregation.

The two sat on opposite sides of the dean's table, regarding each other attentively. Johnsen was pale and had something nervous about his manner, which seemed to betoken a wish to bring the interview to a close.

Dean Sparre sat leaning back in his armchair, and in his hand he held a large ivory paper-knife, which he used to emphasize his words; not, indeed, for the purpose of gesticulating or striking on the table, but every now and then, when he came to some particular point, he drew the knife up and down on the sheets of paper which lay before him.

To speak the thoughts plainly before the congregation was certainly desirable in itself, and entirely in accordance with Scripture. But it was quite easy to imagine that a man might want to make other confessions which should not be for every ear. The Church had, therefore, another and more restricted form of confession, which was not only just as much in accordance with Scripture, but might often be still better adapted to ease the troubled heart.

Johnsen got up to take his leave. He felt a great wish to speak before the congregation. It was, in his opinion, of the greatest importance that he should have a perfectly clear idea of his own views, and that there should be nothing obscure or insincere between him and his hearers.

The dean also got up, and shook hands on wishing him good-bye. He gave his young friend his best wishes for his undertaking, and hoped he would bear in mind that he, as dean, was always ready to assist him in every way, if he should at any time feel the need of his services.

"You will bear this in mind, my young friend, will you not?" said the old dean, with a fatherly look.

Johnsen muttered something about thanks as he hurried out of the room. He was no longer in the frame of mind in which he had been during the last few weeks. The peaceful, genial air of the dean's study, with its well-filled bookshelves, had had a wonderful effect upon him, as had also the dean, with his manner, which was at the same time so mild and so earnest. The mind of the young clergyman seemed, as it were, softened by an influence which he did not clearly understand, and the power of which he was not willing to recognize.

After a long walk, Johnsen at length arrived in the large field which lay beyond Sandsgaard. From this position he could look down into the garden and premises near the house. He could follow with his eye the broad path where Rachel and he had so often walked together, and their conversation seemed to come before him with the greatest distinctness. For a long time he stood there gazing, until he felt strong again in his resolve. What would he not have given to have seen her, if only for a moment! But he felt he could not approach the house. He would not allow any other feeling to mingle with the holy determination with which his thoughts were filled, and with an heroic effort he turned away, and bent his steps towards the town. His mind had now regained its former tone.

The church was filled to overflowing that Sunday on which Mr. Johnsen was to preach his first sermon. There are always plenty of people who are glad of the opportunity of hearing a new preacher, and this number was increased by the interest which was felt in the earnest young man who had attracted so much attention.

Mrs. Garman sat with her daughter in the family seat, in which were also Fanny and Madeleine. Dean Sparre, with his wife and daughter Barbara, were in the front row of the pew which belonged to them; while behind were Pastor Martens with the other Miss Sparres; and behind, again, Mrs. Rasmussen, the chaplain's housekeeper.

The congregation was so large that the voices swelled as when the Christmas hymn is sung, and as the preacher wended his way towards the pulpit, the heads of all the singers were turned as if to follow him.

As Johnsen ascended the narrow winding stair where no eye could see him, he felt a momentary weakness, as if he must almost sink under his burden, and he never afterwards clearly remembered how he had managed to get up the last few steps which led to the pulpit; but when he at length reached his place, and the hundred eyes were again fixed on him, he forced himself, with that energy which was peculiar to him, to conquer his feelings. He looked so calm that many people averred that they had never seen a young clergyman more at home in the pulpit.

Johnsen had sharp eyes, and could recognize many of the faces below him; but he was conscious of Rachel's presence, as she sat opposite to him in the Garmans' pew, more by an instinctive feeling than because he actually saw her. He was, in fact, obliged to avert his eyes from her direction, lest the sight should unman him. The part of the church in which the women sat was immediately under him, just below the pulpit, while the private pews were in a kind of gallery opposite. As the congregation sang the last verse of the psalm, he gazed deliberately over all the upturned eyes. Some were piercing, some curious, some pious and devotional, while some appeared as deep and unfathomable as if he were looking into unknown depths.

After an introductory prayer, he read his text in a clear and composed voice, after which he began a short and clear explanation of the passage. It was only in the last part of the sermon that he really intended to go into more personal matters, and the nearer he approached them the less confidence he seemed to feel. When he had begun his sermon, he had fixed his eyes on a certain point, which he sought every time he lifted his eyes from his notes; and this point, although he had not remarked it at first, was Dean Sparre's head. The snowy hair and the white collar stood out in the sharpest contrast against the dark background, and the more the speaker gazed at this noble face, the more he seemed to dread the conclusion. He was already close upon the point where he was first to begin to speak about sincerity, and the necessity of a perfectly truthful existence, and although he could not exactly tell the reason, he could not but feel that the stirring discourse he had set himself to deliver, was but little in keeping with that bright and peaceful smile, and with that commanding countenance so full of earnestness and harmony.

His head seemed to go round, and not another word could he utter. There was a deathlike stillness in the church, as he wiped his brow with his handkerchief.

But when he again raised his head, he made an effort, and, looking beyond the dean in his need, he sought her who was really the cause of his standing where he did. He was not disappointed, for the moment his eyes met the calm and determined face, a change seemed to come over him. Her eye rested upon him with an inquiring and almost anxious expression, which he well understood.

She should not be disappointed of her trust in him, and with renewed strength, and without a tremor in his voice, he began upon the last part of his discourse. Ever higher and fuller rang his voice, until its sonorous tone filled the church, and was re-echoed from the vaulted roof. The congregation followed him with attention, while some of the old women were moved to tears. And now a sensation of uneasiness seemed to pass through those who composed the great assembly. It was indeed an extraordinary sermon, with its earnest entreaties to be thoroughly upright and sincere, and with its reckless condemnation of all forms and ceremonies, all of which were but of secondary consideration. It seemed too bold, too exaggerated.

He seemed anxious to confess his sceptical opinions, in holding which he did not stand alone. He was only alone in confessing them. He knew only too well that fine web of soothing compromise, with which people were in the habit of deadening their consciences. He knew it still better, too, from his own point of view as a clergyman, who even more than others was bound to live in the full glare of truth, even though he might be despised, hated, and persecuted by an unreasoning world. If he followed the beaten track, whither would it lead? To a position of comfort and respectability, in which the first duty was to throw a veil over one's own heart and those of others: to suppress all doubt and inquiry, and to deaden all real life in the individual, so that the whole machine might continue its regular movements without noise or friction. But truth was a two-edged sword, sharp and shining as crystal. When the light of truth broke into the heart of man, it caused an agony as piercing as when a woman brings her child into the world.

But, instead of this, was a man to lead a life of slumber, shut in by falsehood and form, without force or courage; giving no sign of firmness or power, but stuffed and padded like the hammers of a piano?

He was so carried away by his thoughts that he forgot his notes and said many things he would never have dared to write; and after the last thundering outburst, he concluded with a short and burning prayer for himself and for all, to have power to defy the falsehood by which man was bound, and to live a life of sincerity.

He then went on in an entirely changed voice with the rest of the service; but Rachel particularly noticed that he left out the prayer for the arms of the country, by land and sea; and now, as he read the prayers in a calm, quiet voice, the assembly seemed to breathe more freely, as if after a storm.

Among the men could be heard whispers, and the prevailing idea seemed to be that the sermon was a complete scandal; while those who had to do with the law were of opinion that he would be cited before the Consistorial Court. Among the women the feeling seemed rather undecided, and many inquiring glances were thrown towards where the men were sitting, in the hope of divining what the opinion would be, either of a husband, or a brother, or, in fact, of that particular person of the opposite sex, according to whose decision each woman was in the habit of forming her own.

Most eyes, however, sought the dean, who sat as he had done during the whole sermon, slightly leaning back on his seat, and holding a large hymn-book, which was a gift from his previous congregation, between his hands. From the upper windows on the other side of the church a subdued light fell on his form. The face had the same exalted and peaceful expression; not a sign of uneasiness or annoyance had passed over it during the whole sermon, which was not without a soothing effect upon the congregation. The feeling of restlessness and excitement was universal, but most people seemed inclined to defer, their final judgment.

Pastor Martens had left the pew immediately after the sermon, for he had to conduct the Communion Service. While he performed it, his somewhat unmusical voice trembled with inward emotion. There could be no doubt whatever as to what were the inspector's real opinions.

The chaplain could not help being rather pleased at the satisfaction the dean would now be obliged to render him, for it had been quite against the chaplain's wish and advice, that Johnsen was allowed to preach at the morning service. It would have been more advisable to have given him a first trial either at a Bible-reading, or at most at the evening service. But now the murder was out, and he had shown his feeling of antagonism to the Church before the whole congregation. What would the dean do? The affair would naturally have to be reported.

As soon as the service was over, Martens left the altar and hurried into the sacristy, into which he had already seen the dean enter.

"What do you say to that, sir?" he cried breathlessly, as he shut the door after him.

Dean Sparre was sitting in his armchair, reading the hymn-book he had in his hand. At the chaplain's question he raised his head with an expression of mild reproof at the disturbance, and said abstractedly, "To what are you alluding?"

"Why, the sermon; of course I allude to the sermon; it is perfectly scandalous!" cried the chaplain, excitedly.

"Well, certainly," answered the dean, "I cannot say that it was a good sermon, taken as a whole, but if you take into consideration--"

"But really, sir--" interrupted the chaplain.

"It appears to me, and it is not the first time I have noticed it, my dear Martens, that you do not quite get on with our new fellow-worker; but is it not to us that he ought really to look for support?"

The chaplain cast down his eyes; there was some extraordinary power about his superior. Not an instant before he had formed his opinion quite clearly, but the moment he found himself face to face with the dean's genial countenance, all his ideas seemed to change.

"It grieves me to be obliged to speak to you thus, my dear Martens, but I do so with the best intentions; and, then, we are alone."

"But don't you think, sir, that he was far too bold?" asked the chaplain.

"Yes, clearly, clearly so," assented the dean, in a friendly tone. "He was unguarded, like all beginners; perhaps the most unguarded I have heard. But then we know quite well that the same thing often occurred in our own time. It would be quite unreasonable to expect the Spirit's full maturity in the young."

This remark caused Martens involuntarily to think of his own first attempt. He answered, however, "But he maintained that we ministers, above all others, are living a life of falsehood, shut in by meaningless forms."

"Exaggeration! a wild and dangerous exaggeration! In that I quite agree with you, my dear Martens. But, on the other hand, which of us can deny that a ceremonial, be it ever so beautiful and full of meaning, still in the course of time, when it is frequently repeated, loses something of its influence over us? But who will dare cast the first stone? Is it not youth, as we see, who has not yet experienced the wear of that continuous labour which strives to be true to the end? And then naturally we get exaggeration--dangerous exaggeration. But," continued the dean, "before everything, let us agree to look upon his sermon in the right light, for the opinion of many will be formed upon ours, and if we now allow this young man to slip out of our hands he will, likely enough, be entirely lost for the good work; and I must say I have great hopes of him. I feel sure that in his right place, which would be in a large town--for instance, in Christiania--he will make a name for himself in the Church, and I venture to think that his labours will bear abundant fruit."

Martens again looked up at the dean as he pronounced these words, and for the first time he now perceived what it was that made his manner so irresistible. It was the smile, that changing and varying smile, which yet never entirely left the noble features. It seemed to mingle in all he said, like a warm and soothing sunbeam; and as the chaplain constrained himself to alter his opinion under its influence, he felt that the muscles of his mouth involuntarily assumed the dean's expression.

Madame Rasmussen could not conceal her astonishment at the moderation with which the chaplain spoke of Johnsen's sermon. She was herself in the highest degree shocked, and when Mr. Martens told her that, in his opinion, Mr. Johnsen would be likely to become a clergyman of considerable note in Christiania some day, she almost thought that he was carrying his forbearance too far. Still she could not but like Pastor Martens, who had now lived with her for two years without a single ill word having passed between them. Madame Rasmussen was a young widow, plump, good-looking, and light-hearted. She had no children, and it was quite a pleasure to her to manage for the chaplain--to prepare his little dishes, and to keep his things in order. She was the only person in the whole town who really knew that Martens wore a wig. This was not, however, a thing to be spoken about, and nobody else was admitted into the secret.

As Mrs. Garman drove home from church with Rachel and Madeleine, she spoke disapprovingly of Johnsen's sermon. She considered that it was highly improper for a young man to be so forward and daring; but it was quite in accordance with the spirit of the times, as Pastor Martens had explained on the previous Sunday.

"Ah, Pastor Martens is quite a different man, is he not?" asked Mrs. Garman, addressing Madeleine, as Rachel made no reply.

"Yes--oh yes!" answered Madeleine, abstractedly. She was wondering all the time where Delphin could have come from so suddenly, when he appeared close to her and Fanny in the crowd at the church door He had greeted her in a most friendly way, but when they got to the carriage they found that both he and Fanny had vanished without saying good-bye.

Rachel let her mother talk away, as was her wont. She was all the time meditating on the importance of the event which had just taken place, and was wondering how Johnsen would come out of it all. It was quite clear that her mother's was the prevailing opinion, and it was but too probable that with most people the ill feeling would take a still more bitter form. She could picture him to herself calm and steadfast in the midst of it all. Here at length she had found a truly courageous man.

During dinner Delphin gave his own rendering of some extracts from the sermon, with as much spirit as his fear of Mrs. Garman would allow, and the performance afforded Uncle Richard great amusement. Rachel thought it best to contain her feelings, for she knew that conversation with Mr. Delphin on a serious subject was nothing else than an impossibility. Madeleine, on the contrary, could not help laughing. She always found Delphin very amusing, and at the same time so good-natured. She had latterly been almost annoyed with Fanny because she treated Delphin coolly and distantly. But Delphin seemed scarcely to notice her conduct; on the contrary, he seemed even in better spirits than before. He really was a good fellow.

Several people also thought that Morten Garman was a good fellow, to allow Delphin to carry on with Fanny without interference. It was not easy to know if Morten saw anything or not, and whether his confidence in his wife, or his own bad conscience, caused his indifference.

Rachel passed the Monday and Tuesday in an anxious state of mind. Something, she thought, must happen. The feeling against Johnsen was strong, but it must surely take some more decided form. She knew that he would come to see her, happen what might, and she expected him.

CHAPTER XII.

Fanny and Madeleine had accepted an invitation for the Wednesday in the same week. Rachel had simply refused without giving a reason, but people were now used to her manner.

"I have such a dreadful headache!" sighed Fanny, as she came into Madeleine's room, who was getting ready to go out. Madeleine had come into the town on the Sunday evening.

"Poor Fanny!" said Madeleine, feelingly; "have you got that headache again?"

"Yes, it came just as if it were on purpose, at the very moment I was going to change my dress. Oh, how bad it is!"

"I think you have had a great many of these headaches lately, Fanny; you ought to speak to the doctor."

"It is no use," answered Fanny, endeavouring to cool her forehead by pressing a little hand-glass against it. "The only thing that does me any good is fresh air and perfect quiet. Oh, the noise here from the street is dreadful! To think that I have to spend the whole evening in a hot room! I can't bear it; it will be too much for me!"

"You shan't go out at all when you are so unwell," said Madeleine, decidedly. "I will make such a nice excuse for you."

"Oh, if I could only stop at home, or, even better still, if I could get to Sandsgaard; it is so quiet there!" said Fanny, with a sigh.

"Yes, that is just what you shall do," cried Madeleine. "You take the carriage when it has left me, and drive out there. I believe it is clearing up, and we shall have a lovely quiet moonlight evening."

"Yes; I don't much mind what the weather is," said Fanny, with a sickly smile. "But do you think it will do for me--"

"You need not trouble about that. I will make such charming and plausible excuses for you, that you will really feel quite rewarded for all the trouble you have had in teaching me the ways of society. Look now, I will begin like this;" and Madeleine, who had now got on her dress, curtsied and smiled, and began a most pathetic story about dear Fanny's dreadful headache. Fanny began to laugh, until it gave her head so much pain that she could not help crying out. She, however, allowed herself to be persuaded, and Madeleine drove off alone.

Madeleine now began to find herself at home in her new life. Fanny was so good and kind to her, that the young girl at last got the better of her shyness, and told her friend the whole story about Per, and the rest of her doings at home.

Fanny did not laugh at her in the least; on the contrary, she said that she quite envied Madeleine the romantic little episode, which would be a sweet recollection for the rest of her life. But when Madeleine timidly said that she considered it more than a recollection, and that she regarded herself as really engaged, she met with such a determined opposition that she did not know what to think. "Young girls, often have these absurd adventures," said Fanny, "when they are not old enough to know better." She had herself been madly in love with a chimney-sweep--a common chimney-sweep, just think of that!

The more Madeleine became accustomed to town life the easier she found it to deaden her recollections of the past. But however successful she was in burying them out of sight for the time, they would recur whenever she was alone. But she refused to listen to them; they could never become realities. Still, she never cared to go home to Bratvold with her father, even for a few days. She seemed to dread looking on the sea again.

All that day Rachel had waited in vain; she was beginning to be uneasy. Why did he not come to see her--she who had been so much the cause of his enterprise? He must know how anxious she was to talk with him, and to thank him. It was surely impossible for him to think that she also believed that he had gone too far. Should he not come to-morrow, she would write to him.

There was but little conversation that evening at dinner. The Consul was as precise and polite as he generally was when he was alone with the ladies. Fanny, who had come in hopes of curing her headache, was silent and suffering. By ten o'clock the whole house was perfectly quiet, but Rachel was still sitting in her room, lost in thought. She could not read, but several times she took up a pen to write, she scarcely knew what. She never accomplished her intention, and at last she put out the light, and sat down and gazed over the fjord, which lay spark-ling in the moonlight. If, forsaken by every one, he now came to her and prayed for even more than her friendship, for this too she was prepared, and had finally decided on her answer. He was a man, and a courageous one, and she was deter-mined to follow him. What a joy it had been to her to meet such a man! But why was she out of spirits now?

Rachel sat by the window till she heard the carriage which brought home Madeleine, and then hurriedly undressed and went to bed.

As Madeleine was driving home the carriage stopped for a moment in front of the club, while a boy spoke a few words to the coachman.

The driver that evening was old Per Karl, who many years ago had come from Denmark with a pair of horses for the young Consul. Both he and the horses were long past their work; but whenever he could get the opportunity, he was only too pleased to get the old blacks into the carriage, and himself upon the box. This had been the case this evening, when it was only the good-natured Miss Madeleine for whom the carriage was going, and she was always perfectly satisfied, as the old Jutlander well knew, even if the pace was not very terrific.

Per Karl now turned round and said to Madeleine, "What shall we do, miss? Now there will be a bother. Mr. Morten is going to drive out with us, and when he sees we have got the old horses he will be angry."

A few moments afterwards Morten came out, and, after many apologies for the delay, took his place by Madeleine's side. He said he thought he would go out and see how Fanny was, she looked so very unwell; and besides, what a lovely moonlight evening it was for a drive! He sat himself down comfortably in the carriage, and had just taken a long whiff of his cigar, when all at once he leant forward and said, "Stop! what was that?"

One of the horses had made a slight stumble, and the jar was felt in the carriage.

"I declare, it is those old horses and Per Karl!" cried Morten, partly standing up. "What is the meaning of this?"

"Oh!" muttered Per Karl, who was quite ready to defend himself, "there is nothing the matter with the old horses; but, of course, if we had known we were going to have you in the carriage, sir--"

"Rubbish! You know perfectly well the old horses were not to be used any more. I will tell my father, and have them shot to-morrow, as sure as ever it comes."

Morten was very fond of horses; and besides, he was just in that excited and obstinate mood in which people sometimes are, when they have been dining at their club.

Madeleine tried to pacify her cousin, but it only made him all the worse.

"Just look how lame that one is--the left-hand one!"

"You mean the near one, sir."

"Go to the devil with your near and off! I mean the left-hand one, the mare; both her fore legs are as round as apples. Why, I saw that in the spring."

"Not both of them," answered the old coachman, doggedly.

"Yes, they are; but I will have this looked to. I will have a stop put to it, once for all," said Morten, decidedly. He was just in the humour to take everything very much in earnest.

As soon as they arrived, he scarcely gave himself time to help Madeleine out of the carriage, so anxious was he to examine the mare's fore legs; and she heard the voices disputing and wrangling away in the direction of the stable, as she went into the house.

Madeleine's window looked to the westward, and when she reached her room she found it open. She was going to shut it, but the sea looked so peaceful down below in the clear moonlight, that she knelt down on the window-seat, and remained gazing at the lovely scene. The moon had just reached the point at which it began to shine upon her window, and the shadow fell obliquely from the corner of the house, just beyond the hedge below, thus leaving a triangular space in darkness close underneath. As Madeleine leant out she could see that Miss Cordsen's window was also open. She was just going to call to the old lady, with whom she was on the most friendly terms, but on consideration she thought it would be nicer to enjoy the delightful moonlight evening alone.

In that part of the garden the paths were to a great extent overgrown by the spreading trees. The little pond, which had once been full of carp, and where even now some remained, only no one seemed to notice them, was fringed with tall rushes. On the other side was the old summer-house, almost hidden among the shrubs, which were now never clipped. The fact is, that part of the garden which was now most cared for was that which lay just in front of the house, and the part we are now speaking of was left pretty much to itself. Along the inside of the garden-wall there stood a row of aspen trees, whose leaves were beginning to turn yellow and strew themselves on the paths. Almost all the other trees still kept their foliage, although it was already September. The mountain ash berries were beginning to redden, and shone in heavy clusters among the leaves, while here and there a leaf was to be seen turning from red to yellow. The beech trees, which had been planted in the time of the young Consul's grandfather, spread out their branches far and wide. The shining dark green foliage hung in rich festoons nearly to the ground, and the long shoots were fringed with masses of tufted beech-nuts.

A mysterious silence reigned in the garden, while the moonlight came rippling noiselessly through the leaves and stealing down the trunks, forming patches of radiance on the grass, which were sharply defined by the edges of the dark shadows. Goldfinches, bullfinches, a few thrushes, and other autumn birds, were sitting in the aspen trees. They were mostly occupied in quietly pluming their feathers, and only some of the young birds, which had been hatched that spring, were hopping about from branch to branch. The parents sat watching them, thinking, doubtless, how delightful it was to be young and innocent. All nature seemed to have reached maturity, and the restless activity of spring was forgotten. The birds were now calm and sober enough. The cocks and hens sat peacefully side by side, no advances were made or encouraged. Love-making, with all its follies, was at an end for that year. Only the curious dragon-flies, with their four long wings and taper bodies, were still busy with their love-dances over the pond. August had been so rainy and windy that they seemed anxious to make the most of the still autumn evening. The males were sitting dotted about among the reeds, peering on every side with their prominent eyes, and when one approached another too closely, the two would rush at each other till their transparent wings, like delicate plates of silver, and their scaly bodies, made a tiny rustling when they met in conflict. Then all was still again among the rushes, until the arrival of a female dragon-fly. She would come slowly and carelessly humming along from some other part of the garden, and when she got near the pond would change her course, turn off, and fly back again. Her little heart was doubtless beating high; but casting aside her fears, she at length took courage, and sped on over the pond. Away started five or six males, dashing at each other like knights in helm and harness, and battling confusedly amid the clash of tiny weapons. But the happy victor soon bid adieu to the conflict, and sailed past the others to the side of his lovely prize. Their wings met for a moment in mimic combat, and then away they glided in close embrace far over the heads of the discomfited champions, each aiding other with fairy wings, to seek a lonely spot far away among the rushes.

A plaintive air, sung by some shrill girlish voices in the West End, was wafted over by the light evening breeze. It was so still that Madeleine could follow every word:

"I now myself must sever,
My little friend, from thee.
Let naught oppress thee ever;
Soon home again I'll be."

She felt more than usually depressed, and now, just as it had happened after church on Sunday, Delphin's image seemed suddenly to spring up into her thoughts. Where he came from she knew not. A web of confused reveries seemed to weave themselves in her soul, just as the moon shed its mysterious network of shadows over the grass.

Her attention was all at once attracted by a noise in the garden. She certainly fancied that she heard the door of the summer-house creak on its rusty hinges. At the same moment she heard Morten's heavy tread on the stone steps leading up to the front door: he must be returning from the stable. It was time to go to bed, but still she remained at the window, looking towards the summer-house. She now discovered two forms that were going slowly down the path which led to the wicket in the garden wall. This path was fringed on both sides by high overgrown hedges, and she could only see the heads every now and then as they passed. In the idea that it was one of the maids with her sweetheart, she was just going to shut the window. It was surely nothing which concerned her.

The pair had just reached the place at which two paths crossed each other, which was illuminated by a broad patch of moonlight. Madeleine could not help being curious to see who it might be, and still stood leaning out of the window, holding on to the fastening of the sun-blind. The lovers stood still for a moment, as if they felt that there was danger in passing the place. At length they took courage, and sped hastily by. But not hastily enough--Madeleine had recognized them both. Her pulse seemed to stop and her heart to sink within her, and without uttering a sound she slipped down on the floor under the window. In the passage, outside her door, she heard Morten go grumbling back from the bedroom which he and Fanny usually occupied, and in which she was not to be found.

Madeleine's head became clear in a moment In another instant he would be down the staircase, out in the garden, and then--They must be saved, but why she did not know, nor how; but save them she must. Her first idea was to close the window with a bang, but she did not dare to stand up. In her need she saw the water-bottle on the table. She seized it, and, without lifting her head, put it on the window-sill. She gave it a push, and a second after she heard the crash of the glass, and the splash of the water on the paving-stones with which the house was surrounded. She lay still, crouched in a heap under the window.

A light hurried step and the rustle of a dress were heard over the lawn. All was so still, and her nerves were in such a state of tension, that Madeleine could hear one of the French windows carefully opened and closed again. The step came upstairs, and as it passed her door she heard Morten's voice say, "I am sure you never thought that I should come out this evening;" and Fanny's answer, "Oh, one feels that sort of thing instinctively!"

Madeleine breathed again. It was indeed Fanny's voice, in its most insinuating and deceitful tones.

A short time afterwards she got up and closed her window, and withdrawing into the farthest corner of the room, she hastily undressed and crept into bed. Her tears flowed the whole time, but she was utterly crushed, and soon fell into a heavy slumber.

A good hour after Madeleine had gone to sleep, her door opened noiselessly, and a tall shadowy form glided into the chamber. The form placed a water-bottle upon the table. The moon had reached the point at which it shone obliquely into the window, and down upon the bed where Madeleine was sleeping. The apparition drew the curtains more closely, and the while a beam of moonlight passed over its features. They were furrowed with innumerable small wrinkles, and a night-cap with starched strings was knotted tightly under the chin.

Noiselessly as it had entered, the apparition glided out again, and the door closed.

CHAPTER XIII.

The next day it rained in torrents. Morten drove into the town immediately after breakfast. Madeleine lay in bed with a fever. Rachel went in to see her, but she found her in such a curious state that she wished to send for the doctor. Miss Cordsen, however, was of opinion that it would be better to let her have perfect rest, and that with time she would soon come round. Rachel would all the same have sent for the doctor, if she had not forgotten it almost before she got downstairs; she was so taken up with her own thoughts. Would another day pass without his coming?

A carriage drove up to the door. Mrs. Garman, who had just finished a little private breakfast in her own room, put down her paper and said, "Is it possible? Can it be visitors in this weather?"

Rachel felt that she was blushing. She had recognized his voice in the hall, and to conceal her emotion, she sat down at the piano and aimlessly struck a few chords.

The door opened and in came Dean Sparre, followed by Mr. Johnsen. Rachel turned round on the music-stool, bringing her hand down with a crash on some of the bass notes of the piano. Her eye never wandered from Johnsen, as if she expected every moment that he would begin to speak, and give some explanation as to why he came in such company.

Dean Sparre gave a cordial greeting to the ladies, at the same time mildly reproaching Rachel for not having paid them a visit at the deanery. He had a great many messages for her from his "little girls."

Mrs. Garman became reconciled as soon as she saw who were the visitors. There was nothing she enjoyed more than a gossip with clergymen.

The conversation first turned upon the disagreeable weather, but Rachel's eyes never once moved from the inspector. He did not look in her direction; his face was pale, and his lips closely pressed together.

"We particularly wished, my young friend and I," at last began the dean, "to pay this visit at your house together. There are many things that can be explained, and many misunderstandings which can be avoided, if one only has an opportunity of talking a matter thoroughly over."

The dean paused and looked at Mr. Johnsen, who made a momentary effort to speak, in which he signally failed.

"It would be most unfortunate," continued the dean, "if a few ill-considered remarks should leave an impression on our congregation that there was any want of agreement, or rather, I should say, difference of opinion, among those who have to work together in the service of the Church."

Rachel had left her seat, and was now standing before Mr. Johnsen. "Is that your opinion?"

"My dear Rachel!" interrupted Mrs. Garman. Rachel's eccentricities really exceeded all bounds.

"Is that your opinion?" repeated Rachel, with the severity of a judge condemning a criminal.

Johnsen raised his head nervously and looked at her. "Allow me to explain, Miss Garman," he began. But he could not withstand the penetrating glance of those clear blue eyes, and hung down his head, and stopped in the middle of his sentence. Rachel turned round, and without saying another word left the room.

"I must really, gentlemen," said Mrs. Garman, "beg you to excuse my daughter. Rachel's conduct is sometimes so very extraordinary; in fact, I don't understand it at all."

"The behaviour of youth, my dear Mrs. Garman," said the dean, blandly, "is undoubtedly somewhat strange in these days; but we ought to consider how times have changed." And the pressure of his soft persuasive hand was so soothing, that when they were gone, Mrs. Garman felt almost as much edified as if she had been listening to a sermon.

That the dean, in the course of three or four days, had been able to bring about this entire change in the inspector, was for Martens a new source of wonder and admiration; and every one could not but feel greatly relieved when they saw the two going about and paying their visits together.

The whole of that memorable Sunday Johnsen had spent in pacing up and down his room, repeating to himself different parts of his sermon. Some of his thoughts he had managed to express clearly enough, while others might have been a little more incisive; but on the whole he was satisfied. He was not satisfied in the sense that he thought he had accomplished a great work, but he was so far satisfied that he now felt that he had room to breathe. Wind in one's sails, even if it is a storm, is preferable to a dead calm. What emotions he must have stirred in many a careless soul! How many of his hearers might not now be struggling with the mighty thoughts which he had thrown amongst them? In the mean time he looked out upon the street, and he felt almost inclined to wonder that the town showed its usual Sunday calm. In the afternoon he expected the dean; he felt certain he would come, and he had a speech ready with which to receive him. Give way he would not, rather resign his position; and besides, he knew of one who had promised him her friendship, if all others should turn their backs on him. And now as the day went on, and the shadows of evening began to fall, and no dean appeared, she came more and more into the foreground of his thoughts. He imagined her by his side, battling with him against the whole world, and full of hope and courage he laid down to rest.

When he awoke the next morning, he heard the wind whistling, and the rain pattering on the window-panes. Empty drays were driving at a trot down the street under his windows, and the busy Monday was again alive, on that dingy autumn morning. He had to be in the school before eight o'clock, and begin the work of the day with a prayer and a hymn. Yesterday his ordinary duties had scarcely entered his thoughts; but when the faint odour of the children's clothes as they came wet to school, their inharmonious singing, and that flagging indifference with which the school week opens after Saturday and Sunday's holiday, rose in his imagination, his everyday work appeared more than he could bear.

What was it to him? While he was sitting at his breakfast, and was just thinking of sending the maid down to the school to say he was unwell, a knock was heard at the door, and Dean Sparre entered the room. Johnsen at once endeavoured to recollect what he had yesterday arranged to say to the dean; but at that early hour, and in the presence of that perplexing smile, he might just as well have tried to sing "Lohengrin" without notes as to bring to his recollection his ideas of the day before.

The dean went straight to the point without any parley, but quite from a different point of view to which Johnsen had expected. He was of opinion, in fact, without making any further assumption, that Johnsen was in love with, and even perhaps engaged to, Rachel Garman, and that in his sermon of yesterday he had been expressing her ideas, which, although they were certainly original, were still somewhat distorted. At the same time, he was quite ready to allow that Miss Garman was no doubt a lady of first-rate ability.

All the efforts that Johnsen made to get the dean out of this line of thought were entirely thrown away; neither could he make it clear to him that his assumption of the possibility of his being engaged to Rachel was incorrect.

The dean listened with much patience and with perfect good nature to what he had to say, and took up the argument where he had left it. At last he said, calmly and plainly, "Are you not in love with this woman?"

Johnsen's first idea was to answer no; but he failed in the effort, hesitated, and said, "I don't know."

From that moment the dean had completed his task. Johnsen tried to break off the conversation by looking at the clock, which was now nearly eight.

"You are thinking of your school, like a conscientious man, are you not?" said the dean. "But you need not be anxious about it. I have been in and told them that you would be unable to attend. Mr. Pallesen will take your place this morning."

Johnsen sat down again, entirely crestfallen. He felt that he had been hopelessly outwitted and beaten. The dean's sonorous voice still rolled on. He did not directly attack any particular point in the sermon--not at all; but he showed how earthly love, although it was but the type of a heavenly one, was often apt to lead us mortals into error. This he knew of his own experience. He did not wish to make himself out better than he was, but he felt that it was of the highest importance for all, and especially for the young, to be constantly on their guard against the danger. Johnsen could see for himself to what lengths he had allowed himself to be carried yesterday.

"There is, however, one thing," continued the dean, "in which you show very great merit, my dear young friend, and for this very reason I have had, and I may say still have, great hopes of you. What I speak of is your integrity, and the natural leaning towards truth and sincerity, which seems to pervade your whole nature. But, my dear friend, how can a man claim to be sincere when he comes forward and cries, 'I love truth beyond everything, and my heart is full of love for what is elevated and pure,' and then it appears all the time that the love with which his heart was full is nothing more than an earthly love for the woman who has put these thoughts into his mind? Now, can you deny that this was your case yesterday?"

Johnsen could not exactly deny the accusation, and the dean seized upon the half-confession he had made, and continued his homily, without betraying a sign of weariness. And when he at last took his leave, which was not till nearly twelve o'clock, he said, "I will look in again this afternoon. Your thoughts are doubtless so much occupied that you will not go out to-day, and perhaps it would look quite as well if you stayed at home."

The next day also Johnsen remained in his room, and the dean paid him a visit, both morning and afternoon. At length, all at once, his conversion was accomplished. In a moment it seemed clear to him by how little he had escaped getting on the wrong path, and now all the apprehensions which he had felt on his first visit to Sandsgaard again reappeared. He felt how near he had been to forgetting and abandoning his mission--that mission among the poor, which was really his duty; but now his eyes were opened, and that very affection, the strength of which he had now only begun to recognize, he would bring as a peace-offering for his shortcoming, and for having so nearly been untrue to himself and to his calling.

He sprang up and grasped the dean's hand. "Thank you! thank you! You have saved me!" His eyes flashed, and his broad, powerful bosom seemed to swell. At that moment the dean might have sent him to certain death, and he would have obeyed.

As they drove back from Sandsgaard, the dean narrowly observed his young friend. The visit at the Garmans' had not passed off quite so successfully as some of the others which they had paid, where the inspector's calm and genuine manner had made a favourable impression. The dean thought, however, that it was better not to carry things too far, now that they seemed to have taken a good direction. They did not, therefore, pay any more visits, but drove home to the dean's to get a cup of chocolate, which Miss Barbara had prepared for them.

Miss Cordsen had now two patients to attend to, for Rachel had also kept her room for some days. The old lady went to and fro between the two. It was not easy to discover how much she comprehended of it all. Her mouth, surrounded by its innumerable wrinkles, was so tightly closed that gossip was, for her, out of the question. Calmly and methodically did Miss Cordsen carry on her duties. Both upstairs and down were to be seen her well-starched cap-strings, and the faint, old-fashioned smell of lavender seemed to hang in her very clothes.

Rachel sat for hours looking before her, without caring to do anything. To think that this should be the end of all her hopes! Was it, then, impossible to find a man with courage in his heart, and blood in his veins? She felt that she was precluded from any line of action that would really satisfy her, condemned as she was to a life of daily drudgery; but her thoughts became more and more embittered, first against him who had deceived her, and finally against the whole human race.

Madeleine, on the contrary, had no feelings of this nature; but she had a feeling of dread, which seemed daily to increase. She felt that the duplicity of her friend was so great, so enormous, that it quite passed her imagination; and then the thought that it must be he--he, to whom alone, among all this world of strangers, she felt herself attracted on the very ground of his sincerity! Again and again these thoughts arose within her and tortured her. She felt as if her foothold must be insecure for evermore. A stain of impurity seemed to have passed over her life, which made her timid and apprehensive of all these so-called friends who had thus misunderstood and deceived her.

The morning after that night she was awakened by Fanny, who came into her room in her dressing-gown before it was quite light. The truth was, Fanny had not slept very soundly, tormented as she was the whole time by her fears, and by wondering from whence the warning came. It was quite certain that it must have proceeded either from Miss Cordsen or Madeleine, for the windows of both rooms were open. If it were Madeleine, the plot had become so involved that she did not dare to think of it. If it were Miss Cordsen, it was bad enough, but still not so desperate. From the sound she guessed that it must be a glass of water, or something of that sort, and as soon as day began to dawn she got up and left her room in the hope of clearing up the mystery. Madeleine sat up as she heard Fanny come in.

"I beg pardon, Madeleine. I came to see if you could give me a glass of water. There is a spider in our water-bottle."

She drew back the curtains, and there, sure enough, stood the water-bottle with its glass. Fanny gave a sigh of relief, and left Madeleine still gazing in astonishment. It was more than she could understand.

CHAPTER XIV.

The autumn rains had now begun in earnest. Day after day the water came down in streams, and at night it could be heard pattering on the window-panes, and dripping from the eaves, every time one woke.

At first the rain came for a long time from the south-west, but there was nothing wonderful in that, for the south-west is a rainy quarter. But when it rained for a whole fortnight with a north wind, people who were weatherwise maintained that if it once began to rain steadily from the north, there would be no end to it.

One morning the wind ceased, but the clouds lay heavy and lowering overhead; and now the weatherwise averred, with much shaking of heads, that it would be worse than ever. The morning, however, actually passed without rain, and the air grew lighter and clearer; but just as the aspect began to improve, the drizzle again commenced.

The rain now set in with renewed vigour, with all its pleasing varieties of shower and deluge; but the worst form it took was when it poured persistently and unmercifully from morning to night.

The new moons came in with rain and went out with rain, and every day of the calendar was alike wet. The wind veered about to every point of the compass, and heaped up banks of fog out to sea, and heavy masses of cloud up in the mountains, which finally drifted together, and poured down their contents in torrents all along the west coast.

And now the storms began in earnest, and went soughing through the trees in the avenue, and whistling in the rigging of the vessels that were laid up for the winter.

In the old house at Sandsgaard each separate wind had its own pet corner, to which it returned with delight every autumn. The north wind came howling along between the warehouses; the south wind took the wet leaves from the garden and hurled them in handfuls against the window-panes; the east wind whirled down the chimneys till all the rooms were full of smoke; while the pet amusement of the west wind was to make a clatter with all the loose tiles on the roof, during the whole livelong night.

The Consul kept going and looking at the barometer, and tapping it to see if the quicksilver was rising or falling: but, to tell the truth, it did not seem to make much matter which it did; for the sky, the clouds, the rain, and the storm had all got into such a jumble, that the weather continued equally abominable, week after week, during the whole winter.

In the ship-yard work went on but slowly, for Garman and Worse were not so new-fangled as to build under cover; but Mr. Robson still thought that he would be ready by the appointed day, although the weather certainly was "the very devil!"

But the person who most of all anathematized the weather, and indeed the whole west coast, and everything that belonged to it, was our friend Mr. Aalbom. When he left his house in the morning, the wind and rain would persist in beating in his face, and when he came out of school, they were so obliging as to follow him right up again to his very door. When he had gone part of the way down the avenue, the wind managed to blow down on the top of his umbrella, which, after many struggles, it finally pressed down until his hat got jammed in among the ribs. Then all at once it began the same tactics from below, and blew up under the umbrella, and between the master's long legs, filling out the closely buttoned waterproof, until it bid fair to blow it away altogether.

All October and November went on much in the same fashion, and people who were given to jokes began to say that they had quite forgotten the sun's appearance.

CHAPTER XV.

At last, one day well on in December, the dreadful weather seemed to have worn itself out for a time. The sky was perfectly clear, and not even the smallest cloud was to be seen which could give rise to apprehension. During the night there had been a few degrees of frost, and the roads, which had for a long time been nearly impassable, became all at once hard and dry. On the puddles lay the first ice, as thin and clear as glass, and the meadows were hoary with frost.

The chaplain was on his way to Sandsgaard, with his newly acquired smile on his features. The lovely weather enlivened him, and made his thoughts cheerful and full of hope; for the chaplain was going a-wooing.

It was fully two years since Martens had lost his first wife; he had really regretted his loss, but now it was a long time ago. It would have been quite improper, and not at all in accordance with the views of the congregation, for so young a widower to remain single longer than was absolutely required by the ordinary rules of society. Now, the chaplain knew just as well as any one that a particular charm attaches to an unmarried clergyman--that is, for a time; and he also fully agreed with Dean Sparre, when he said a short time previously, "If a congregation is to have the peaceful, comforting feeling that their souls are well cared for, they should have the example of a peaceful, homely life before their eyes, in the form of a motherly wife at the rectory, and even better still, a family of happy children."

And besides, Pastor Martens was really in love. Madeleine Garman had long ago, in fact as soon as ever she left Bratvold, taken possession of his heart by her modest and natural demeanour; and no worldly expectations mingled in the chaplain's affections. He knew that Richard Garman had not a shilling, and he was sufficiently free from prejudice to disbelieve the general report that Madeleine's father had never been properly married to her mother. In Madeleine he hoped to find the retiring and simple-minded woman for whom he was seeking, and latterly, since her manners had become even more quiet, he had paid her greater attention, and it appeared to him that she met him in a modest and womanly manner.

On his arrival at Sandsgaard, he met Mrs. Garman in her room, and to her he entrusted his secret. At first she did not seem to take to the idea, but on second thoughts she appeared more favourably disposed. She considered that sooner or later something of the kind must happen, and it was perhaps just as well that the chaplain, who was already so dear to her should become a member of the family. She therefore said, when she had made up her mind--

"Well, Mr. Martens, if you really think that Madeleine will make you a good wife in the eyes of God and man, I have nothing to do but give you my very best wishes on the choice you have made. You will find Madeleine in the green-room."

Pastor Martens went off to the green-room, and returned after a quarter of an hour had elapsed; but Mrs. Garman's astonishment defies description, when she learnt that he had met with a refusal.

"Tell me," she groaned--"tell me every word. Oh, the poor misguided child!"

"I am afraid I cannot tell you every word that passed, Mrs. Garman," answered Martens, pale with emotion; "I am too much shocked and--"

"And surprised too, I am sure," said Mrs. Garman, concluding his sentence; "yes, that I can readily believe. What is the matter with the child? What reason did she give?"

"She did not say much," answered the pastor; "she seemed to be almost afraid of me. She went off to the door and began to cry, and said--"

"What--what did she say?"

"She simply kept repeating 'no,'" answered the chaplain, quite crestfallen.

Mrs. Garman could not disguise her astonishment.

The bright sunshine had not the same enlivening effect upon the pastor as he returned to his lodgings. He, however, managed to control both his feelings and his countenance. This was a trial that he would have to receive with humility. The only thing that annoyed him was, that he had said anything about it to Mrs. Garman.

Mr. Martens's proposal was the only thing that was wanted to complete the life of wretchedness, which Madeleine had passed ever since that moonlight autumn evening; and yet the chaplain was to a certain extent right, when he thought that Madeleine had met him with some degree of warmth. There was, in fact, something in the almost fatherly manner with which he treated her, something which seemed to soothe her affrighted heart. She had a longing to be able to feel confidence in somebody, and the calm, earnest clergyman seemed to her so different from all those for whom she had such an abhorrence, since she had made her fatal discovery. And now he, too, was to come to her with the same story; told, certainly, in a different way--that she was quite willing to allow; but still the gist of it was the same--the very same whichever way she turned.

Mrs. Garman took her most severely to task for having so unreasonably and foolishly rejected such a man as Pastor Martens; and at length, what with one thing and another, the poor girl quite lost her health, and the doctor had as much as he could do to pull her through an obstinate attack of low fever.

George Delphin had soon got to know from Fanny that it was old Miss Cordsen who had seen them in the garden, and given them the timely warning. This was for him a greater relief than Fanny expected; for, after the first feeling of pride and delight at having gained his lovely prize, Delphin had felt more and more compunction in his inmost heart every time he thought of Madeleine. He was not willing to break off with Fanny--this was more than he dared to do; but, careless and clever as he was, he thought that he would be able for the present to keep up the double game with both.

He could make up his mind when the time came, and he would make up his mind, too, if he could win Madeleine, and if he thought she was worth the price of breaking off with the lovely Fanny. But within a few days after that evening on which they had been so careless, his eyes began to be opened. Fanny was not at Sandsgaard that day, for little Christian Frederick had got the measles, and Delphin, therefore, attempted to talk with Madeleine in the good-natured and patronizing way which he had hitherto done. But a single look from her frightened eyes was enough for him; he could not endure her glance, and became silent, and immediately after dinner made an excuse for taking his leave. He had promised to look in at Fanny's during the afternoon, and he found her expecting him, as she came from the child's sick-room in a charming demi-toilette. When he came in, she ran forwards with her hands stretched out to meet him. Delphin did not take them, but said with a serious air--

"I know now who it was that saw us that evening; it was not Miss Cordsen."

"That is what I have long suspected," answered Fanny, with a smile; "but I did not wish to alarm you. Besides, Madeleine is far too stupid to allow of her doing us any harm."

At that moment he was almost afraid of her. He felt he could not remain with her any longer, although she besought him to do so.

Fanny stood watching him as he went down the street, biting her lips to restrain her feelings; but the tears stood in her eyes, and she kept a convulsive hold on the curtains, behind which she was concealing herself. For the conquest she had made, which had also on her side been at first only mere vanity, had ended by becoming a serious matter. She really loved him, and could now see clearly exactly how the situation lay.

Christmas came and passed. The ordinary festivities of the season went on as usual at the Garmans'; but this year they were less merry than usual. There were several members of the family who each had to bear his own separate sorrow; and little Christian Frederick, the only hope of the family, was lying at home, slowly recovering from the measles. Uncle Richard never seemed to gain quite his usual Christmas spirits, for Madeleine's appearance caused him considerable anxiety. Since he had no longer been able to keep her under his eye by means of the big telescope, she had quite got beyond his ken amongst all the others with whom she constantly mixed, and whenever they happened by chance to find themselves alone together, Madeleine did nothing but cry, and that was more than her father could bear.

Morten was dreading the settling of the year's accounts with his father. That part of the business which was carried on in the town, and which was regarded as a kind of offshoot from Garman and Worse, had to be most carefully examined on account of a large amount of private business and debts, which the son had incurred during the past year. His housekeeping account, which his father always wished to see, had also to be worked out carefully by itself. But the worst of it all was, that when they were sitting together in the Consul's office, Morten could never get rid of the feeling, that however he might twist and wriggle, the clear blue eyes still seemed to pierce through his every manoeuvre; and the part he had to play was very painful to him. As soon as they had reckoned up the result of the year, the Consul put his finger on the gross receipts and said, "These are far too small."

"Times have been very bad," answered Morten. "I feel sure that by next year-_"

"The times have not been so bad," interrupted the father, "but that a house with the capital with which we have to work ought to have managed to earn double. In my father's time we earned twice as much with half our present capital."

"Yes; but times were quite different in those days, father."

"And people were quite different too," answered the Consul, severely. "In those days we were contented to move with caution and foresight, without ruining our credit by mixing with a lot of speculators in all kinds of doubtful undertakings."

Morten felt the rebuke, and answered, "I did not think Garman and Worse set such store by its credit in those days."

"The house is no longer what it has been," said the young Consul dryly, closing the thick ledger. He then held out his hand to Morten over the table, and said, "Best wishes for the new year."

"The same to you, father," said Morten, as their eyes met for a moment.

The young Consul thought upon the time when he himself stood where Morten was now standing, and when the old Consul sat in the armchair. How utterly different everything was in the old days! However, the year's account was over, and Morten was glad of it.

After Christmas there was a succession of balls and parties in the town. At Sandsgaard only one large ball was given every year, and that was on the old Consul's birthday, which fell on the 15th of May.

Madeleine did not go out that winter, neither did she pay any more visits to Fanny. Rachel was, as usual, quite incomprehensible. Sometimes she would answer her well-known "No, thanks," and sometimes she would take it into her head to make herself smart, go to a dance, and be either pleasant or the contrary, just as the fit took her.

The disappointment she had experienced at the hands of Mr. Johnsen made her more bitter than ever; but she never gave him another thought. She had done her best for him, as she said to herself, and now that it was over, she heard with the greatest indifference that his Bible explanations at the prayer-meeting were so wonderfully successful; but in her innermost heart Rachel often felt a void, which sometimes made her uneasy. It seemed as if she was indifferent to everything. She felt no pleasure in anything; and it was generally when she was in this mood that she felt most inclined to go to a ball.

In February there was a dance given at the Club, at which both Rachel and

Fanny were present. Fanny was dressed entirely in blue, even to her shoes, fan, and blue flowers in her hair; but her eyes were bluer than all.

> "Ein meer von blauen Gedanken
> Ergiesst sich über mein Herz,"

as Delphin said when he came into the room. The pleasure caused her by this compliment had to suffice her for the whole evening. She could no longer hide from herself that Delphin was in danger of slipping out of her hands; but she never reproached him, for she felt instinctively that as soon as anything of the kind arose between them, all would be over, and part from him she could not.

Jacob Worse danced a waltz with Rachel, and during the pauses he tried several times to lead the conversation on to the injustice she had done him in calling him a coward. At first she avoided the subject, which was, indeed, too serious a one for the ballroom; but Worse was persistent--it was not very often that he had the opportunity of speaking with her--and at last Rachel promised him half jestingly to give him an answer when the dance was over.

As they were sitting by themselves in a corner of one of the rooms leading off the ballroom, and while the dancing was still going on, she said, "I must beg your pardon for what I said the other day. You are not a bit more cowardly than the rest of them."

"If we could manage to define exactly what you mean by cowardice," said Jacob Worse.

"But you know perfectly well."

"Well, then, is not this about your idea? When a man, either in politics, or in religion, or in any other serious matter, is not at all in accordance with the general tone of the society in which he lives--then, if he holds his tongue, it can be from no other cause than from what you are pleased to call cowardice."

"That is exactly my opinion, and I maintain it is correct."

"But, on the other hand, I am sure you must allow," continued Jacob Worse, "that all opposition has not the same weight. In many cases it might do more harm--"

"Oh, I know that miserable, cowardly excuse!" broke in Rachel, abruptly. "'What is the good,' you say, 'of even my best endeavours when I work alone?' and then you lie down and go to sleep. That is indeed cowardice *par excellence.*"

"I must, however, tell you, Miss Rachel," answered Jacob Worse, who was beginning to lose his self-control, "that there is many a man who during his whole life is painfully conscious that he has not the power of making his views felt, or has even the opportunity of bringing them before the world. But it is not in courage that such a man is wanting--far from it."

"I could almost believe that you were speaking of yourself," said Rachel, with indifference.

"Yes, and so I am!" answered he, hurriedly. "I have always been one of those heavy, slow-thinking people, but I have a quality which that kind of person would be better without. I am hasty. From my boyhood I have known it, and have kept it under to the best of my ability. But, notwithstanding my efforts, this hastiness sometimes gets the better of me, just when I am most in want of a little cool reflection. I lose my head, the words begin to flow like a torrent, and I listen to them myself almost with terror. Yes, you have heard me yourself on one memorable occasion, Miss Rachel," he added with a smile, "and I am sure you will confess that a man of my nature is but little suited to engage in a struggle with prejudice. For, for such a struggle, patience and coolness are imperative."

"It is quite possible that the attributes of which you speak are most desirable," answered Rachel, "but still it seems quite clear to me that every man who has a conviction is bound to act up to it. How much he can accomplish is not the question he must ask himself, but he is bound to make the attempt."

"I will just tell you how my first attempt turned out," said Jacob Worse. "When I came home, which is now about two or three years ago, still breathing the comparative freedom of other lands, the first thing in our own country which attracted my attention was the exceptionally bad social condition of our labourers and mechanics. Their houses and food, the bringing-up of their children, their teaching and education, in fact, everything which belonged to them, fell far short of what I thought it ought to be."

"I have often thought upon the same subject," rejoined Rachel. "But father says it is the fault of the people themselves; they are so greatly opposed to change."

"That is one of your most excellent father's worst prejudices. However, I began by getting up a society, which with us is no easy matter. All went well at first, and then a president had to be chosen. Some one suggested myself, a proposition to which all the others agreed, which was quite natural. I thus became president, and took no little trouble in instructing the people as to what questions were important for them, and what were their requirements. Then I began to hear a whisper here and there that it was a curious thing that the president of the society had never been properly elected. I did not take much notice of these whispers, but still I suggested that there should be an election. The day came, and some one else was chosen in my place."

"It was Mr. Martens, was it not?" asked Rachel.

"Yes; you are quite right. I was greatly astonished, and did not attempt to conceal my feelings. Martens had not attended a single one of our meetings before the afternoon on which he was elected. I found the whole thing quite incomprehensible. However, in our state of society, it is not difficult to get to know anything if you only give yourself the trouble to make a few inquiries; and so I soon got a clear knowledge that the person who had got up the whole thing was the dean. So one day I called upon him."

"No! I never heard of that!" cried Rachel. "What did the dean say?"

"Nothing. The answer he gave me amounted to nothing. Not that I wish you to understand that he held his tongue. On the contrary, he talked incessantly in his best-modulated voice, and was smiling, friendly, in fact, almost appreciative, but not a single word fell from his lips that was really to the point. Do what I would, I could not get him to discuss a single question, or to give me a reason as to why he had got me turned out of the workman's society, and put his chaplain in my place. He denied nothing and confessed nothing, and the end of it was--there, again, my misfortune--I got so annoyed to see him leaning back in his chair, with his white hair and everlasting smile, that I got into one of my worst tempers and poured out a regular volley of thunder at him."

"Well, and the dean--did he lose his temper?" asked Rachel.

Worse laughed. "I might just as well have tried to get a spark out of wood, as to get him to lose his temper. No; the dean was bland as ever, and when I left he shook my hand, and hoped he might soon have the pleasure of seeing me again. But afterwards I got well paid out for that visit."

"How was that?" she asked.

"Well, you see, since then I seem to have been under a ban, which shows itself in all sorts of little ways--in business, in society, everywhere. My mother, poor thing, hears it in her shop from her customers, and it always takes the same annoying form: regret about modern disbelief, and free-thinking, and so on; and I am certain that most people regard it as a stroke of wonderful good luck, that I was prevented in good time from corrupting--yes, no less than corrupting--our noble work-people. So I said to myself, 'Since there is such a wide difference between my opinions and those of the people whom I wish to assist, and since my nature is what it is, there is nothing else to be done but for me to keep myself thoroughly occupied with my work, and hold my peace.'"

"Peace! Yes, there it is again!" said Rachel. "But no, no! I am sure you are not right."

"Well, let me speak to you about yourself, Miss Garman," said Jacob Worse, becoming more courageous. "Neither I nor any one else of your acquaintance will be able to comply fully with the conditions you lay down. But I know one person who has the power, and that, Miss Garman, is yourself. You have all the qualifications we others lack."

"I! a woman! and, worse than all, a lady!" said Rachel, looking at him with the greatest astonishment. "And how, if I may ask?"

"You must write!"

Rachel hesitated, and looked at him suspiciously. "That is not the first time I have heard this. More than one person has mentioned it to me before. I suppose it is that authorship is reckoned as one of the bad habits of an emancipated woman."

Jacob Worse again began to lose his self-command. "I don't mind your calling me a coward, Miss Garman. But when you think, or pretend to think, that I am not speaking more seriously than some of these--"

"No, no; sit down, I beg you," said Rachel, anxiously, putting her hand on his arm. "I did not mean any harm, but I am so suspicious. I beg pardon. There, now, don't think any more about it. You really do think, then, that I ought to write?"

"I am quite sure you ought," answered Worse, who soon became quiet again. "You have so much originality and so much energy, that you will be able to overcome every difficulty, and in courage you are certainly not wanting."

Amid the whirl of the dance around them, these encouraging words sounded doubly strange in her ears, and seemed to open out new vistas before her.

"But what have I got to write about? What do I know that the world does not know already? No, you really must be wrong, Mr. Worse. It is beyond me;" and she looked down at her dress, and could not help feeling that Worse was becoming rather dull.

"It is not very easy to say beforehand what your subject ought to be," said he; "but it is clear that there are endless things that the world can only learn from a woman, and which it seems to be expecting to hear. For you it is but to have the will. You are now passing through a crisis in your life, and you have such a fund of energy--"

"You seem to be treating me more like a chemical equivalent than like a human being, not to say like a lady," said Rachel, laughing.

"Let us be thankful that you have so little of the lady about you," said Jacob Worse, bluntly.

The dance now began for which Rachel was otherwise engaged, and her partner came and carried her off.

Jacob Worse stood watching her for a few minutes. He then got his coat and went home.

He perfectly understood that by awakening these thoughts in her, he would make the fulfilment of what was really the dream of his life become more distant than ever. But he felt convinced that Rachel's splendid abilities would be entirely thrown away in her present narrow sphere; and he felt, too, that he was perfectly honest to himself, when he said that he would not hinder her from taking the path she ought to follow, even if he thereby destroyed his own greatest happiness. But when he got home and was alone in his own quiet room, he was even more dispirited. He could not but see that when Rachel came to have a proper estimate of her own powers, she would find her present home too narrow for her, and a marriage such as he could offer would be quite unworthy of her.

He saw a light in the rooms at the back of the house. It was not much past eleven; so he went over to his mother, whom he found in her dressing-gown, busied in arranging her small remnant of hair for the night.

It was not astonishing that the worthy Mrs. Worse's eyes kindled with pride when she saw her tall, handsome son come in, dressed as he had been for the ball: but when he threw himself on the sofa, and hid his face in his hands, and said, "Oh, mother! mother!" just as he had done in his boyhood when he had done something foolish, Mrs. Worse shook her clenched fist against some imaginary foe in the corner of the room, and muttered, "Is it decent to send me home a son in such a plight?"

She did not, however, say the words aloud, but went over and took his head upon her lap, and, as she passed her fingers through his hair, she said with her unwavering constancy, "There, my dear boy, only keep yourself calm, and it will all come right, somehow or another."

Rachel would also have been glad enough to have been taken home at once; but Mrs. Garman had heard that the new cook had something new in *filets*, and they therefore had to wait until after supper.

CHAPTER XVI.

At length winter went stealing off to the northward, like a weary monster, leaving its long train of dirty white snow patches along the hedges, and its neutral-tinted ice pitted all over with small holes, upon the pools. The spring followed closely on its heels, and had work enough to make the earth look green again, and deck it out in all its finery for a little time, until the monster came creeping southward again with its wreaths of new-fallen snow, and its dark-blue ice shining like polished steel.

It was the 14th of May, and Uncle Richard was riding on Don Juan along the road from Bratvold. To-morrow was the great day at Sandsgaard. The ship was to be launched in the morning, and in the evening was to be given the yearly ball.

The old gentleman was deep in thought, and Don Juan went pacing slowly along, turning his well-shaped head on every side, while the south wind that came swelling up along the coast persisted in lifting the locks of his long mane and throwing them on the wrong side, and played with the forelock on his brow.

The road led over swelling ground covered with heather, past well-stocked farms, over moors, and desolate wastes thickly strewn with boulders. Not a tree was to be seen as far as the eye could reach, and it reached far, both out to sea and over the country, which sloped gradually up to the mountains many a mile inland.

What a wealth of life seemed bursting from the thawing earth! How many balmy odours seemed to rise; how many changing colours; how many wreaths of mist were gliding over the pools, and hanging in the rushes, or spreading themselves over the moorland; while the clear sunny air was ringing with the song of larks singing in emulation! There were the plovers racing after each other, the sandpipers, the snipes, starlings, and ducks. A whole life of joyous bustle; while out to the westward could be seen the line of bright yellow sand standing out against the dark-blue sea.

Uncle Richard saw but little of all this as he went along. Things had not gone well with him during the winter. While at home, Madeleine was constantly in his thoughts; and when he went to Sandsgaard and saw her, it did not tend to make him more cheerful.

She had told him about Pastor Martens's proposal to her; but there was nothing to worry over in that, thought the *attaché*, especially as she had refused the offer. There must be some other cause for her depression, and to-day he had made up his mind to talk to Christian Frederick, who always gave such good advice. He had also determined that he would at length take courage, and ask his brother how money matters stood between them. It was really too bad not to have a clear knowledge of one's own affairs.

At Sandsgaard he found the whole house in an uproar. On the second floor the furniture was being moved, dusting was going on, and candles were being put in the chandeliers. Downstairs the table was already laid for supper; only the old gentlemen's bedrooms and the offices were respected; and in the window of the still-room he noticed jellies and blancmanges, which had been put there to cool.

"Oh dear me! what a bustle it all is!" said Mrs. Garman, faintly.

She had had her armchair moved into a room at the side of the kitchen, where the dishing-up was done.

Here she remained the whole day, and had samples of everything that was cooked in the kitchen brought to her. The kitchen-maids were as nervous as if they had been undergoing an examination.

Miss Cordsen was everywhere, prim and noiseless as usual, and without wasting a word, she gave an eye to the vast amount of knives and forks, lights and silver, glass and china. Everything was arranged in her experienced head, from the ladies' cloak-room to the supper for the musicians.

But if there was a busy stir in the house, it was even greater down at the ship-yard. Tom Robson had kept his promise, and the ship stood trim and ready, "as a bride," as he put it. And now the whole staff of workmen were occupied in getting everything in order for the morrow, and clearing out the yard, so that it might look tidy and neat when all the visitors came to see the ship "go."

"What time will it be high water, Mr. Robson?" asked the young Consul, as he and Uncle Richard were making an inspection of the ship-yard in the afternoon.

"At half-past ten, sir," answered the foreman.

"Very well, then, let me see that you have everything ready to-morrow at half-past ten, on the stroke, you understand--at half-past ten on the stroke."

"All right, sir!" said Mr. Robson, touching his cap.

But Tom Robson was not going to leave anything till the morning. That evening he had every intention of making a night of it, and Martin had already got the money to make some extensive purchases. There would be time enough to sleep it off before half-past ten. He was careful to have everything ready that evening. The ways were carefully smeared with tallow and soft soap, and put in their places; the props were all ready to be removed; and everything that might get in the way in the harbour, was hauled out of the way and secured to its moorings.

The ship lay with her stern towards the water, and her stem slightly raised above it. Under her bows lay all the material for use the next day. The spare pieces of timber that were to be put under her, and the wedges which were to be driven in to raise her forward, were ready to hand, as were the jacks and levers. Everything, in fact, down to the long-handled mauls was in its place.

Gabriel followed at Tom's heels all day. He wanted to take in everything clearly, and succeeded fully in so doing. Only one thing, the ship's name, that he was so anxious to know, still remained a secret, which Tom would not betray. And Tom himself it was who, in accordance with the Consul's orders, had spiked on the name-board when it was nearly dark.

The company at Anders Begmand's had been busy that evening, especially Tom Robson, and by the time it was about ten o'clock he was pretty well tipsy. Woodlouse was no better; but Torpander kept as sober as usual, looking towards the door every time he heard a noise. With the darkness a fresh breeze began to blow up from the south-west, which swept over the open ground above Sands-gaard and down on to the fjord. It made the old cottage shake again when the wind came back in eddies from the hill behind it, and Torpander got up every moment, thinking that the door was opening, to the endless amusement of Mr. Robson.

Martin drank in silence, and looked even more gloomy than usual. The whole winter he had been out of work. Tom Robson had lent him money, and that made him even more morose, for he was proud after his own fashion, and gratitude was not in his nature.

At last Marianne came. Torpander greeted her in his usual respectful manner, to which she answered with a faint smile. She looked almost ready to fall from weariness, as she passed hurriedly through the room. "Hulloa!" cried Tom, who only saw her when she had reached the kitchen door, "here comes my sweetheart! Marianne, my darling! the ship is ready now, and Tom Robson has got some money. Let's have the wedding; to-night, if you like! Come along!" cried he, struggling to get over the bench.

Martin thrust him back. "Will you let my sister alone?"

"I suppose she is not good enough for an honest seaman, because of that infernal young Gar----"

He did not get any farther, for Martin aimed a blow at him and struck him behind the ear. Marianne hastily left the room. Torpander now threw himself courageously on his ancient enemy from the other side, and a frightful scuffle ensued.

Tom Robson put himself in position like an English boxer, drunk as he was, and squared his arms and elbows for the fray.

At first he made a few feints at Martin, which were not meant to be serious. But when he had received a few blows which were really painful, he sprang away from the table so as to get more room. Torpander had not the least idea of using his fists, but hammered away like a blacksmith with his long skinny arms, either at Tom or else in the air, just as it might happen. Mr. Robson gave him a tap every now and then which made his bones rattle again, but on the whole he allowed the Swede to hammer away at his back as much as he liked.

Woodlouse looked on for some time with the greatest satisfaction, until the idea struck him that he would clear the room. He accomplished his object with the greatest perseverance, and what with butting with his head and pushing his heavy body between the combatants, he at length managed to get the whole lot turned out of doors. Begmand threw their hats after them, and shut the door.

The fresh wind had a cooling effect on them all, and on Woodlouse's suggestion a truce was concluded. In order to ratify this, it was arranged that they should go to Tom Robson's house, and have another dram and a bit of English cheese.

They then clambered up the steep path at the back of Begmand's house, Tom Robson leading, and as he was helping himself with his hands up the steepest places, he chanced to get hold of a loose stone, which, in pure drunken wantonness, he threw at Marianne's window, where he happened to see a light. The stone struck with such force, just where the bars of the window-frame crossed, that all the four panes were smashed, and the glass came clattering down.

"That was Tom Robson!" yelled Martin, who was the last. "Let me get up to him! Out of the way! Only let me get my hands on him!" and he worked his way past the others, and got up to Tom, just as he had reached the top of the slope where the flat meadow began.

Martin went at him with such violence that the other had not time to put himself in position. Blow after blow rained down on him, until he fell to the ground half stupefied. Martin threw himself upon him, put his knees on his breast, and struck him in the face, and then continued hitting and kicking at random until he could do so no longer.

The others now came up, but did not get between the combatants. Martin was now perfectly wild, and went on in front, swinging his arms, cursing and swearing horribly. Tom Robson came limping behind; but no sooner did Martin catch sight of him, than he threw himself upon him a second time, until he again lay apparently dead upon the meadow. They thus continued their way over the field, but just as Martin was making a third attack upon Tom, a tall, slender boy came springing over the field, and put himself in front of Martin. It was Gabriel Garman.

"Will you leave him alone, Martin?" he cried, breathless from running.

"Oh!" cried Martin, "here is one of the bloodsuckers! You have just come at the right time. I will wreak my vengeance on you, you infernal young scoundrel!"

But just as he was on the point of attacking Gabriel his arms were seized from behind.

"Are you mad, Martin? It's Gabriel, the Consul's son. You are out of your senses, lad!" cried Woodlouse. Both he and the Swede threw themselves upon Martin, and held him fast. Martin yelled and struggled, until he at length fell back, wearied with his efforts, and lay still.

Tom Robson did not know much about what was going on, but managed, however, to stumble up to his house, which was close by.

"You have no occasion to be afraid, Mr. Gabriel," said Woodlouse, in a fawning tone; "we have got him tight."

"That is what you ought to have done before," answered Gabriel. "I should have been able to look after myself."

He was so slight and slender that Martin could have crushed him, mad as he was; but Woodlouse could not help saying, as he went down the slope, "There is good blood in them."

Martin, whom they had now let go, raised his head. "Blood, do you say? Yes, there's blood in them--the blood of the poor that they have sucked from father to son. And all that blood have they turned to gold--shining, blood-red gold; but," added he, mysteriously, "I will tap the gold out of them--I will--till it shines as red as blood all over Sandsgaard! Just wait a minute!" And off he rushed down the slope with the activity of a deer. Woodlouse and the Swede looked at each other meaningly, and each went his way without saying a word.

After the window had been broken, Marianne quickly put out the light. She took her petticoat, and tried to stop up the window, but the wind was blowing so hard that she could not manage to make it tight. She shivered with the cold as she stood, and hurriedly got into bed. But every time a blast came she felt the cold draught, and could not get warm.

In the room below she heard her grandfather stumbling about, drinking up what was left in the glasses. Marianne clasped her hands, and prayed that she might die; but in the night she got up, and felt herself throbbing with heat and shivering with fever. She thought she could hear a tumult, and the sound of many voices.

CHAPTER XVII.

Mrs. Garman had already gone to bed after her long and tiring day. Madeleine had also slipped out of the way, as she always tried to do when Fanny came. Both Fanny and Morten were at Sandsgaard that evening. The latter behaved to Madeleine just as before, and was so smiling and kind that Madeleine had often to ask herself if she had not, after all, been dreaming on that moonlight evening.

It was nearly eleven o'clock, and Gabriel had just returned from his expedition to the field above the West End. He had heard a noise up there when he had gone out to see how the wind was.

The Consul and Uncle Richard were playing chess. Morten, Fanny, and Rachel were talking of to-morrow's ball, and they every now and then addressed themselves to Miss Cordsen, who was sitting by the fireside polishing the silver.

"It is a south wind, is it not, Gabriel?" said the Consul, as he listened to the sough of the wind through the trees.

"South-west, and blowing fresh, father," answered Gabriel.

"Good!" said the Consul. "It won't do us any harm if only the wind doesn't get round to the northward, because that drives the sea right in on to the yard."

The ladies were getting up to say good night, and Morten was just going to brew himself another glass of toddy, when excited voices were heard below. Some one came hurriedly up the staircase, the door opened, and in rushed Anders Begmand. His face was as white as it could be for sweat and pitch, his stiff hair was standing on end, while, hat in hand and with his eyes fixed on the young Consul, he began--"The--the--the"--quicker and quicker. It was quite plain that it was something of great importance, and his face grew as red as fire with the effort. "The--the--the--"

"Sing, will you?" shouted the young Consul, stamping on the floor.

Begmand began singing to a merry little air, "A fire's broken out in the pitch-house!"

At the same moment some one in the yard below shouted at the top of his voice, "Fire! fire!"

Morten tore aside the blind, and the red glare could be seen on the dewy panes. Every one sprang to the window.

"Silence!" cried the young Consul, while every one paused and looked at him. The little man was standing as erect as an arrow, his eyes calm and clear, and his lower jaw projecting as usual; and as if conscious that he was the chief of the house, he said, "A fire has broken out in the building-yard. You, Morten, go and get the two engines from the warehouse. The keys are hanging in the men's bed-room. Take the fire-buckets with you."

Morten dashed off.

"Dick, you must go up to the second floor in the same building. There's a large sail there; put it in the sea, and stretch it over the roof of the storehouse. You understand? The storehouse must be saved, or else--"

Uncle Richard was already out of the door with Anders Begmand.

"Gabriel! you run up to the farm! Gabriel!" cried the Consul. But there was no Gabriel to be seen; he had already vanished through another door.

"Oh! what a wretched boy it is!" said the young Consul, in spite of himself.

There was something uncanny about the black smoke, and the dark red flame, which seemed every moment to get a surer foothold, and to gather strength without a soul to oppose them. Gabriel noticed nothing: he saw only the red glare on the ship, which loomed against the dark grey sky, and off he ran like a madman over the field above the house. When he saw the ship was in danger, Tom Robson was his first and only thought, and he went straight into the house where he was so well known.

"Mr. Robson! Tom! Tom!" he shouted into the dark room, which smelt like an old rum-cask. "She's on fire, Tom! The ship's on fire!"

He groped his way to the bed, and gave Mr. Robson a good shaking. The landlady, a slatternly sailor's wife, now entered with a light. Only a few minutes before, she had managed to get Tom undressed, somehow or another.

"Oh no! can that be Mr. Gabriel?" said she, drawing her night-dress closer to her. "Is it a fire? Mr. Robson!" she cried, and helped Gabriel to shake him.

"What's the matter?" muttered he in English, turning round his face, all bruised and bloody as he was.

"Oh no, no!" whined the woman, "how beastly drunk he is! Isn't it a shame for such a fine fellow to make himself just like a pig? Tom! Tom! Oh dear me, how tipsy he is!"

Without a moment's hesitation, Gabriel dashed the contents of the basin in his face. Mr. Robson sputtered and blew, and raising himself on his left arm, swung the right feebly over his head, and shouted, "Three cheers for Morten Garman! Hip--hip---" But before he got to "Hurrah," he fell back on his side and was snoring again. Gabriel left the room; there was nothing to be done with Tom.

The wind was sweeping down over the meadow, and driving the thick smoke from the pitch-house out over the fjord. All round the house it was as light as day. Long tongues of flame were flying far away over the fields, shedding their glare here and there on the front of a whitewashed house, while up above on the level ground it was still dark, under the shadow of the vessel. And now a glitter was seen, and a rumble was heard in the direction of the town. The fire brigade was on its way. And from the farmhouses which lay near, down over the fields, but chiefly in the avenue leading from the town, people were to be seen running, first singly, then two or three, then several together, until the crowd in the avenue appeared like a close black mass, dotted here and there with red-and-white specks. When Gabriel got down again to the house he was at his wits' ends, and, leaning against the garden wall, he sobbed aloud.

Some one came skirting along the wall; it was the schoolmaster, Aalbom. He recognized Gabriel, and stopped. "Isn't it what I always said?" cried he, triumphantly. "You are a regular Laban, standing here blubbering. You might at any rate manage to lend a hand with the water, you lout!"

Gabriel sprang up, as if seized with a sudden inspiration, pushed the master aside, and dashed down towards the building-yard.

"An ill-mannered cub," muttered Aalbom, as he continued his way to get a good place from which to see the fire.

Rachel was naturally most anxious to make herself useful, but there was nothing for her to do. She therefore stood on the steps in front of the house, and watched the crowd streaming up from the town, while the fire threw its ever-increasing glare down the highroad, which was now thronged with people. Suddenly she heard a voice she recognized. "Out of the way! Let the engines pass! Look out there--the engines! Out of the way!" The crowd opened, and out of the throng came two rows of men, dragging the red-painted fire-engine by a long rope. Jacob Worse was running in front, shouting and giving his orders. He gave her a hurried greeting as he passed, and away rumbled the engine towards the ship-yard. It struck Rachel that his face was the only one that showed any feeling of sympathy or sorrow; all the rest appeared indifferent, and some showed, openly enough, that they thought the fire glorious sport. Rachel turned away and went into the house.

All this time the young Consul was standing at the corner window, on the north side of the small sitting-room. The pitch-house was now blazing inside; the flames came bursting out of the door, and followed the line of melted pitch which flowed along the ground. The thick wooden walls were glowing with the heat, and he could see the people shrink back when they got too near them. The wind was blowing so strongly, that it beat down the smoke and shrouded the engines and spectators from his view, but upon the roof of the storehouse he could see Uncle Richard, in company with some other forms, working away with the wet sail. The storehouse was only a few yards distant from the pitch-house, and was thus so close under the stern of the ship that she was as good as lost, if the fire once happened to catch the former building.

The Consul could see that they had got the sail drawn over the roof; but at that instant the tiled roof of the pitch-house fell in, and the flames suddenly shot high into the air, and were borne by the wind right down on to the storehouse. The *attaché*, and those that were with him, had to get down from the roof on the other side as best they might.

A step was heard running up the stairs and through the passage.

"Father! father!" It was Morten, who dashed in breathless and dripping. "Father, we must have some powder; the storehouse must be blown up!"

"Nonsense!" answered the Consul, drily. "Why, it is right under the very stern of the ship."

"Well, I don't know," answered Morten, "but something must be done. I don't see much good in those old fire-engines."

The young Consul drew himself up; he seemed to hear an echo of all the disagreements there had been between them. It was the old story, the new against the old, and he answered shortly and coldly--

"I am still the head of the firm. Go back and do your duty, as I directed."

Morten turned and left the room with an air of defiance. The idea of using powder had taken his fancy, although it was not his own. An engineer had been standing behind Morten with his hands in his pockets, after the manner of engineers, and had said, as engineers do say, "If I had my way, I'm blest if I wouldn't do different to this."

"What would you do?" asked Morten.

"Powder!" answered the engineer, curtly, as engineers have a habit of answering.

It was hard for Morten to give up his powder, and he muttered many ugly oaths as he went down the staircase.

When the Consul again looked out of the window after Morten had gone, he involuntarily seized the damask curtains tightly in his grasp, for the change which had taken place in these few minutes was only too apparent. The wet sail had already turned black, and in another minute was beginning to shrivel; while the whole of one side of the storehouse burst into a bright yellow flame, which came streaming down over the roof, flashing amid the thick smoke, and long fiery tongues began to lick underneath the vessel.

The Consul knew what there was in the building--tow, paint, oil, tar. The ship was hopelessly lost; the good ship of which he was even more proud than any one suspected.

After the first feeling of despair, he began to calculate in his head. The loss was heavy, very heavy. The business would be crippled for a long time, and the firm would receive an ugly blow.

And yet it was not this which seemed to crush the determined little man, until it almost made his knees quiver. This ship was to him more than a mere sum of money. It was a work he had undertaken in honour of "the old" against "the new;" against the advice of his son, and with his father always in his thoughts, under whose eye he almost seemed to be working. And now all was thus to come to such an untimely end.

The large engine belonging to the town managed to reach up just so high as to keep the ship's side wet as far as the gold stripe which surrounded her; but in under the stern the water could not get properly to work, and small points of flame soon began to break out, and the Consul could now see that the fire had caught the stern-post.

The side of the ship which was towards the fire became so hot that the steam rose from it every time the thin stream of water swept over it. And now all at once a large part became covered with small sparkling flames, just as if sheets of gold leaf had been thrown against it, which crackled in the wind, and at last got fast hold in the oakum seams between the planking. The hose played upon them and swept them away; in another moment they were there again. They broke out in other places, ever gaining ground, taking fast hold with their thousand tiny feet until they got up to the gold band, and even beyond it; and see! the flames now seemed to take a spring, and seize upon the name-board, and the shining letters stood out amidst the flames. It could be read by all. The Consul saw it. There it stood: *Morten W. Garman*. It was the old Consul's name--his ship--and now what was its fate?

"Look at the young Consul; how pale he is!" said one of the spectators to his neighbour.

"Where? Where is he? I don't see him."

"He was standing close by the corner window. He looked as pale as death. I wonder if he was insured?"

But the young Consul lay stretched upon the floor, and had pulled down the heavy damask curtains with him in his fall.

Miss Cordsen came into the room. When she saw the Consul, she pressed her hand to her heart, but not a sound escaped her lips. For a moment she stood collecting her thoughts, then she knelt down, freed the curtain from his grasp, and lifted him in her long bony arms.

He was not heavy, and she managed to raise herself with her burden. At this moment her glance fell on the mirror opposite. A shudder passed through her, and it was with difficulty she kept herself from falling. A whirlwind of recollections swept through her brain as he lay on her shoulder; and she bore him along, an aged and withered man. But she pressed her lips together, and drawing herself up, she carried him along like a child; and, as all the doors were open, she was able to get as far as the staircase. There she called to one of the maids, who came to her assistance.

CHAPTER XVIII.

After Uncle Richard had been driven from the roof of the storehouse, and could see that all hope was over, he went off to take his turn at the engines. He worked at the pumps with all his-might and main, as if to deaden his sorrow; but now and again he looked towards the house and thought, "Poor Christian Frederick!"

Jacob Worse was directing the operations, and had had the planking, which surrounded the building-yard on the side where the warehouses lay, pulled down in order to get room for the engines. He managed to get some order among the men who were handing the water, and drove the idle spectators up into the yard near the house. As he happened to pass Uncle Richard, the latter asked him, "Do you think there is any hope, Worse?"

"No!" answered Worse, in a low tone; "I am working in sheer desperation."

"So am I," said the *attaché*, with a nod; "but think of poor Christian Frederick."

Just then a murmur went through the crowd, who could read the name of the vessel--*Marten W. Garman.*

"Why, that's the old Consul's name," said several voices.

Uncle Richard had already heard the name from his brother, and, looking up, he saw the name of their father standing out in its gold letters amidst the flames, which were curling up the vessel's side. Jacob Worse seized the nozzle of the hose, and with one sweep forced the water to such a height that the fire was quenched for the moment.

But now it was plain to all that the ship's fate was sealed, and even if there were some among the spectators who might owe Garman and Worse a grudge, still they could not but feel that it was a pity for the proud ship to be thus doomed to destruction.

Morten had returned after his interview with his father, and was standing close by Uncle Richard. Every eye was fixed on the ship. The fire increased every second, and with a loud roar the flames burst out above the roof of the storehouse, and at each blast of wind the conflagration waxed higher and higher, until the heat by the engines became almost intolerable. The more furiously the fire raged, the more silent grew the crowd. No orders were heard, and the shouts of encouragement from the seamen died away; while the strokes of the pump no longer fell with the same determined regularity. Even Jacob Worse lost heart.

But now a shout is heard from a small boy belonging to the West End, who had climbed up into the rigging of a coaster which lay off one of the warehouses. "She's giving way! She's off! Hurrah! She's off!"

A murmur of disapproval went through the crowd at this ill-timed joke. But see! it almost seems as if the joke were a reality. The excitement increases every moment, and with it are heard cries of hope and fear. Yes!--no!--yes! she really is moving. She's off! The pumps are deserted amidst breathless expectation, while the sound of voices waxes higher and higher, not only in the yard itself, but among the crowd who surround it, till it becomes a cheer, a joyous cry of hundreds; men, women, boys, all shouting they know not what, till all is mingled in one tumultuous roar.

For see! she's starting. The huge dark mass begins to move; and inch by inch, with ever-increasing speed, the massive hull glides out through the flames; her shining sides disappear foot by foot through the smoke; the golden band flashes in the glare, and high as if in triumph does the bow rear itself heavenwards, while the stern dives deep into the waves. Then is heard a hissing and a crackling as if a hundred glowing irons had been cast into the water, as the burning stern cleaves its way into the billows, which come foaming up over the sides, and in under the counter, while the tiny flames which were flickering along the seams are quenched by the rush of air.

The wind, which got more power now that the ship was away, swept down on to the still burning buildings, and, spreading out over the ground, hid from view the vessel, which was gliding out into the harbour, by a curtain of dark smoke fringed with flame; and in the midst of the place where she had stood, which looked vast indeed now she was gone, stood a little band of bent and tar-stained men, fanning their faces with their caps. In the midst of the band was seen the form of a tall and slender youth, his face glowing red in the light of the fire.

"Gabriel!" shouted Uncle Richard. "Gabriel!" was repeated by a hundred voices. The *attaché* elbowed his way towards him, followed by some of the crowd, who, however, stopped and formed a respectful ring round the hero of the day. Uncle Richard gave Gabriel a hearty embrace, and then turning round to the crowd he cried, "Three cheers for Gabriel Garman! Hurrah!" He was about to wave his hat, when he discovered that he was bareheaded.

"Hurrah!" shouted the spectators with a mighty cheer; they were just in the humour for cheering.

"Three cheers for the carpenters!" shouted Gabriel; but his boy's voice broke into a discordant scream in the effort. But it did not matter; a wild hurrah was given for the shipwrights, another for the ship, and another for the firm. There was cheering and rejoicing without end.

"Come with me," said Gabriel to the workmen. "Father was going to give you a breakfast, but now it will have to be a supper."

The shipwrights laughed heartily at this joke, but the laughter was even louder when Uncle Richard added, "I think you have earned your breakfast as well." They thought the remark so wonderfully witty, that they laughed as if they would never stop, and the joke about "Uncle Richard's breakfast" was a proverb both with them and their successors ever after.

In the mean time, the storehouse, and everything the yard contained which was burnable, was on fire. The flames began stealing down the ways, but no one took any notice of them. The ship was saved. Nothing else was of much consequence, and fortunately the wind was blowing off the land. Morten was busy setting a watch for the night, and the engines were kept ready in case the wind might change.

As Uncle Richard and Gabriel were walking back arm-in-arm to the house, the latter had to relate how it had all happened. Gabriel told his uncle how he had found the shipwrights all beginning to assemble under the ship, and so he had thought he had better take command.

"Take command!" cried Uncle Richard; "why, what a boy you are, Gabriel!" And then Gabriel went on to explain how they got the ways in their places, loosened the cradle, and wedged up the fore part of the vessel; then the stays were hastily removed; it was Begmand who had taken away the last from the stern amidst the fire and smoke, and so away went the ship just in the nick of time. Tom Robson ought really to have all the praise, since everything was ready to hand, and in the most perfect order.

Rachel came to meet them on the steps; she went straight up to Uncle Richard and whispered in his ear, "Be calm, uncle; don't let us spoil Gabriel's evening. Father has had a stroke. He is in bed, and the doctor is here."

The *attaché* entered without saying a word, and Rachel threw her arms round her brother's neck and said, "Who would have thought of your being such a clever boy, Gabriel?"

"Boy!" said Gabriel.

"Or man, I shall have to say in future," answered Rachel, with a smile. "But what have you done with your workmen?"

They were not far behind; and Rachel distributed among them beer, wine, sausages, bacon, white bread, and other delicacies, until Gabriel remarked, "You are much more liberal than Miss Cordsen; but had you not got some chickens for the ball?"

Yes, indeed! She had forgotten the ball. Rachel's feelings were so pained by seeing Gabriel in such high spirits, that she could not contain them any longer, so she said quietly, "Gabriel, there will be no ball to-morrow. Father is ill."

Gabriel had not to ask why. He saw it was something serious. The workmen were standing by the steps, laden with the good things, and uncertain where they should take them.

"Come, let us go back to the ship-yard," said Gabriel; "we shall be all to ourselves there, and besides, it will be nice and warm."

Rachel could hear from his voice that there were tears in his eyes, and the thought occurred to her, how he had grown from a boy to a man in the last few hours.

The storehouse had now fallen in, and the ruins were still burning on the ground. The yard, thanks to Mr. Robson, had been so well cleared, that the watchmen had but little difficulty in keeping the fire isolated. After midnight the wind lulled, and the thick clouds of smoke soared up into the air, and were driven slowly over the fjord.

As the ship took the water, she drove across the wind a little way from the shore, and fouled an old brig belonging to the firm; and for the rest of the night was heard the shouting and singing of the numerous volunteers, who were hard at work clearing the vessels, and mooring the newly launched one.

The shipwrights sat comfortably in the yard, just near enough to the fire to feel its warmth. They had got far more than they could fairly take on board, and, every now and then, they treated one of the watchmen to something as he passed.

The only flaw in their pleasure was that Gabriel could not be with them. He had been obliged to tell them that the Consul was ill, and that he must, therefore, remain in the house. No one thought of accusing Gabriel of pride, and they all drank his health, and as many other healths as they could find an excuse for, in bumpers of the wine to which they were so little accustomed. Of the food which had been given to them, they ate as much as they could, and when they could eat no more, they divided the remainder by lot, just as they shared the shavings for their fires, laughing the whole time heartily at the sport. Then away they all wandered homewards to the West End, carrying sausages, chickens, bottles of wine, and other delicacies. The sun was just rising over the corner of the mountain to the east of the town, and lit up the window-panes of the cottages, till it looked as if the whole West End was illuminated.

That morning there was not a wife who had the heart to find fault with her husband because he had had a little drop too much. Eating and drinking went on merrily, combined with gossiping and running from house to house. The children sat up in bed, blinking at the sunlight, and stuffing themselves with sausages, still half in doubt whether it was real tangible sausage they were eating, or whether it was not one of those lovely dreams which sometimes visit the hungry.

The sun was shining over the bay of Sandsgaard, where the new ship now lay securely moored with hawsers both ahead and astern. The sounds of activity from West End could be heard far out into the fjord.

In Begmand's cottage Marianne lay raving in delirium, and the neighbour who attended her said she had the fever. Anders, who had burnt himself on the side of the face at the fire, was sitting with her, a handkerchief tied round his head.

The townspeople managed to get home by degrees. Some pretended that they did not see the sun, and went to bed. Others stayed up, and went yawning about all day. More than half the town had been at Sandsgaard that night, or else on the heights above the house, looking on the fire.

One of the few people who had not been at the fire was our friend Woodlouse. When he and the Swede parted, after the fight between Martin and Robson, he went straight off to his home in the town. As he passed the first house, he met some people who were running, and deaf as he was, he heard the two cannon-shots which gave warning of a fire. When he got to the church, he saw that the door was open, and that there was a light in the place from whence the bells were pulled. Woodlouse looked in and saw a pair of legs, now bending, now straightening again, now going up, and now down. From what he saw, he drew the conclusion that some one was tolling the big bell. He observed carefully what time it was by the church clock, and as he went along, he was already making up his mind how he should answer the inquiries of the police, for he fully expected the cause of the fire would be the subject for investigation.

CHAPTER XIX.

Consul Garman was in bed, now three days after the fire. The left side was almost powerless; but the doctor said there was still a chance of recovery, since the patient had managed to get through the first few days. The Consul had not hitherto spoken a word, but the eyes moved occasionally, and especially the right one, for the left was half closed, and the mouth remained crooked.

Uncle Richard sat constantly by the bed, watching his brother, until their eyes happened to meet, when he would look away with an expression that was meant to be unconcerned, for the doctor had particularly said that the patient was not to be excited.

When the *attaché* was alone with his brother, he was always anxious lest he should begin to speak, and it so happened that he began to do so one day just after the doctor had been, as if he had been waiting for him to leave the room.

"Richard," said he all at once, "there will have to be a great many changes."

"There, now he is off!" thought the *attaché*.

The Consul waited a little before he continued. "It was a heavy loss, which will affect us all. The ship was not insured."

"Yes; but, you see," answered Uncle Richard, in a tone that was most unbecoming in its frivolity, "it is extraordinary what may possibly happen; in the case of a ship, for instance."

The Consul regarded him expectantly.

"How shall I get on?" thought his brother, looking round vainly for assistance.

"What do you mean, Richard?"

"Yes, he is a wonderful boy, Gabriel is," said the *attaché*, trying to smile. "I don't mean in school, but I mean--well, I hardly know; well, he knows a good deal about ship-building."

"What's the matter with Gabriel?" asked the Consul, quickly.

"Oh, nothing is the matter with Gabriel; he is all right--quite right. Did you think there was anything wrong?"

At this moment Rachel entered the room, and Uncle Richard gave a sigh of relief.

Rachel saw in a moment that her father had begun to talk, and went over to the bed.

"Tell me all about it, Rachel," said the invalid. "I should like to tell you the whole story, father; everything has turned out so well. But I am not sure that you could bear the surprise--and such a joyful surprise, too." As she said these words she looked at him calmly.

The invalid began to get impatient, and Rachel took hold of his hand as she continued her story. "You see, the ship was ready for launching, quite ready, and so away she went just at the very nick of time--without being burnt, you understand--out into the fjord; and now she is quite safe, and everything is all right. Now, father, you know it all."

"But what about Gabriel?" said the Consul, looking at his brother.

"Oh, it was Gabriel who managed everything, because Tom Robson never came," said Rachel.

"Drunk, you know; drunk as a lord. In bed all the time. Dead drunk--don't you see?" said Uncle Richard, explaining his words with signs and gestures.

"There, now, father, you mustn't ask any more questions," said Rachel, decidedly. "Now we have told you the whole story."

Her father looked at her, and she could just feel the light pressure of his hand on hers. She then took Uncle Richard with her out of the sick-room, and gave him strict orders not to be there alone in future; an injunction which he found most unreasonable.

Miss Cordsen's time was fully occupied, both with the invalid, who would have none but her and Rachel near him, and also with getting everything into order again after the preparation for the ball. In those few days, however, the old lady formed a far higher opinion of Rachel than she had hitherto done.

Pastor Martens had not had an opportunity of speaking to Madeleine by herself since his proposal. But at this time of anxiety and excitement he came very frequently to Sandsgaard. Mrs. Garman kept her bed, for what reason it was not easy to know; and so it chanced that several times, when he came, no one but Madeleine happened to be in the room. At first she was very shy and timid, but when she found that he was not in the least offended with her, she could not help appreciating his conduct. Of all others, he was certainly the person who showed her the most attention; for her father's thoughts were entirely engrossed with her uncle's illness.

A few days after this, when the Consul had been quiet for some time, he said to Rachel, "Send Gabriel in here."

Mr. Garman gave Gabriel his right hand, which he was now able to move a little. "Thanks, my boy; you have saved us from a heavy loss, and shown yourself a man. If what I hear from Rachel is true, that you would prefer to give up your studies--"

"Not without you wish it, father," stammered the boy.

"I should wish you to go to the commercial school in Dresden, and then take your place in the firm, when you have gained sufficient instruction."

"Father! father!" cried Gabriel, bending down over the Consul's hand.

"There, my boy, let me see that you are able to work, and then you may turn out good for something after all. And now will you do me the favour of finding another name for the ship? For I wish her to have a new one," said the Consul, calmly.

This great honour was almost too much for Gabriel, but with a sudden inspiration he cried, "*Phoenix!*"

A faint smile flitted over the right side of the Consul's face. "Very well; we will call her *Phoenix*. And will you see the name painted on her stern?"

As Gabriel left the room he met Miss Cordsen. He threw his arms round her neck, and began hugging and kissing her, repeating all the time, incoherently, the words, "*Phoenix*--Dresden--the firm."

Miss Cordsen scolded and struggled. She was afraid to scream; but he was too strong for her, and the old lady had to resign herself to her fate. At length he ran off, and Miss Cordsen was left, arranging her cap-strings, and saying to herself, "They are all alike, one and all." But when Gabriel ran across the yard, and, meeting the fat kitchen-maid Bertha, gave her a friendly slap on the back, the old lady clapped her hands together, and exclaimed, "Well, I declare, he is the worst of the whole lot!"

The Consul had several long interviews with Morten, who put on an air of importance before the clerks and workpeople. But his feelings, when he took his father's place in the old armchair in the office, are not easily described.

Fanny saw little of her husband, and noticed him even less. Her connection with Delphin had obtained a power over her, which she could not previously have believed possible, and she strove by every means at her command to keep him fast. But since the day on which Delphin had discovered that Madeleine knew of his intimacy with Fanny, his position became almost unbearable. He would gladly have done with it, but had not the will, and he lacked the courage to leave the place, and be quit of it all for ever. And so deeper and deeper he fell into the snare. He was weary of lying and living a life of shame, but the effort required was more than he could command. And often, when conversation flagged, he felt instinctively that she knew what was passing in his mind; as if their secret was determined to make its voice heard, although Fanny kissed him, and went on talking and laughing incessantly in order to deafen it.

One thing was a source of wonder to every one, and that was, how lukewarm the authorities were in endeavouring to discover how the fire had arisen; for that it was malicious no one doubted for a moment. It is true there were a few inquiries made at long intervals, but nothing came to light. This was not, however, much to be wondered at, considering that it was only a pack of old women and children from the West End who were questioned, while those to whom suspicion really attached were allowed to go unexamined.

Anders Begmand had been brought up, but the magistrate stated that his evidence could not be received, on the ground of his mental deficiency and general infirmity. So there the matter ended.

Woodlouse's expectation was not fulfilled; neither he, nor the Swede, nor Martin were examined, and after a few ill-natured remarks in the papers, the affair died out and was forgotten. But in the West End, and indeed also in the town amongst the lower orders, people would smile and shake their heads mysteriously when the matter was mentioned. They might say what they liked about Garman and Worse in other ways, but the firm must be allowed the credit generally of not placing their people in an uncomfortable position. And since the ship had so fortunately been saved, there was no more use in raking up the matter any further. Every one knew the story about Marianne, so now the best thing for both parties was to cry quits, and start fair for the future. It was all very well for the police magistrate to sit there looking so serious, bullying and questioning as if he meant to get at the point; but this was really only for the sake of appearances. One thing was perfectly plain--that it must all end as the grand folks chose it should; and when Garman and Worse were determined that nothing should come out, the magistrate might do whatever he liked, but he would certainly never discover anything.

This kind of thing might be unpleasant enough sometimes, but in this particular instance it was most fortunate, and the lesson to be learnt from it all was--if, indeed, there was any one who did not know it already--that it is as well to be on good terms with grand folks, even if it does cost something.

But no one would have anything to do with Martin. He had escaped scot-free from those common enemies of mankind, the law and the police, but he was a marked man, even among his own friends, and they did not scruple to let him know plainly, that the sooner he packed himself off out of the country the better.

CHAPTER XX.

There was no hope of the young Consul's recovery. For a fortnight he had been wavering to and fro. Sometimes it appeared as if the right side would prevail, but then the left got the upper hand again; and each time the paralysis seemed to get a firmer hold.

Miss Cordsen heard the doctor say to Richard, "He may perhaps linger for a few hours, but he cannot live through the night." The old lady remained for a few minutes in the sick-room, and then went upstairs. Her own apartment was a picture of old-fashioned neatness. Carpets and chairs carefully covered, boxes locked, nothing lying about; everything trim, well cared for, and shielded from prying eyes.

There arose an odour of clean linen and lavender she opened the press, and in a little secret drawer behind a bundle of well-starched nightcaps, there lay carefully wrapped up, a miniature portrait in a black frame. It represented a young man dressed in a green frock-coat, with a broad velvet collar. The hair was slightly red, and brushed back in the fashion of the time, in two locks in front of the ears. The eyes were blue and clear, and the under jaw was slightly projecting. Miss Cordsen sat a long time gazing at the portrait, and tear after tear dropped down among the other secrets which lay cherished in the old press among the linen and dry lavender.

Uncle Richard sat gazing at his brother. The doctor's words had deprived him of all hope, but even yet he could not bring himself to believe that the end could be so near.

"It will soon be all over, Richard," said the invalid, in a feeble voice.

The *attaché* sat down by the side of the bed, and after a short struggle broke into tears, and laid his head on the coverlid.

"Here am I, so strong and well," he sobbed, "and can't do even the smallest thing to help you! I have never been anything to you but a trouble and a burden."

"Nonsense, Dick!" answered the Consul; "you have been everything to me--you and the business. But I have something for which to ask your forgiveness before I die."

"My forgiveness?" Uncle Richard thought he was wandering, and looked up.

"Yes," said the Consul, as what was almost a smile passed over the half-stiffened features. "I have made a fool of you. Your account does not exist. It was only a joke. Are you angry with me?"

How could he possibly be angry? He laid his face down again on the withered hand, and as he lay there in his sorrow, with his curly head buried in the pillows, he looked almost like a great shaggy Newfoundland.

The doctor came into the room.

"I really cannot permit your brother to lie so close to you--it will interfere with your breathing; and if you don't wish--"

"My brother," said the young Consul, interrupting him in a voice which bore some resemblance to his business voice. "I wish my brother, Mr. Richard Garman, to remain exactly where he is." He then added with an effort, "Will you summon my family?"

The doctor left the room, and a few minutes afterwards the invalid drew a long breath, and said, "Good-bye, Dick! How many happy days we have had together since our childhood! You shall have all the Burgundy. I have arranged it all. I should have wished to have left you better off, but--" A movement came over the features, which feebly reminded Richard of the gesture he used when adjusting his chin in his neckcloth, and he said slowly and almost noiselessly, "The house is no longer what it has been."

These were the last words he spoke, for before the doctor had got the family assembled in the sick-chamber, the young Consul was dead; calm and precise as he had lived.

CHAPTER XXI.

The same morning Torpander was seen, going along the road which led to Sandsgaard. Contrary to his usual custom, he had taken a holiday that Monday. On his head he wore a grey felt hat of the particular shape which was called in the trade "the mercantile." The hatter had assured him that it had been originally made for Mr. Morten Garman, but that it was unfortunately just a trifle too small. The hat, however, exactly fitted Torpander, and dear as it was, he bought it; and he could not help noticing the coincidence, that he was that day wearing a hat which Morten Garman had rejected. He had also bought a coat for the occasion, not quite new, it is true, but of a most unusual light-brown hue. The trousers were the worst part of the costume, but the coat was long enough, in a great measure, to hide them. Torpander could well enough have bought trousers as well, but he did not wish to trench too deeply on his savings, before he saw how it fared with him that day. If all went well she should have everything he possessed, and if it went badly he would return at once to Sweden, for he could bear the suspense no longer. He had not, truth to say, great hopes as to his ultimate success. He had heard a report that Marianne was unwell, but perhaps she was upset by the disgrace which Martin had brought upon the family. The fact that he was making his proposal at that particular time might be a point in his favour; but no, he could not help feeling that such happiness was almost bewildering.

It was a lovely sunshiny day, and the tall light-brown form went briskly on its way, moving its arms unconsciously, as if rehearsing the scene which was shortly to follow. In the left-hand pocket of his coat he had a silk handkerchief, which had long been his dream, of a bright orange colour with a light-blue border, and of which the corner was seen protruding from his pocket. It was not at all his intention to put the handkerchief to its legitimate use; for that purpose he had a red cotton one, adorned with Abraham Lincoln's portrait. The silk handkerchief was to be used only for effect, and every time he met any one in the avenue before whom he thought it worth while to show off, and that was nearly every passer-by, he drew the brilliant handkerchief from his pocket, raised it carefully to his face, and let it fall again. He derived the greatest satisfaction from feeling the rough surface of the silk cling to the hard skin on the inside of his hands.

At the building-yard he met Martin, who was coming hastily along in the opposite direction.

"Is your sister at home?" asked Torpander.

"Yes, you will find her at home," answered Martin, with an ominous smile.

In the yard close to the house at Sandsgaard, Martin met Pastor Martens, who was on his way from the town, dressed in cassock and ruff.

Martin touched his cap. "Will you come and see my sister, sir? She is at the point of death."

"Who is your sister?" asked the pastor.

"Marianne, sir; Anders Begmand's granddaughter."

"Oh yes, I remember now," answered the pastor, who knew her history perfectly well. "But I cannot come just now; I have to go in here first. Consul Garman is also on his death-bed. But I will come afterwards."

"Oh yes, this is just what I might have expected," muttered Martin, turning to go away.

"Wait a moment, young man," cried the pastor. "If you think that time presses, I will go and see your sister. It's the last house, is it not?" Upon which he went on past Sandsgaard, and on towards West End.

Martin was astonished, if not almost disappointed. The pastor meanwhile continued his way, which he did not find very pleasant when he had to pass among the cottages. Ragged urchins waylaid him, the girls and the old women put their heads out of the doors and gaped after him, while a group of children who were grovelling on the shore cheered him lustily. Wherever he turned, all reeked of filth and poverty.

As Torpander could get nothing out of Anders Begmand, whom he found huddled up in a corner of the room, he went upstairs and knocked at Marianne's door. No one said "Come in," and he therefore ventured to open the door slightly and look into the room.

Poor man! he was so appalled that he could scarcely keep his feet. There she lay, his own beloved Marianne; her mouth half open, and moaning incessantly. Her cheeks, which were sunken, were of an ashy white, and in the dark hollows round her eyes were standing small drops of perspiration. He had no idea that her state was so hopeless; and this was the time he had chosen for making his proposal! Marianne lifted her eyes. She knew him--of that he felt assured, for she smiled faintly with her own heavenly smile; but he could not help remarking how conspicuous her teeth appeared. She could no longer speak, but her large eyes moved several times from him to the window, and he thought that she was asking for something. Torpander went to the window, which was a new one Tom Robson had had made, and laid his hand on the fastening. She smiled again, and as he opened the window, he could see a look of thankfulness pass over her features. The midday sun, which was shining over the hill at the back of the house and falling obliquely on the window, threw a ray of light for a short distance into the room. Away in the town the bells were tolling for a funeral, and their sound, which was re-echoed from the hill, was soft and subdued in its tone.

Marianne turned towards the light; her eyes were shining brilliantly, and a delicate shade of red mantled her cheeks. Torpander thought he had never seen her look so lovely.

When Pastor Martens entered the room, he was as much struck by the appearance of the dying woman as Torpander had been, but in quite a different manner. It was impossible she could be so near death; and he could not help feeling annoyed with Martin, who had thus exaggerated his sister's danger, and had perhaps been the cause of his arriving too late at Consul Garman's death-bed. The extraordinary figure dressed in the long light-brown coat, which kept ever and anon bowing to him, did not tend to calm his feelings, and it is possible that something of his annoyance showed itself in the words which he now addressed to Marianne.

The clergyman was standing by the bed in such a position as to shield the light of the window from Marianne, who was gazing at him with her large eyes. He did not wish to be severe, but it was well known that the woman at whose death-bed he was standing, was fallen. At the close of such a life, it was only his duty to speak of sin and its bitter consequences. Marianne's eyes began to wander uneasily as she turned them, now on the clergyman, and now on Torpander. At length she made an effort, and turned her face in the other direction.

The pastor did not intend to finish his discourse without holding out a hope of reconciliation with God, even after such a life of sin; but while he continued speaking about repentance and forgiveness, the neighbour, who had been at her dinner, entered the room.

The woman went to the foot of the bed, but when she looked at Marianne's face she said quietly, "I beg your pardon, sir, but she is dead."

"Dead!" said the minister, rising hastily from his chair. "It is most extraordinary!" He took up his hat, said good-bye, and left the room.

The woman took Marianne's hands and folded them decently across her breast; she then put her arms under the bedclothes and straightened the legs, so that the corpse should not stiffen with the knees bent. The mouth was slightly open. She shut it, but the chin fell again. Torpander could see what the woman was looking for, and handed her his silk handkerchief. How rejoiced he was that he had not used it! The woman regarded the handkerchief suspiciously, but when she saw that it was perfectly clean, she folded it neatly and tied it round Marianne's head.

Torpander stood gazing at the little weary face, bound round with his lovely silk handkerchief, and he felt at length as if he had some part in her. He had received her last look, her last smile, and as a reward she had accepted his first and last gift. After all, his courtship had had the best ending he could possibly have hoped for. He bent his head, and wept silently in Abraham Lincoln's portrait.

Begmand came upstairs, and sat gazing at the body. Since the fire he had not been altogether himself.

"Shall I go to Zacharias the carpenter, and order the coffin?" asked the woman. But as she did not get any answer, she went off and ordered the coffin on her own account. It was not to be any more ornamental than was usual in the West End.

Meanwhile Pastor Martens was continuing his journey. Marianne's death had made a most disagreeable impression upon him, which probably added to his former ill humour.

The women, both old and young, were again on the look-out for him. A clergyman was not often to be seen in West End. The boys, who had found a dead cat on the shore, and which the eldest was dragging after him, came marching along like little soldiers. Behind them followed a tiny little creature not higher than one's knee, with his mother's wooden shoes on his feet, and wearing a paper cap on his head. The whole band was in high spirits, and sang with a ringing voice a national air, according to the comic version which was in use in West End:

> "Yes, we love our country;
> Yes, indeed we do!
> He who dares deny it,
> We will let him know!"

The pastor had to pass the children, whose song went through his head. The cat, of which he just caught a glimpse, was half putrid, and its skin was hanging in rags. Parson Martens pressed his handkerchief to his mouth; he was afraid that the unhealthy atmosphere would be injurious to his health.

He hurried out of West End and up to the house, as fast as his cassock, and having to pick his way among the dirty puddles, would allow; but he came too late. The Consul had already been dead half an hour, and so Pastor Martens turned and went back to the town. It was very hot walking in the long black garment, and already well past dinner-time.

Madame Rasmussen came running to meet him. "My dear Mr. Martens, dinner. Why, it's half-past two! Why, how exhausted you look!"

"Let us rejoice, Madame Rasmussen," answered the clergyman, with a bland smile, "when we are thought worthy to endure trials."

He was indeed a heavenly man, was the pastor. How pious and amiable he looked as he sat at table! No one could ever have suspected that he wore a wig.

Madame Rasmussen sat down to embroider some cushions to put in the window, for the chaplain could not bear the slightest draught.

CHAPTER XXII.

Consul Garman's death caused a great sensation in the town. The wonderful escape of the ship was already material enough for several weeks' gossip; and now there came this death, with all its immediate circumstances and possible consequences. The whole town was fairly buzzing with stories and gossip.

The business men gave each other a knowing wink. The old man at Sandsgaard had been a hard nut to crack, but now they would have more elbow-room, and Morten was not so dangerous.

The preparations for the funeral were on the grandest scale. The body was to be taken from Sandsgaard and laid in the church, where Dean Sparre was to deliver a discourse, while the chaplain was to conduct the funeral service at the cemetery.

All the different guilds were to follow with their banners, and the town band was busy practising till late at night. A regular committee of management was formed, and there was almost as much stir as if it was the 17th of May.[2]

Jacob Worse did not take any part in all this. He truly regretted the Consul, who had always been almost like a father to him.

Mrs. Worse was more annoyed than sorry. "It was too bad, it was really too bad," she grumbled, "of the Consul to go and die!" She was sure that he would have arranged the match, such a sensible man as he was; but now that there were nothing but a lot of women in the house--for the *attaché* was little better than an old woman himself--And so on, and so on, thought the old lady, and she wondered that Rachel, who had such a clever father, had not inherited a little more sense.

Sandsgaard was silent and desolate from top to bottom. The body lay upstairs in the little room on the north side, and white curtains were hanging in front of all the windows of the second story. Not a sound was heard, except the monotonous step of one, who went pacing unceasingly to and fro in the empty rooms. Thus had Uncle Richard been wandering every day since his brother's death. Restlessly he passed in and out of one room after another, then up and down the long ballroom; now and again into the room where the body lay, ever to and fro, in and out, the whole livelong day, and far into the night.

Rachel was more grieved at the loss of her father than she could have believed possible during his lifetime. But a change had lately taken place in her nature; she, who was so exacting towards others, was now brought to examine herself, and could see how much there was in her own nature which required reform. She

[2] Anniversary of the declaration of the Norwegian Independence in 1814.

could now see plainly enough, that it was principally her own fault that she and her father had not understood each other better. It was only during his illness, that they had both come to know how many ideas they had in common, and what they might have been to each other. Now it was too late, and she looked back on her wasted life with regret; for Jacob Worse's idea seemed to her quite impracticable.

The day before the funeral, Madeleine was sitting in the room which looked on to the garden. It was a raw, cold spring morning, with a drizzling rain from the south-west, and she had been obliged to close the window. Upstairs she could hear her father's heavy footfall, which came nearer, passed overhead, and then became lost in the distance. Never had she felt so oppressed, sick at heart, and lonely as in that house, in which there reigned the silence which always seems to accompany death.

A knock was heard at the door, and Pastor Martens entered the room. Mrs. Garman had particularly invited him to pay them a visit every day.

"Good morning, Miss Madeleine. How do you feel to-day?"

"Thanks," answered she, "I am pretty well; I mean about as well as I usually am."

"That means, I am afraid, not particularly well," said the clergyman, sympathetically. "If I were your doctor I should order you to go somewhere for a change this summer."

He still kept his hat in his hand, and remained standing near the window which led into the garden. Madeleine was sitting on the end of the sofa at the other end of the room.

"This is a gloomy day for so late in the spring," observed Mr. Martens, looking into the garden; "and a house like this, to which Death has brought his sad tidings, is a mournful place."

She listened to him, keeping her eyes fixed on the ground, and without returning a word.

"A house like this," he continued, "in which death is lying, is a picture of the lives of many of us. How many of us carry death at our hearts! Some hope or another that for us has long passed away, or some bitter disappointment that we have buried in the depths of our soul."

He could see that she bent her head lower over the sofa, and he went on speaking earnestly and soothingly, and almost to himself.

"Since it is a good thing for us not to be alone; since it is good for us to have some one to cling to, when the bitter experiences of life cast their shadows over us, so--"

Madeleine suddenly burst into tears, and her sobs reached his ears.

"I beg your pardon," said he, coming close to the sofa. "I was but following the bent of my own thoughts, and I fear I have made you unhappy, when my object ought rather to have been to endeavour to cheer you. Poor child!"

Her sobbing had now become so violent that she did not any longer try to conceal her emotion.

"Dear Miss Madeleine," said the pastor, seating himself on the sofa at a little distance from her, "I am sure you are not well--I have observed it for some time; and you may imagine how painful it is for me to see you thus suffering, without having any right to offer you my assistance."

"You have always been so good to me," sobbed Madeleine. "But no one can help me, I am so wretched--so wretched!"

"Do not indulge such thoughts, my dear young lady; do not allow yourself to think that any feeling of wretchedness is so great that it cannot be mitigated. Intercourse with the friend who understands our nature has a wonderfully soothing power over the sick heart. And for that very reason," added he, with a sigh, "I feel it doubly painful that you will not allow me to be such a friend to you."

"I cannot," stammered Madeleine in dismay. "Do not be angry with me. I do not mean to be ungrateful. You are the only one--But I am so nervous--I don't understand it all. But don't be angry with me;" and she held her hand a little nearer to him.

Pastor Martens took the hand, and pressed it gently between his own.

"You know I mean to be kind to you, Miss Madeleine," said he, in an earnest and soothing tone.

"Yes, yes, I know you do. But do you believe--" and her eye rested on him with an earnest expression.

"I am afraid your mind is disturbed; but I hope that I may be able to be a trustworthy guide for you through life. You have been unwilling to accept me, and I will not importune you; but I must tell you that everything I have is at your service."

"But if I am unable--but if it is too much for me. No, I cannot!" she replied, hiding her face in her hands.

His voice was kind, almost fatherly in its tone, as he moved nearer to her and said, "Tell me, Madeleine, do not you feel as if it was almost a dispensation of Providence? When I asked you for your hand, you rejected my offer hastily--without consideration, may I venture to say? That hand now lies in mine." She made an attempt to withdraw it, but he held it fast. "Here are we again brought together. Is it not as if you were destined to be mine--you who are so lonely and forsaken amongst your own relations? You do feel lonely, Madeleine, do you not?"

"Oh yes; I do feel lonely--so dreadfully lonely," said she, disconsolately; and whether he now drew her to him, or whether she gave way of herself, she now lay with her head on his shoulder, wearied and helpless. And, as his voice sounded bland and soothing in her ears, she seemed to recover her breath, as if after a long period of oppression.

In a moment she was on her feet: he had ventured to kiss her brow. He also rose, but still retained his grasp of her hand.

"We will not tell any one about it to-day," he said reassuringly, "because of the affliction which has come upon your family. But we had better go to Mrs. Garman, and ask her blessing. With respect to your father----"

"No! no!" she cried; "father must not know anything about it! Oh, heavens! what have I done?" she murmured, holding her hand before her eyes.

A bland smile passed over his face as he took her arm in his. "You are still a little discomposed, child, but it will soon pass away." He then led her to Mrs. Garman's room.

"Could not we wait till to-morrow? My head is so painful," entreated Madeleine.

"We will only just show ourselves to your aunt," said he, quietly but decidedly, as he opened the door.

They found Mrs. Garman in her room, sitting comfortably in her armchair. Before her she had a tray, on which stood a bottle of water and a small straw-covered flask of curaçoa. On a plate was some chicken, which had been cut into small pieces and neatly arranged round the edge, and in the middle was a little shape of asparagus butter, garnished with some chopped parsley.

When Madeleine and the pastor entered the room, she was just in the act of holding a piece of chicken on a fork and dipping it into the butter, but when she saw them she put down her fork with an air of indifference, and said, "I hope, Madeleine, you will not forget to thank the Lord for thus changing your obstinate heart; and for you, Mr. Martens, I will hope and pray that you will never have to repent the step you have taken."

For a moment Madeleine's eyes seemed to flash, but Mr. Martens hastened to observe, "My dear Madeleine is quite overcome. Would you not rather go to your room? We shall meet again to-morrow."

Madeline felt really thankful for his suggestion, and gave him a feeble smile as he followed her to the door.

When the pastor had gone, Mrs. Garman could not help thinking how differently people behave as soon as they are engaged. She suspected that she would not find the chaplain's society so agreeable for the future.

Pastor Martens was so overjoyed that he could scarcely take his usual midday nap. Later in the day it began to clear up; it was only a sea-fog which had come up during the night, as is frequently the case in the spring. Everything appeared radiant and bright to Martens as he came along the street from the jeweller's, where he had been to order the ring, but he took care not to show his feelings; it would not do to look too pleased on the day before the funeral of his intended's uncle.

In the market-place he met Mr. Johnsen.

"You are coming to the funeral to-morrow?" said Martens, insensibly leading the conversation into the direction of his own thoughts.

"No," answered Johnsen, drily; "I have to give an address at the Mission Bazaar."

"What, between twelve and two? Why, the whole town will be following the funeral."

"It is for the women, my address," said the inspector, as he continued his way.

"Well," thought Martens, "he is indeed changed! Prayer-meetings, missions, Bible-readings--quite a different kind of work!" said the chaplain mysteriously to himself. His feelings were almost too much for him.

A little farther up the street he met Delphin on horseback. There was such an unusual expression on the clergyman's face, that Delphin pulled up his horse and called out, "Good morning, Mr. Martens! Is it the thought of the discourse you have to deliver to-morrow that makes you look so pleased?"

"Discourse! discourse!" thought the chaplain. He had never prepared it. It was well indeed he had been thus reminded. However, he answered, "If notwithstanding my--or perhaps I ought to say our--sorrow, I do look rather more cheerful than I ought under the circumstances, I only do so from something which has happened to myself. It is purely on personal grounds."

"And may I venture to ask what the circumstances are which make you look so happy?" asked Delphin, carelessly.

"Well, it ought not really to be told to any one to-day, but I think I may venture to tell you," said the pastor, in a calm voice. "I have proposed to a lady, and have had the good fortune to be accepted."

"Indeed? I congratulate you!" cried the other gaily. "I think, too, I can guess who it is." His thoughts turned on Madam Rasmussen.

"Yes, I dare say you can," answered Martens, quietly. "It is Miss Garman--Madeleine, I mean."

"It's a lie!" shouted Delphin, grasping his riding-whip.

The pastor cautiously took two or three steps backwards on the footpath, raised his hat, and continued his way.

But Delphin rode off rapidly down the road, and away past Sandsgaard, ever faster and faster, till his steed was covered with foam. He had ridden four miles without noticing where he was going. The coast became flat and sandy, the patches of cultivation ceased, and the open sea lay before him. The sun shone on the blue expanse, while far out lay the mist like a wall, as if ready to return again at night.

Delphin put his horse up at a farmhouse, and went on foot over the sand. The vast and peaceful ocean seemed to attract him. He felt a longing to be alone with his thoughts, longer, indeed, than was his usual custom. George Delphin was not often given to serious thought--his nature was too frivolous and unstable; but to-day he felt that there must be a reckoning, and on the very verge of the sea he threw himself on the sand, which was now warmed by the afternoon sun. At first his thoughts surged like the billows over which he gazed. He was furious with

Pastor Martens. Who could have believed that he, George Delphin, should have suffered himself to be supplanted by a chaplain, and, more than that, a widower? And Madeleine! how could she have accepted him? And the more his thoughts turned upon her, the more he felt how truly he loved her.

How different it might have been! Yes, many things might have been different in his life, when he came to review it fairly. His thoughts then fell upon Jacob Worse, who had lately quite given him up. It had often happened to Delphin that people did not remain friends with him long. It was only Fanny who did not give him up. He made one more effort to bring up her image in his thoughts, in all its most enchanting beauty, but he failed in the effort. Madeleine seemed to overshadow everything. Then his thoughts reverted to Martens, and his agony returned. He seemed no longer to have any aim in life, which had been so utterly wasted, useless and desolate, and he began to regard himself with loathing, friendless as he was, and thus entangled in an intrigue with one for whom he had no affection, and despised by her whose love he really longed for.

All this time the mist was stealing in light wreaths over the shore; it came gliding beyond the line of the waves, and on over the sand. It paused for an instant at the man who was thus lying in despair, then stole on further, and finally settled behind the sand-hills. The grey wall of mist had now attained such a height that it obscured the evening sun, so that the landscape became all at once cold and grey, whilst the fog went scudding along, denser and denser every moment.

Delphin stretched himself on the sand, wearied with his long ride and his bitter thoughts. The long white breakers came curling ever nearer and nearer, as they broke on the beach with their subdued and monotonous roar.

He could not but think how easy it would be to have done with the life altogether, which now seemed to him of so little worth. He had but to roll himself down the sandy slope, and the waves would take his body into their embrace, and, after rocking him on their bosom, perhaps bear him far away and leave him on a distant shore. But he felt full well that he had not the courage; and as he lay there, thus pondering over his past life, he fell into a reverie, while the breakers murmured their monotonous song, and the mist, which was borne up on the light evening breeze, breathed over him cold and chill.

The landscape assumed a general tone of grey. The mist stole on, still more close and compact, and the form of him who lay by the waves became more and more indistinct. At last he was gone; the sea raised her mantle and wiped him out, while the fog drifted inland thick as a wall, and, reaching the first dwellings, swept round the corners of the houses, and sent cold gusts in at the open doors and windows.

But swifter than the mist, closer and ever more penetrating, swept the report of the chaplain's engagement through the town. It crept in through cracks and keyholes, filled houses from cellar to garret, and stood so thick in the street that it stopped the traffic.

"Have you heard the news? They are engaged? Guess! where? who? Miss Garman; I heard it an hour ago! Have you heard the news? It's the chaplain who is engaged! Well, I am surprised! They might have waited till after the funeral. Are you sure? He has been at the jeweller's! Have you heard the news?"

Thus it spread, buzz, buzz, from house to house; and when at length the weary town went to its bed, there was certainly not a soul who had not heard of the engagement from at least five separate people. It was a wonderful time, rich in important events.

But just as one sometimes sees a little brawling and muddy brook flowing into a clear stream, and following along in its course, but ever keeping its little band of dirty brown water separate from the translucent river, even so there followed with the news of the great event, a little whisper of uncomfortable gossip. It always accompanied the main story, cropping up everywhere, whispered, muttered, doubted, but never contradicted; and this little bit of intelligence was, that Pastor Martens wore a wig. It was scarcely credible, but it was undeniable; Madame Rasmussen herself was the authority.

CHAPTER XXIII.

Like all wise rulers, who feel that they ought to mark the epoch of their arrival at power with certain merciful actions, Morten had given permission to Per Karl to drive the hearse with the old blacks, which were, however, condemned to be shot on the following day.

The old coachman had got them into "funeral trim," as he said, and for three days had groomed them incessantly. The last night he had passed in the stable, so that they should not lie down and spoil their coats. They were therefore shining as they never shone before, when, at eleven o'clock on Saturday morning, they drew up with the hearse at the door.

There are three kinds of hearses, so that one has the option of driving to the churchyard just as one travels by rail--in a first, second, or third class carriage. Unless, indeed, one manages to quit life in such an abject state of poverty, that one has to get one's self carried on foot by one's friends. Consul Garman drove first class, in a carriage adorned with angels' heads and silver trappings. Per Karl sat under the black canopy, with crape round his hat, and looking with pride and sadness on his old blacks.

When the coffin, which was adorned with flowers and white drapery, was carried down from upstairs, Miss Cordsen stood at the foot of the staircase, with the servants assembled in a group behind her. The old lady folded her hands on her breast, and bowed low as they bore him past; she then went up to her room, and locked the door.

The ladies of the family followed in the close carriage with Uncle Richard, so as to be present at the ceremony in the church. Morten and Gabriel were in the open carriage. The whole staff of workmen belonging to the firm, and many of the townspeople who were not contented with following from the church to the grave, joined the procession on foot when the hearse set itself in motion. The spring sunshine was reflected from the silver trappings and angels' heads, and from the sleek and well-groomed horses, who were going on their last drive with a step full of pride and solemnity. It happened most awkwardly that Marianne had also to be buried that day. Martin had tried his best to prevent the *contretemps*, but the answer which he had received from the authorities was, that it was impossible to make an exception on his account; that the present arrangement would be most convenient for all parties, and particularly so, because it would save the clergyman a double journey to the cemetery; besides, there would be only the simple funeral service, and no address would be given.

Very well, then; since there would be no address the funeral would take place on Saturday, between twelve and two.

Outside Begmand's cottage a group of young seafaring men were assembling. There were a few relations from the town, and some of Marianne's acquaintances, such as Tom Robson, Torpander, and Woodlouse. Anders Begmand was not there: no amount of persuasion could prevent him from following the Consul's funeral.

At Marianne's funeral there was no undertaker to regulate the pace of the procession, and the young sailors stepped out briskly with the coffin. They thus managed to arrive at the town just as the Consul's remains were being carried into the church. Now, it would scarcely do for them to go through the town along the road leading to the cemetery, which was strewn with green leaves, and with lilac and laburnum blossoms, for Mr. Garman. There was, therefore, nothing for it but to wait until the service was over. It was hot work carrying a coffin, dressed in Sunday clothes, and they therefore put down their burden on the steps of a cottage hard by, whilst several of them took off their jackets in order to get a bit cooler.

On the opposite side of the street there was a small beerhouse. There were several of them to whom a pint of beer would have been very grateful, and who had the money in their pockets to pay for it; but perhaps it would hardly do.

The sailors stood talking together, and turning their quids in their mouths; dry in the throat were they, and opposite was the open door of the beerhouse, with jugs and bottles on the counter. It looked so cool and moist in there, and the street was perfectly empty, for all the world was crowding to the cemetery. At length one slunk across the street and sneaked in; two more followed. It seemed but too probable that all the bearers would give way to the same temptation; so Tom Robson went over to the group, and, putting a five-kroner note into the hand of the eldest, said, "There! you can drink that, but on condition that only two go in at a time."

The stipulation was agreed to without a murmur, and they took their turns in the most orderly way. A great many pints of beer go to a five-kroner note. Martin and Tom Robson resolutely turned their backs on the temptation. Woodlouse resisted it for a long time, but in the end he was obliged to give way. Torpander was sitting on a stone at the corner of the cottage, gazing at the coffin. His silk handkerchief had, in accordance with his earnest request, been allowed to follow Marianne to the grave; and on the lid of the coffin, over her heart, lay a garland which had cost him three kroner. This was the only adornment the coffin possessed, for most of the flowers from the West End had been bought by the townspeople for the Consul's funeral. Marianne would otherwise have had plenty.

At length the people began to stream out of the church; those who were with Marianne had to wait till the main procession arrived at the cemetery. The seamen then, after moistening their palms in the usual way, went on with their burden with renewed vigour. There was no change from the five-kroner note.

No one could remember to have seen so long a funeral procession as that which followed the young Consul. It reached almost from the church door, to the gate of the cemetery, which lay in a distant part of the town. As they began to move slowly along the road, a whole crowd of hats came into view, hats of all kinds and shapes. There was Morten's new hat fresh from Paris, and the well-known broad brim of Dean Sparre. There were hats of the old chimney-pot shape, with scarcely any brim at all, while others had brims which hung over almost like the roof of a Swiss cottage. Some hats had a red tinge when they came into the glare of the sunshine, while others were brushed as smooth as velvet. Twenty years' changing fashions were blended together like a packet of "mixed drops." Only old Anders was still constant to his cap, which was covered with pitch as usual. A crowd of boys and children followed on both sides of the road, and the cemetery, which lay on the slope of the hill, was already thronged at the part near the Garmans' tomb.

At the entrance of the churchyard were planted two large flag-staves decorated with wreaths; the flags, which were at half-mast, hung down to the ground, waving gently in the light breeze. The town band was now allowed a moment's rest. The whole way from the church it had played incessantly an indescribable air; and it was only in the evening, when an account appeared in the papers, that the air was recognized as Chopin's Funeral March.

The precentor, with his choristers, "Satan's clerks," as he used to call them when he was annoyed, begun to intone a psalm. The coffin was lifted from the hearse, and carried through the cemetery, by the principal merchants of the town.

It was a magnificent spectacle, as the long funeral procession, with here and there a uniform, and its many flower-decorated banners, moved majestically along through the seething crowd of women and children, which stood closely packed on and among the graves on both sides of the path.

The funeral party now assembled round the grave, into which the coffin was lowered. The merchants who had carried it looked relieved when he was laid to rest; he had been an equally heavy burden to them both in death and in life. The singing ceased, and a silence ensued, as the clergyman ascended the little heap of earth which had been thrown up at the side of the grave.

During the latter part of the preparation of his discourse, the chaplain had felt keenly in what a difficult position he was placed in regard to the deceased. Since his engagement with Madeleine, his first duty was to be strictly impartial, and not to allow himself to be led into any flattering expressions, which would be quite out of place from the lips of one who had, in point of fact, become one of the family.

The dean had, in his discourse in the church, dwelt entirely on the merits of the deceased, as a fellow-citizen and as a good man of business, who had, almost like a father, found daily bread for hundreds, and who had shed happiness and prosperity all around him. The chaplain began his address as follows:--

"My sorrowing friends, when we look into this grave--six feet long and six feet deep, when we look at this dark coffin, when we think of this body which is going to decay, we naturally, my dear friends, say to ourselves, 'Here lies a man of riches, of great riches.' But let us search the depths of our own hearts. For where is now the glitter of that wealth which dazzles the eyes of so many? Where is now the influence which to us, short-sighted mortals, appears to attach to earthly prosperity? Here in this dark tomb, six feet long and six feet deep, it is buried from our sight.

"Oh, my friends! let us learn the lesson which is taught by this silent tomb. Here all is finished, here is the end of all inequality, which is, after all, but the result of sin. Here, in the calm peace of the churchyard, they rest side by side, rich and poor, high and low, all alike before the majesty of death. All that is perishable on earth is swept aside like a used garment. Six feet of earth, that is all; it is the same for each one of us."

The gentle spring breeze breathed on the silk banners of the various guilds, lifting the heavy folds out from the staff, and making a glad rustle in the silk. And the same breeze also carried the words over the cemetery, to the old crones who were sitting on the tombstones, and the girls and women who were grouped along the slope. Yes, even to the far distant edge of the cemetery did the wind bear the eloquent discourse, so that the words could be distinctly heard at the grave in which Marianne was about to be laid. And those words about equality and the evanescence of worldly wealth, were indeed words of comfort for the poor, as well as for the rich. But those who stood by Marianne's grave scarcely listened to them--not even Torpander, who stood gazing intently at his solitary wreath, which lay on the simple coffin.

Woodlouse was guiltless of inattention, for he could not hear; but instead, he made his observations and gave vent to his philosophical reflections as was his wont.

There lay, in the gravelly heap which had been thrown up from the grave, a few bones and skulls. The story was, that that part of the churchyard, which was especially devoted to the poor, had been a burying-place at some former period, and the graves which had not been paid for for twenty years were, after the lapse of that time, again made use of, according to the rule and custom of the Church. It was thus no unusual thing to find coffins while a new grave was being dug, which fell to pieces under the spade. The bodies had been packed closely, and often several had been placed in the same grave.

It was, however, a scandal that the bones should be allowed to lie out in the light of day, until the new corpse came to be buried. Abraham the sexton had his orders, to take such bones at once to the house which was appointed for them, and which was a mere shed in one corner of the cemetery, where it was left to each skull to discover the bones belonging to it as best it might. But when any of the officials found fault with Abraham for his neglect, he would stand leaning on his spade, and cocking his red nose knowingly on one side, would answer with a smile, "Well, you see, what are we to do? The poor are just as much trouble in death as they are in life. They never will die like respectable people, one by one, now and again; but they all die at the same time, you see, and then come out here and want to get buried. Particularly all through the winter, when the ground is hard, and then in the early spring, what are we to do? It is really too bad. Yes, at those seasons they bring such shoals of children--ah, preserve us from the children!--yes, and grown-up people too, for that matter; and they all want graves just at the wrong time of year! They always choose the wrong time! It would not be so bad if one could only skimp the measurements a bit; but, you see, no one is so particular as the poor about the measurements. Six feet long and six feet deep--they will have it, never an inch less. And so, you see, it is not always so easy to get these bones out of sight in time for one of these pauper funerals. No, no! it is quite true what I say. The poor are just as much trouble in death as they are in life!"

There was once a new manager of the cemetery who wished to get rid of Abraham, who caused general indignation when he went tumbling about tipsy among the graves. But the dean said, "What is to become of the poor man? He will remain as a burden either to you or to me; and besides, he has been with us as long as I have been here, and I have always been able to bear with his sad infirmity. It would really go to my heart to drive him away." And so the public were content to keep Abraham as an evidence of Dean Sparre's kindness of heart.

As Woodlouse stood looking at the bones, he was absorbed in philosophical meditation, and he could not help thinking that there was a sort of air of defiance in the grin, with which one of the skulls returned his gaze. It struck him that this skull might perhaps be thinking how peaceful it was to rest here in the sacred earth of the churchyard. But surely it was just as peaceful over there in the house in which the bones were placed; and if neither church nor provost, chaplain nor sexton, gravedigger nor organist, bell-ringer nor acolyte, no, not one of them had got his due, it was quite impossible that it should be otherwise. And when he came to consider further, he thought that he could discover in these bare bones and these bleached skulls, an expression he knew only too well in life; a kind of cleared-out expression, which seems to cling to those who have not paid their debts.

Meanwhile Pastor Martens's sonorous voice echoed over the cemetery as he was approaching the end of his discourse. "The six feet of earth" was repeated again and again, like the refrain upon which a good composer will hang a whole symphony; and each time it seemed to make a deeper impression. The account in the evening papers might perhaps be slightly exaggerated, when it said that not an eye was dry; but certain is it that many wept, and not only women, but men also. Some even of the merchants, who had carried the coffin, were seen using their pocket-handkerchiefs.

It was really an extraordinary address. Just at the commencement it had caused an uneasy feeling, when Martens began to speak about the great riches of the deceased. There was some apprehension lest he should make some ill-timed application of the parable of the camel and the needle's eye; but the speaker had just managed to say the right thing. There is nothing which gives the poor so much pleasure, as to hear how little power really belongs to earthly wealth, and how little there is to grudge when it comes to the last. And so this allusion to "the six feet of earth" had a good effect throughout.

When the funeral discourse was over, Abraham came forward with the box which was to hold the earth to be thrown on the coffin.

Struggling with his inmost feelings, the pastor seized the box, filled it with mould, and uncovered his head. Off in a moment came all the various hats, and just as many various heads were disclosed to view. Some were smooth, some were rough, some had long hair, and on others the hair was clipped as close as the top of a hair trunk, while here and there appeared a skull as smooth as a billiard ball.

The clergyman threw the earth into the grave, deeply moved, and almost mechanically, as if the task were too much for him. The loose mould could be heard rustling down on the flowers and silk ribbons. One more short and thrilling prayer was heard; the service was over, and the hats appeared again.

The bandsmen, who had been standing in a group among the mourners, keeping their instruments under their coats, so that they might not get cold, suddenly broke out into music, at a mysterious sign from the bandmaster. The effect was striking. Just as when a stone is thrown into the water, and the ripples roll outwards in an ever-widening circle, so did the mighty waves of sound drive back the bystanders in all directions, until there was quite an open place around the players. The undertaker turned the opportunity to advantage, and took his place at the head of the procession, which returned in the same order as it came.

At a short distance behind the musicians, came the precentor with his choristers. He was terribly annoyed by the band, and in a great state of anxiety, lest the sorrowing relatives of the deceased should not notice, how much extra trouble he had taken with the singing.

The undertaker, on the contrary, was extremely pleased with the band, which had made such a nice clear space for him, and when he got home to his wife he said, "Even if the drums of my ears are nearly broken, I must say I fully appreciate the effect of a brass band. Nothing can be more opportune, when one has to lead a procession through a large crowd at a respectable funeral."

At a short distance from the grave, the clergyman left the *cortége* and went in a different direction across the cemetery. As soon as he was out of sight of the crowd, he took a short cut over the graves, which in that part of the cemetery were low and overgrown with grass, and every now and then he held up his cassock, and stepped over one which lay in his path.

Abraham the sexton had got an extra lurch on, in honour of the grand funeral, and came stumbling along after the pastor, carrying the black box, which was the same that was used for all burials, without distinction.

When the pastor arrived at Marianne's grave, he found Anders Begmand and some others from the West End, who had already been in the Consul's procession. The chaplain took off his hat and wiped his brow, as he stood looking round for Abraham. The others also uncovered their heads. At length Abraham came up, and the three handfuls of earth fell, hurriedly and mechanically, on the simple coffin. "Of earth thou art, to earth thou shalt return, and from the earth thou shalt rise again. Amen."

The pastor went scrambling along farther over the graves. There were still some other poor people to be buried, and it was getting late.

CHAPTER XXIV.

The young Consul's death did not bring with it any great changes, either in the household or in the business. Everything was in such a solid and well-regulated condition, that it kept on going like a good machine. The new driver had as much as he could manage, and there were some who thought that the more delicate parts of the complicated mechanism would be likely to suffer under his hands.

At the same time, no one could say of Morten that he did not bring great energy to bear on his new duties. Now, indeed, it was almost impossible to find him; he was continually on the go between the town and Sandsgaard. His carriage might be seen waiting at the most unlikely corners, or all of a sudden he would pop up out of a boat at the quay, tear off to the office, call out something to the bookkeeper, and flash out of the door again. But when the bookkeeper hurried after him, to ask what the instructions were, all he saw was a glimpse of the dogcart as it turned the corner.

The business men in the town used to say, quietly among themselves, that it was easier to work against Morten than with him. Garman and Worse's predominance began to grow weaker, and what had been the central power was now distributed in several hands. The year which followed was not a prosperous one for shippers; most of the ships belonging to the firm had been working either at a loss or at a very small profit. The most successful was the *Phoenix*, which had been put on the guano trade. She still continued to be a favourite, and her voyages were followed with great interest in the newspapers. The poet of the town had written some verses in her honour:--

> "Rock proud, thou fire's daughter,
> Thy flame-enshrouded helm!"

It was doubtless this allusion to the helm, which had been most in danger at the time of the fire, which caused the success of the poem, and insured it a permanent position in all the concerts.

In accordance with the express wishes of the deceased, Jacob Worse had been chosen as guardian for Rachel and Gabriel. Mrs. Garman was still to remain in the position of partner, with Morten as manager of the business. For each of the younger children a considerable sum was set apart; a sum, in fact, which was just about equal to that with which Morten had entered the firm.

Rachel had thus to go to Jacob Worse for an explanation of her affairs, for she wanted to have a clear idea of what she really possessed, and what her exact position was. Worse answered her in a calm and measured business tone.

"Well, then, this money," said she, one day, in Worse's office, "is my own, and is entirely under my own control?"

"Yes, in addition to your share in the business," added Worse, in explanation; "and if your mother should die, your part of her property will come to you at the division which will follow. It will then depend upon you or your future husband--"

"My future husband will surely allow me to manage my own property," said Rachel.

"It is to be hoped he will; but, as you perhaps know, in the event of your marrying, you will lose the entire control."

"Then I will never marry!"

"I am of opinion myself that you might do something better than marriage," said Jacob Worse.

Rachel observed him closely, but failed to fathom his thoughts.

"How I envy you your clear intelligent head!" said she, somewhat scornfully. "You lay out for yourself some plan or another in life, and then your object is forthwith accomplished. You quietly follow your plans, and in the same way you expect that those to whom you give your advice, will follow it without wavering. You are just like father. You really are too precise."

"I regard that as the greatest compliment I have ever received," answered Worse, smiling.

"But father was in many respects an old-fashioned and somewhat prejudiced man. It was just these very modern ideas that you find so attractive, which were to him strange or even positively distasteful." She made this remark more for the purpose of drawing out Worse than because she wished to disparage her father.

"Consul Garman," said Worse, rising from his chair, "was a dissatisfied man. His whole life was an ill-concealed struggle between the old and the new. He placed extraordinary confidence in me, and I found in him ideas, which no one would have expected to meet with in such a precise and old-fashioned man of business. But to reconcile the two incongruous currents was beyond his power; the immature and impetuous want of exactitude of modern times was repugnant to his nature; and when his great sense of justice forced him to recognize certain fundamental truths, it was still always a source of annoyance to him to be obliged to do so. It appears to me that he sought a counteracting influence to all this, in his boundless admiration for old Consul Garman."

"But was not my grandfather a remarkable man? Don't you think so?" asked Rachel, with interest.

"I will tell you my opinion, Miss Garman. He was a man who lived in a time to which he was suited, and in which, on the whole, existence was far more easy."

"You mean to say, then, that existence was easier in those times than in the present?"

"Yes, I am sure of it," continued Worse, pacing hurriedly up and down the room, as was his custom when he was excited. "Do you not see how existence becomes more difficult with each year as it passes? New discoveries and experiences are springing up every hour, and doubts and inquiry are burrowing under, and undermining the whole fabric. Revered and well-grounded truths are falling to the ground, and those who are too timid to advance with the times, are gathering confusedly about the rotten framework, supporting, preserving, and terrified, denouncing youth, and predicting the destruction of society. Your grandfather stood on the very summit of the cultivation of his day, living as he did in a state of society which was peaceful and conscious of its security, with aristocratic intelligence above and aristocratic ignorance below. Your father, on the other hand, had grown to manhood when the movement reached us, and he had already a fixed understanding as to his own line in life, when the new ideas came streaming in upon him. Then followed the long and painful struggle. But we who are a generation younger, and who enter upon life from school, with the old maxims only half rooted in our minds, feel the whole fabric tottering. Doubt and uncertainty reign on every side, and we find ourselves now in a state of eager expectation, and now plunged in gloomy apprehension. Wheresoever we place our foot, the ground gives way beneath us, and if we wish to sit down and rest awhile, the chair is drawn from under us by some invisible hand. Thus are we whirled to and fro in a struggle for which we were never prepared, and in which numbers of us miserably perish. Fathers scold and threaten, while mothers weep because we have forsaken the traditions of our childhood. Bitter words and party names are caught up in the continuous strife, and find their way into family life; the one no longer understands the motives of the other; we stand railing at each other in the pitchy darkness; no distinction is made between sincere conviction and restless love of change. All strive blindly together, whilst society becomes interwoven with a tissue of hostility, mistrust, falsehood, and hypocrisy."

Rachel looked at him with open eyes, and at length she exclaimed, "I cannot imagine how you can be content with your present existence, so silent and so reserved, when such a tumult of thought is passing through your brain."

Jacob Worse stopped, and his face grew calm as he said, "I have a simple remedy, which I have learnt from my mother, and which your father also employed--and that is, work. To keep at it from morning to evening; to begin the day with a large packet of foreign letters here on my desk, and to leave off in the evening, tired but content--content for that day. That is my remedy--that keeps the life in me; so far it suffices; higher I cannot attain."

"I said a short time ago that I envied you your calm and logical mind. I now regret the tone in which the words were spoken. I often, somehow or another, I don't know why, but I often find myself speaking to you somewhat--" She faltered, and her face became suffused with blushes.

"Somewhat plainly, you mean," said Worse, smiling.

"May I hope it is because you think me worthy of your confidence?"

She looked at him again, but his eyes were now fixed on the map which hung over her head.

"Well," said Rachel, "perhaps that is the reason; but what I really envy you is your love of work, or, I should say, not so much the love of work--for that I have myself--but your having discovered an employment which keeps you calm. But you are able to work, that's where it is," she added, meditatively.

"My opinion about you, Miss Garman, has always been, that the aimless life a lady in your position is obliged to lead here at home, must sooner or later become unbearable to you."

"I cannot work," said she in a crestfallen tone.

"Well, but at least you can try."

"How am I to begin? You remember that time when father would not receive my offer of assistance."

"Your father did not understand you; nor will you find it easy to discover satisfactory employment in your own country. But travel, look around you. You are rich and independent, and there are other lands where work is to be had, and in them you ought to find suitable occupation."

"Do you really advise me to travel elsewhere, Mr. Worse?" said Rachel.

"Yes; that is to say--yes, I think it would be best for you. Here you have little opportunity of development, and, to speak plainly, I think you ought to travel." As he said the last words he regained his self-possession, and could now look her in the face calmly, and without flinching.

"But where shall I go--a lonely woman without friends? I am afraid you over-estimate my powers," said Rachel, with a reluctant air. It was as if she did not fancy his advising her to go away.

"I may as well tell you what I think now," he began, hurriedly. "I have some acquaintances in Paris. In fact, an American firm--Barnett Brothers they are called-- who have a house in Paris; and Mr. Frederick Barnett is a personal friend of mine."

"You seem to have been arranging to get rid of me for some time," said Rachel; "why, you have the whole plan ready prepared."

He showed some signs of confusion, for it was a scheme he had carefully considered, but which he had always hoped he would not have to put into execution.

"Yes," answered he, endeavouring to laugh; "as your guardian, it is my duty to assist you, to the best of my ability, to arrange for your future."

"But are you going to send me to Paris alone?"

"No; I have been thinking of offering you Svendsen as an escort. You surely know old Svendsen, my bookkeeper? He has been several times in Paris, and is a most trustworthy man. I am sure you will be contented with Mr. Barnett's house, which is more like an English one. And that, I think, will suit you better than a purely French household."

"Does your friend take boarders?" asked Rachel, quickly.

"Not as a rule, as far as I know. You will thus find it more expensive than at an ordinary *pension;* but I am almost certain that both Mr. and Mrs. Barnett, who is a French lady, are the sort of people you will like. And it is exactly in the American society of Paris that you will have the best opportunity of finding employment if you wish for it. At any rate, you can stay some time in Mr. Barnett's house, until you find something else you prefer."

His tone was deliberate and decided, as if he already regarded the matter as finally settled; and when Rachel got up to take her leave she found that her mind was already made up, without being conscious of how she had arrived at her conclusion. She looked forward to a new and more active life, with mingled feelings of expectation and pleasure. But at the same time she was somewhat hurt--no, not hurt, but sad--no, not exactly sad, either; but she could not help thinking it was extraordinary, that he should show himself so eager to get her away.

Jacob Worse followed her to the door leading into the street, but when she had gone he did not go back to the office, but crossed over the yard to his mother's.

A month later, Gabriel and Rachel set off under the escort of old Svendsen; Gabriel to Dresden, and Rachel to Paris. Madeleine also quitted Sandsgaard. Her intended had arranged, with the assistance of the doctor, that she should go to the baths of Modum, where Martens's mother, who was the widow of a clergyman from the east coast, was to take care of her.

Uncle Richard was utterly confounded when he heard Madeleine was going to marry a clergyman, and he had a kind of dim feeling that he would have done better to have kept her under the observation of the big telescope. But the old gentleman, who had never been very strong-minded, had become still more feeble in his sorrow, and now that he could no longer go to Christian Frederick for advice, he gave way in everything.

As for Madeleine herself, the exhaustion which followed her illness had produced a feeling of indifference; and now that the important step had once been taken, she allowed herself to be led without offering any opposition, and did not find it disagreeable, when the pastor took upon himself to think and act for her in everything. But when it came to saying good-bye to her father she gave way, and was carried senseless to the carriage.

Martens soon found that if he wished to educate Madeleine to be a pattern wife after his own heart, he must get her away from Sandsgaard. With the same object in view, he sought, and standing as well as he did with those in authority, soon obtained, a living at some distance in the country; and, a year after his betrothal, he celebrated his marriage at his mother's house.

After his ride along the shore, George Delphin suffered from a dangerous attack of inflammation of the lungs. His illness lasted so long that a substitute had to be provided for the time in the magistrate's office; and as soon as he recovered sufficiently to write, he informed the magistrate that he wished to resign his situation. The magistrate accepted his resignation with alacrity, for George Delphin had never been the kind of man he liked.

During the whole time of the illness, Fanny was in a state of nervous excitement. To visit the invalid, or put herself in any sort of communication with him, was quite out of the question. She had thus to content herself with such news as she could pick up, either accidentally or through Morten; but she dared not ask as many questions as she could have wished. One day when she was standing before the glass, she discovered three small wrinkles at the corner of her left eye. When she laughed, they improved her; but when she was serious, they made her look old. Nothing seemed to suit her any longer, not even mourning, in which she had always looked her best. Fanny, in fact, suffered as much as she was capable of suffering, and one day she received a note from him, in which he said adieu.

"I start to-night, and say farewell thus to spare us both a painful parting. Farewell!" This was all the note contained.

Her lovely complexion turned almost to an ashen grey, but only for a moment. The whole night she lay awake, listening to her husband, who lay breathing heavily by her side; but the next morning found her sitting by her window, as calm and bright as ever. Many of her friends, as she had expected, came to visit her, but she disappointed them all. Delphin's sudden departure was a subject of conversation in which she joined, jesting and laughing as usual. Her friends could perceive no change in her, and yet how much scandal had been talked about her and Delphin! It was a lesson to people to keep their tongues to themselves.

But Fanny herself noticed several changes in her appearance, and was reminded of it every time she saw her reflection in the glass.

In small circles great events seem to come all at once, one after another in startling succession. The worthy town had been quite upset by all those remarkable events, of a joyful, mournful, or mixed nature, which followed after the night of the fire at Sandsgaard; and while busy tongues kept reverting to the materials for gossip thus provided, the years rolled by without anything further taking place.

Tom Robson had taken Martin with him to America, where they disappeared.

Contrary to his intention, Torpander did not travel home to Sweden. He put off his departure from time to time. *Her* grave never seemed pretty enough, and he never felt perfectly certain that it would be kept properly in order. He thus remained where he was, and at last moved over to old Anders Begmand's cottage. The old man's head had become somewhat affected. He received his week's pay every Saturday, without, however, doing any work to earn it. And now Torpander grew to be quite a fixture in the cottage, and the two would sit for many a winter's evening over the fire, repeating to each other the same stories, which never varied year after year, about her who had been, and still continued for both, the very sunshine of their lives.

Uncle Richard soon gave up the lighthouse at Bratvold, and he and Mrs. Garman shared Sandsgaard between them. Downstairs the lady went about in her wheel-chair, and she had had all the thresholds of the doors removed, so that she might be able to have herself rolled into the kitchen.

Upstairs Uncle Richard continued his ceaseless wanderings, in and out, to and fro, just as he had begun on the day after his brother's death. Once only he had had Don Juan saddled; but when he was brought round to the door, the old gentleman, thought he was too fresh for him. He put his hand before his eyes, and had Don Juan taken back again, to the stable.

Summer and winter, day after day, the sound of his footfall overhead never ceased. A long strip of soft carpet had been put down the whole length of the house, partly for warmth, and partly to deaden the sound of his step.

In winter he wore a long coat lined with fur, a fur cap, and a pair of deerskin gloves; and there were some people who confidently maintained that he carried an open umbrella when the weather was wet. In the little room on the north side, there was a cupboard in which a bottle of Burgundy was always kept standing. When the old gentleman got to this point he would pause, drink a glass of the wine, and look thoughtfully in the large mirror. He then shook his head and continued his wanderings.

No change took place in Miss Cordsen. The well-starched cap-strings and the odour of dry lavender still followed her wherever she went; while all the secrets of the family lay carefully preserved, together with her own, to both of which the closely pressed mouth, with its innumerable wrinkles, formed a lock of the safest description.

CHAPTER XXV.

Thus passed six years. According to Martens's prediction, Dean Sparre had been made a bishop. His predecessor in office had been a strict and haughty prelate, and there was, therefore, no little disturbance in the camp when he departed. But from the moment Dean Sparre mounted the vacant seat, all friction ceased, and everything went on evenly and smoothly. It was like covering the hammers of an old piano with new felt. The hitherto sharp tone gives place to a soft and agreeable sound; and after Dean Sparre's patent felt had been introduced into the mechanism, it all worked silently and noiselessly, and gave the greatest pleasure to all parties concerned.

The bishop did not forget his young friend, Inspector Johnsen, of whom he had always had such "good hopes." He obtained for Johnsen a chaplaincy in his cathedral town; and some people were so mischievous as to assert that the bishop's "good hopes" were now fulfilled, for Pastor Johnsen was shortly after engaged to Miss Barbara Sparre.

A great change had taken place in the *ci-devant* school inspector. When the turning-point was once reached, he set to work in his new line in real earnest, as was only to be expected from one of his energetic character. He never dabbled any more in advanced philosophy, and had but little to do with grand society; on the contrary, he grew to be a clergyman to whom the women were particularly attracted. His sermons were always severe, very severe; and those who cared to listen closely, might remark that he never repeated the prayer for the arms of the country by land and by sea.

Down at Mrs. Worse's shop, in the dark corner of the lane, trade went on regularly and well. Little Pitter Nilken had arrived at that stage of shriveldom, at which both fruits and people cannot hold out much longer without a change. He still managed to swing himself over the counter as lightly as a cork when the enemy became too troublesome, and the redoubtable iron ruler had lost none of its gruesome terrors.

Mrs. Worse, on the contrary, had become rather stout in the course of years. Her legs would no longer "balance" her properly, as she said. But still she refused to buy a carriage until all had "come right," which she thought could not be long now.

When all had come right! It required a faith as blind as Mrs. Worse's to reckon on such a possibility. Rachel had now been six years in Paris without saying a word about coming home. What her occupation there really was, Jacob Worse could never discover. Each time he sent her money--and it was marvellous how much she used--he wrote her a few lines. She always answered briefly and reservedly. Through his friend Mr. Barnett he did not learn anything explicit. He only knew that Rachel was still living in the house, and that they were much attached to her. Mrs. Barnett's *salon* was quite a place of assembly for the American colony, among which were many rich and accomplished men. Any day might bring the intelligence of her approaching marriage.

Worse was in the habit of reading the papers every morning as they sat at breakfast in his mother's room. One day Mrs. Worse, who usually occupied herself half the morning with her paper, read out to her son that Pastor Martens had been nominated as clergyman in the town.

"Just fancy! So they are coming westward again!" ejaculated Mrs. Worse. "I should like to know how little Madeleine has got on in married life," sighed the old woman, who knew but too well the uncertainty which marriage brings with it. The news awoke many painful recollections in Worse's breast, and he paced up and down in his office for a long time, before he could bring himself to begin upon the foreign post, which lay in a formidable packet on his desk.

Among the letters there was one from Barnett Brothers in Paris; he knew the handwriting, but the office stamp was missing. As he opened it, it struck him that it was longer than usual. He turned it over hastily. What was this? Rachel Carman's signature stood at the foot of the letter! Jacob Worse read as. follows:--

"DEAR MR. WORSE,

"As I sit down to write to you, and thus carry out a long-formed resolution, I feel so overcome by emotion, that I find it difficult to control myself sufficiently, to express my thoughts *verbatim*. But now, as I have made up my mind, I will endeavour to make my letter clear and concise.

"I have, as you now perhaps perceive, carried on the Norwegian correspondence of Messrs. Barnett Brothers for several years. In my private letters to you I have disguised my handwriting, so as not to betray my secret. I wished, in fact, to see first if I could make myself useful, and am at length satisfied I that I can. I have learnt to adopt your mother's homely maxim--remember me kindly to her--I can work.' In your kind letters, for which receive my best thanks, I have sometimes thought that I could perceive a feeling of astonishment, as to how I could be employing all the money you have sent me. It is placed in our business. I say our business, because Messrs. Barnett Brothers have offered me a share in their Paris house. I have thus attained the object of my ambition in that direction.

"You once gave me some advice. You see, I attack each point separately, so as to prevent confusion, to avoid wasting words, or forgetting anything important. But to return. When you advised me to come forward as an authoress, I did not at that time think that your idea was reasonable. Since then I have, however, thought the subject carefully over, and have indeed made some small attempts that way, and now I beg to thank you for the good advice you gave me. I have indeed much to thank you for.

"Now that I am able to work, I no longer feel so apprehensive about the future.

It is true, as you said long ago, that there are many things which a woman may have to write about, and this is more especially true with us in our own country. I am fortunately in an independent position, *bonheur oblige*, and I have courage, so I will make the attempt. But I must first get home, not only because I am as homesick as a child--for I know perfectly well that when I have been at home for a short time, I shall be anxious to start again on my travels--but I feel that if I am to accomplish anything, I must be among those I wish to help. I also wish to be able to go abroad again, and thus make existence more interesting; but I must at the same time have a *pied à terre* at home, so as to be able to return whenever I may desire to do so. And now comes the great 'but' which is, in fact, the chief point in this letter--and that, Mr. Worse, is yourself.

"I do not wish to return home before I know clearly in what position we stand to each other. Of this I feel convinced, that you have no ill feeling towards me on account of my former behaviour to you. But still I know nothing further; and if there is nothing more to know, I hope we may meet as good friends. If there should be anything further, kindly let me have a few lines.

"There, now! you see how the matter lies; let us now understand each other plainly, and I beg that you will be honourable and straightforward towards me. On one thing you can count for a certainty, which is, that I am, in any case,

Your very sincere friend,
RACHEL GARMAN."

When Jacob Worse had read this letter, he sprang up, seized his hat and umbrella, and went into the clerk's office.

"Has the Hamburg steamer started?"

"No, sir, but the first bell has just rung," was the answer.

"Have you any gold?"

"Yes; that is to say, not very much," answered the cashier.

"Let me have what you have got, and send Thomas over to the bank for some more. A couple of thousand kroner or so will do."

The boy ran off with a bundle of notes and a little canvas bag.

"I am going abroad, Svendsen, for a fortnight or so--I cannot say for certain. Look, here is my address. And with that he snatched the pen from behind Svendsen's ear and wrote across a large sheet of paper, on which the unfortunate man had just begun a magnificent letter:

"*Pavilion Rohan*
"*Paris.*

The second bell was now heard on board the steamer.

"All right, Svendsen. Now you must manage as well as you can; telegraph if you want anything--my keys are in my desk." When he reached the door he turned round and cried, "Yes, I forgot, Svendsen; run over to my mother and tell her--yes, just tell her that it's all 'come right;'" and with that away he ran.

Old Svendsen stood perfectly speechless, staring through the open door, as he rubbed his thumb and forefinger together, which was a habit of his when anything unusually perplexing occurred. Every door was open, a chair upset in the inner office, and Mr. Worse on the road to Paris with a hat and umbrella, Thomas after him in full career with the canvas bag. The cashier was sitting with the coin and notes scattered on the table in front of him, looking as if he had been robbed; and as old Svendsen's eye rested on the ruined letter, he discovered that he had a smudge of ink on one of his fingers. Now, it was thirty years since old Svendsen had had any ink on his fingers. Mr. Worse must have made a splutter with his pen when he snatched it so hurriedly; and as the old bookkeeper's eye wandered from the smudge of ink, to the frightful confusion which reigned in the office, and back again to the smudge, he repeated, slowly and majestically, the magic words which were to awake him from this horrible nightmare: "Tell my mother it has all come right." But matters grew still worse when, a short time afterwards, he presented himself before Mrs. Worse in the back room; for scarcely had he pronounced the fatal words, "It has all come right!" than Mrs. Worse flew at him and kissed him right on his lips.

This kiss, in connection with the smudge of ink, made this day a memorable one for old Svendsen, and he used to reckon from it as an epoch which he could never forget.

The same post brought, among other things, a note for Morten Garman. He opened it, smiled in a singular manner, and sent it upstairs to his wife. Fanny took the two enclosed cards, on one of which was written the name of a lady, which she recognized as belonging to a wealthy family in Christiania, and on the other was the name of George Delphin.

She stood before the looking-glass with his card in her hand, observing narrowly the expression on her face, while the genuine sorrow she had hitherto felt, now turned to mortification and bitterness. There was scarce a shadow to be seen on her brow while these sensations passed through her heart. She had accustomed herself to these exercises before the glass; this was a grand rehearsal, and she bore it bravely. Only the delicate wrinkles round her eyes quivered slightly; but when she smiled again they made her as charming as ever. No emotion should spoil her beauty; and while these six years of pain and sorrow seemed again to burst forth, she stood as lovely and undisturbed as ever, without losing anything of her self-command.

At this moment the doctor entered the room.

"Have you spoken to my husband, doctor?"

"No, Mrs. Garman. Is there anything the matter with him?"

"Has he anything the matter with him! I am really surprised that you should ask such a question," replied Fanny, sharply. "Can you not see that he is weary--overworked? He must go to Carlsbad this year, or his health will suffer severely."

"Oh yes!" said the doctor, good-humouredly, "it might perhaps have a good effect; but you know yourself that his answer always is that he has no time, and so--"

"Bah!" answered Fanny; "as if a doctor ought to listen to rubbish of that sort!"

The doctor went off straight to the office, and succeeded in frightening Morten to such a degree that the journey was arranged for the next week.

Jacob Worse's "disappearance," as it was called, caused a great sensation, and the astonishment did not diminish when a telegram arrived, announcing his engagement to Rachel Garman. At the same time he begged Morten to arrange everything for the wedding, as they intended to be married shortly after their return home.

Morten, after consulting his wife, answered that the doctor had ordered him off to Carlsbad at once; but he proposed to meet them both in Copenhagen, where the wedding might take place. He received an answer assenting to his proposal, and the day was fixed. Although he had not been consulted, Morten was much pleased with the match.

During the last six years, he had often thought upon the advice his father had given him before his death, when he had advised him to take Jacob Worse into partnership. Morten had never mentioned the idea to any one. He could not reconcile himself to such a humiliation. Now the opportunity came of itself, and at a most fortunate time, when he was on the point of starting for abroad. Worse would, therefore, be able to get an insight into everything during his absence, and there were some weak places in the business which were causing Morten much uneasiness. Matters of this nature are more easily got over when they can be explained by letter.

The wedding thus took place in Copenhagen. Gabriel was present at the ceremony. He had been for some time in an office in England, whither they had telegraphed to him from Paris, and he joined them at Cologne. It was already more than half settled, that Gabriel should take Rachel's place with Barnett Brothers in Paris, a prospect at which he was quite overjoyed.

The wedding-breakfast was served at the Hôtel d'Angleterre, in one of the large *salons* looking out on the Kongen's Nytorv. Every one was in the highest spirits, and Morten made a speech in which he remarked, that Garman and Worse would now again become a reality.

"And my old enemy Aalbom?" asked Gabriel at dessert.

"Oh, he is the same as ever," answered Morten. "The other day he made a virulent speech somewhere about the Garman dynasty. He is terribly bitter since we have ceased inviting him to Sandsgaard."

"Poor Aalbom!" said Gabriel, thoughtfully. He was so happy himself, and in such a forgiving mood, that he sat down at a table by the window, and began sketching, with the greatest care and attention, the equestrian statue on the Kongen's Nytorv. The sketch was intended as a present for Mr. Aalbom.

A few days after each went to his own place; Morten and Fanny to Carlsbad,

Gabriel to England to arrange his change of quarters, and the newly married couple home to Norway.

On the quay where the steamers landed their passengers was to be seen a shining new carriage, with a new coachman and a new pair of horses. In the carriage sat Mrs. Worse, wearing a new silk mantle and a new bonnet. She had telegraphed for the whole set-out to Worse's agent in Copenhagen, with whom the money had for some time been lying ready.

On the box of the carriage, huddled up in a heap, sat Mr. Samuelsen. Mrs. Worse's efforts to make him take his place by her side had been unavailing; he thought it was quite bad enough as it was.

A group of small boys were naturally standing round the carriage, partly to see the horses, and partly to have a good look at the dreaded Pitter Nilken. Suddenly one of the young rascals took it into his head to repeat the well-known irritating verse--not exactly singing out loud, but only barely moving his lips. The idea was soon caught up by his comrades, and wherever the unhappy Mr. Samuelsen turned his head he could read the couplet on the busy lips, and follow the song--

"Little Pitter Nilken,
Sitting on his chair"--

It was enough to drive one mad.

"He's always growing smaller
The longer he sits there."

The newly married couple got in, and the carriage rolled off through the town. Mrs. Worse laughed boisterously with tears in her eyes the whole way; she kept bowing in all directions, and her face was radiant with smiles. As they turned into the yard, the new bonnet had slipped so far over to one side that it fell off when the carriage stopped at the door; and as the worthy Mr. Samuelsen jumped down, in his great anxiety to help the ladies to alight, he came with both feet right on top of the bonnet, notwithstanding that he had seen the danger when he was making his spring.

It was quite a business to get Mrs. Worse "balanced" upstairs, she laughed so immoderately. They all laughed; the coachman laughed; the maids laughed; the newly married couple laughed; every one laughed except the unfortunate Mr. Samuelsen, who followed the others upstairs, carrying, with averted eyes, his mistress's bonnet by one string, and dragging the other after him up the staircase. The lovely new bonnet, which was scarcely recognizable as a bonnet any longer!

They had dinner in the young people's apartments, where Mrs. Worse did the fine lady to her own intense satisfaction, and persisted in talking something which she called French. In the evening, when Rachel and her husband returned from a visit from Sandsgaard, the whole party moved over to Mrs. Worse's room at the back of the house.

And there, there was laughing, story-telling, drinking of healths, and rejoicing, until Pitter Nilken was quite overcome, and offered of his own accord to sing "The Knife-Grinder's Courtship"--a song which had been a great favourite in the days of his youth. He sang amidst rounds of applause, in a curious thin voice, which sounded as if he had all at once recovered his boy's treble, and which was high, squeaky, and cracked. He, however, rendered the air with a great deal of feeling, and his eye rested on Mrs. Worse as he sang--

"Maiden, oh list! With those sweet winning glances,
Thy looks nought but goodness and kindness betide!
Oh, couldst thou but smile on my timid advances!
Say, wilt thou be thine own knife-grinder's bride?"

Mrs. Worse beat time with her knitting as she joined in the chorus--

"Whirr! whirr!
Blithely we go. Never say no!
My foot's on the treadle,
which rocks to and fro!"

CHAPTER XXVI.

In the bright sunshine the yellow sand, dotted here and there with patches of bent grass, stretched away to the northward as far as the eye could reach. The coast-line, with its succession of bays and promontories, was here and there enlivened by a cluster of boats, or a flock of gulls, or wild geese, busily at work on the shore, while the sea came curling in with its small crested ripples, which sparkled in the clear sunshine. Over the heather-covered heights, which rolled away far inland, came a carriage, in which were sitting a lady and a gentleman. They had left the post-road, and were making their way along the narrow sandy track which led down towards the village of Bratvold.

It had been much against Madeleine's wish, but as her husband happened to hear from the coachman, that the *détour* only made a difference of about an hour, the order was given to drive down to Bratvold, where they would be able to rest for a little time on the road.

The pastor and his wife were on their way westward, on a visit to the new living, although they would not come into actual residence till August. They wished to take a house, and visit their relations and old acquaintances in the town. Pleased as Madeleine was at the prospect of again seeing her father, she was still far from glad when she heard that her husband was endeavouring to obtain the living. He did so, however, in accordance with the express wish of Bishop Sparre, and it was moreover looked upon as a great piece of advancement. Madeleine had, as usual, made but little opposition to the project. Pastor Martens had at length succeeded in educating her into a wife after his own heart.

As she sat there, somewhat crowded in one corner of the carriage, for her husband had grown rather stout with the lapse of time, she resembled but little that Madeleine whose home had once been among the surroundings they were now approaching. She was not ill, but her look suggested weariness--great weariness. In a large country rectory there is much work to be done, and three children are pretty well to begin with.

For the first few years she was almost in a state of despair, and several times her old violent temper broke out. But her husband had his own particular method of dealing with her. He never lost his temper, and the more Madeleine flared up, the more gentle his answers became, as with a quiet smile he gently placed his hand upon her shoulder.

But when Madeleine began to calm down, he would speak to her in an admonishing tone, and by degrees he succeeded wonderfully in getting her into the groove he desired, until at last she got accustomed to the method.

Pastor Martens's genial and open countenance did not look its best that day. He had, to tell the truth, been dreadfully sea-sick, and so for that reason they had left the steamer, preferring to travel the last part of the journey by land. His sleek face wore a decidedly green hue, and he made a grimace ever and anon, as he looked out of the carriage window towards the element they had quitted.

He was, however, a fortunate man, and he was thankful for it. Madeleine had improved beyond all expectation under his hands. Her violent temper now seldom appeared, and if it did, he was perfectly certain of his method of dealing with it. Many a time he remembered with thankfulness his dear Bishop Sparre, from whom he had learnt so much, and whose fatherly kindness seemed to follow him wherever he went.

The nearer they approached the sea-shore, the broader grew the dark-blue line out to the westward, where the sea lay glittering in the sunshine. Madeleine gazed and gazed, and thoughts of the past came surging up in her heart.

The plovers had their young, and followed after the carriage, swooping down in front of the horses with their well-known cry. Larks in hundreds filled the air with their joyous warble, which went straight to her heart, and the breeze began to waft to her the fresh salt flavour of the sea. There was something in it of seaweed, something of fish, but all was so wonderfully rich in recollection. Madeleine leant towards the breeze and drew in a deep breath; it seemed like a greeting from the sea she knew so well, and which recognized her in return; it was a reminiscence of her short day of love and happiness. She longed to fill her lungs with the pure fresh sea air, so that it might purify all the dark and dusty corners in her fettered soul. All the time she had been away from Bratvold a taint of impurity seemed to have rested on her; and now that she found herself once again face to face with the ocean, she seemed almost ashamed thus to return. Oh that she were lying out there in its cool depths, with the fresh salt billows dashing over her!

The carriage now approached the top of the last hill, and the village of Bratvold, with its lighthouse, burst upon her view. She hid her face in her hands and groaned aloud.

It was probable that her husband had not noticed this sudden outburst. He had kept his eyes turned to the landward side, for he did not yet feel sufficiently strong to bear the sight of the waves as they came rolling in.

"Where shall we put up?" asked the driver. "Per Bratvold's is the best house, but there are several others that will do well enough."

"Let us go to Per's," said the clergyman.

For a long time Madeleine had not been certain whether Martens knew of her adventure with Per; but after a short time of married life, she found that a story does not travel very far, without reaching the clergyman, and without looking up she felt that his eye was resting upon her, with the smile with which he used to bend her to his will.

Per was in the peat-shed when they drove up, and saw her as he peeped through a chink in the boards. The moment he did so, he involuntarily took the quid of tobacco out of his mouth and threw it from him. After waiting a long time, he had begun again to chew tobacco, and after a still longer time he had married. It was thus Per's wife who, with numberless excuses, conducted the clergyman and his lady into the best room. She repeated that it was not what such people were accustomed to. While she went out to find Per, and introduce him to the strangers, the pastor went round the room examining the curiosities it contained. Madeleine sat gazing out of the window. The sight of Per's wife, looking so fresh and happy, had pained her--she knew not why.

"Look here, Lena!" he cried, every time he found something of interest.

Lena was a name of his own invention, and which he had given her in spite of all her entreaties. Lena sounded so homely, and was well suited to a clergyman's wife; while Madeleine had a foreign, French ring, which was quite out of place in a rectory.

In the room were several things worthy of his attention. In the first place there were two pictures, representing Vesuvius by day, and Vesuvius by night; then came a drawing of a coasting vessel called *The Three Sisters of Farsund*; then Frederick VII. with his red uniform and hook nose; and over the bed, which was heaped up with eider-downs as high as one's head, hung a huge horn of plenty, made of white cardboard, and on which was the motto, in gilt paper letters, "Be fruitful and multiply," which had been given them as a wedding-present. On one end of the chest of drawers stood a yellow canary on a red pear, and on the other end a red bullfinch on a yellow pear. The floor was dazzlingly clean and neatly sanded. The window-panes were small, and the glass of different tints; while over one of the windows was nailed a board, on which was painted in gold letters the words "*L'Espérance*," which was the name of the vessel to which it had belonged. At length Per came in. He held out his hand first to the pastor and then to Madeleine, and said, "How do you do?" to both. As Madeleine touched the hard and powerful hand, she involuntarily drew back her own, and turned away without pronouncing the usual greeting. The words seemed to stick in her throat.

At that moment Per's wife entered and asked him in a whisper to cut her a few chips to make the peat fire burn more quickly, as she wished to prepare some coffee. Per went out of the room, and the pastor followed the prosperous little peasant woman to inspect the house.

Madeleine took a few steps to and fro in the room, and then went to the door. As she stood on the stone steps under the porch, she could see down into the little harbour, and her eye could follow the path which led across the flat meadow, and up across the steep slope as far as the lighthouse. There lay her old home, with its solid stone walls, and the lantern with its red-painted cover. She turned away: the sight was more than she could bear. Her ear now caught the sound of Per chopping the wood in the peat-shed, and almost without knowing what she did, she found herself in the shed, standing by his side. He ceased for a moment from his work, raised himself up, and looked beyond her over the sea. Per wore a stiff sailor's beard, and his face had grown older and coarser with the lapse of time, but still every feature was familiar to her. Madeleine made a step towards him and endeavoured to take his hand. In this she was unsuccessful, for he drew it away from her. She could no longer command her feelings, and, throwing her arms round his neck, she laid her head on his breast.

Delphin's remark was perfectly true about the mixture of fish, tobacco, and damp woollen clothing; but she felt that this was her place, and here she ought to rest. At that moment, too, she perceived why the pang had passed through her heart when she met Per's wife. She envied her everything. Husband, home, even her very existence,--all belonged to her. Here was her place, and here the man she loved and understood. Oh, how all her so-called friends had mocked and deceived her! What a life was hers!--a life which consisted only in being the wife of a man she did not love, in keeping his house, and bearing his children, surrounded on every side by an unwholesome atmosphere of form, ceremony, and selfishness.

Closer and closer she clung to the broad breast whereon she lay, and that heart, so well drilled and confined, ran over in one supreme moment of mingled happiness and anguish, while the recollections of her youthful love passed through her sobbing heart.

"It was not my fault--it was not my fault!" she repeated plaintively, like a child who has had the misfortune to break something.

He lifted his hard heavy hand, and laying it on her head, passed it gently over her hair. Now he understood it all, but not a word passed his lips.

"Lena, Lena!" cried the pastor from the door, "you must come and see what I have found. Here are twins. Lena, Lena! where are you? Make haste! What a good wife! Just think, twins the first time!"

It was not easy to tell what Per's thoughts were as he stood again alone looking over the sea. Thus had the billows rolled to and fro in storm and sunshine, whilst he had waited and waited. And this was what he had waited for! He drew a long breath, and his face seemed to grow clearer again as he slowly nodded his head several times towards the ocean.

Per's wife made many apologies, as is but right and proper on such occasions, for the repast, which, however, consisted of coffee, with cream and sugar, bread and butter and cakes, and lastly a dish of small lobsters. She insisted that it was a shame to offer such small lobsters to her guests. It was a pity they had not some larger ones.

But now it was just one of the pastor's favourite theories, and which he always defended with much energy and conviction, namely, that small lobsters are really better and more delicate than large ones. He was, therefore, in the best of humours, and made several innocent jokes with the friendly peasant woman.

Per now came in and begged they would begin their meal, as everything was ready. He then sat down by the side of the fireplace, with his elbows resting on his knees.

The sun shone so brightly through the small window-panes, the room was so clean and comfortable, the table-cloth so white, the cream so yellow, and the small lobsters so red and appetizing, that the pastor felt constrained to improve the occasion.

He chose as his text a fact which he had heard from the woman, namely, that Per had built the house entirely of the wreckage of a French brig, which had been stranded on the coast a little way to the northward. This was the vessel to which the board over the window had belonged.

The pastor dwelt on the uncertainty of human affairs, how often we are disappointed, but how there is a leading thread which seems to run through our existence.

"And look," said he, "on that proud ship, fitted out in the sunny land of France, and bearing a name which points to hope and expectation; for *L'Espérance*, my friends, signifies hope, only to be lost on our desolate coast. So it is with us mortals. How many a vain hope sails out with flag and banner, only to be miserably wrecked in the storms of life! But observe! that which has been dashed to pieces by the tempest, has been refashioned by humble hands into a new dwelling-place. Thus does life spring from death, comfort from desolation, and happiness from shattered hopes, and thus our whole career may be but a patchwork of mere wreckage!"

It was with the last remains of her old impetuosity that Madeleine repeated the words, "Thus live we all!"

At this moment Per got up and went out. His wife could not understand why his behaviour was so unseemly.

Pastor Martens saw it all; but explanations, if any were necessary, might follow later on. It was not worth while to spoil the delightful meal. He handed his wife the cream, as, with a friendly smile, he placed his hand upon her shoulder.

He then set to work on his small lobsters, which he found excellent.

Lector House believes that a society develops through a two-fold approach of continuous learning and adaptation, which is derived from the study of classic literary works spread across the historic timeline of literature records. Therefore, we aim at reviving, repairing and redeveloping all those inaccessible or damaged but historically as well as culturally important literature across subjects so that the future generations may have an opportunity to study and learn from past works to embark upon a journey of creating a better future.

This book is a result of an effort made by Lector House towards making a contribution to the preservation and repair of original ancient works which might hold historical significance to the approach of continuous learning across subjects.

HAPPY READING & LEARNING!

LECTOR HOUSE LLP
E-MAIL: lectorpublishing@gmail.com

9 789353 424619

Lightning Source UK Ltd.
Milton Keynes UK
UKHW011817110922
408691UK00002B/332